Praise for Liz Balmaseda and

Sweet Mary

"With *Sweet Mary,* Balmaseda joins the ranks of suspense writers such as Janet Evanovich and Dean Koontz and brings her own sweet South Florida and Cuban flavor to the story."

—*The Boston Globe*

"Balmaseda goes from star journalist to debut novelist with her sleek ripped-from-the-headlines *Sweet Mary.* . . . A wild ride, not just for Maria but for the reader."

—*The Miami Herald*

"A fast-paced tale of mistaken identity and gutsy vigilante justice. . . . Slick, efficient and spare, this story smokes like a well-rolled cigar."

—*Kirkus Reviews*

"A yearning for justice, Balmaseda's beautifully orchestrated first novel is also a noir journey of self-discovery."

—Bookreporter.com

"Liz Balmaseda is a gifted writer and a keen-eyed journalist, and *Sweet Mary* shimmers with authentic Florida heat. It's not often you find a thriller so richly textured, and so true to the culture and soul of its setting."

—Carl Hiaasen, *New York Times* bestselling author

SWEET MARY

A NOVEL

LIZ BALMASEDA

ATRIA PAPERBACK

New York   London   Toronto   Sydney

ATRIA PAPERBACK
A Division of Simon & Schuster, Inc.
1230 Avenue of the Americas
New York, NY 10020

First Atria Paperback edition June 2010

ATRIA PAPERBACK and colophon are trademarks of Simon & Schuster, Inc.

For information about special discounts for bulk purchases, please contact Simon & Schuster Special Sales at 1-866-506-1949 or business@simonandschuster.com.

The Simon & Schuster Speakers Bureau can bring authors to your live event. For more information or to book an event, contact the Simon & Schuster Speakers Bureau at 1-866-248-3049 or visit our website at www.simonspeakers.com.

Designed by Kyoko Watanabe

Manufactured in the United States of America

10   9   8   7   6   5   4   3   2   1

The Library of Congress has cataloged the hardcover edition as follows:

Balmaseda, Liz.
    Sweet Mary : a novel / Liz Balmaseda. — 1st Atria Books hardcover ed.
        p. cm.
    I. Title.

    PS3602.A627S94 2009
    813.6—dc22   2009003536

ISBN 978-1-4165-4296-4
ISBN 978-1-4165-4297-1 (pbk)
ISBN 978-1-4391-6546-1 (ebook)

This book is dedicated to my family:
Dad, Elaine, Edward, Natalie, Lauren,
Nicholas, and sweet Lola on earth,
and Mami in heaven.

People run away from who they really are—they do it all the time.

—SPECIAL CRIMES INVESTIGATOR
LIEUTENANT EARL WINROCK,
ESPAÑOLA POLICE DEPARTMENT

SWEET MARY

ONE

THE WORST WEEK of my life began like any other late summer week in Miami, stifling hot. The August steam rose from the Everglades and wrapped itself around the city with a vengeance. No ocean breeze or inland gust seemed strong enough to break its stranglehold. The steam became our second skin, a filmy, salty gauze impossible to wash off. I couldn't imagine being one of those plastic types who, despite the 95-degree swelter, insisted on her usual Miami corporate-level quantities of makeup—the SPF, the primer, the base, the bronzer, the inner eye highlighter, the lip plumping gloss, all intended to create that "fresh from the beach" glow. To me, the thought of slipping into a business suit seemed punishing enough without the added torture of having to fabricate evidence of a nonexistent trip to the beach. Besides, who needs makeup when you can get second-degree sunburn from walking the dog for fifteen minutes?

I fool myself into thinking I can deflect the heat by wearing white. Of course, nothing deflects the kind of heat I'm talking about. But I wear white anyway because I like what it says about you. It says you're gutsy. It takes nerve to wear a narrow white skirt cut a few inches above the knee and a crisp white shirt unbuttoned to that exact place where your breasts just begin to rise from your ivory lace balconette. That's my no-fail outfit, the one I wear when I have a monumental deal I need to close pronto.

That's what I wore on the day I took the old cowboy out to the middle of the boonies to show him the Glades Terrace property. I piled this guy—and his maroon-colored poly-blend suit, his diamante-encrusted boots, and his ruby-studded gold bracelet—into my white BMW M6 and tore across westbound Tamiami Trail just before noon. He was a balding man of rugged complexion, Texan, about sixty years old, and he had an air about him I couldn't pinpoint, not at first. Then again, he once won the World Series of Poker, cashing in at $7.3 million, and I imagine one does not win that ungodly WSOP bracelet if one's intentions are easily read. He seemed charming enough, a soft-spoken sort. But I couldn't tell if he was quiet because he was wily, gullible, or even shy. I was hoping for door number two that morning. I needed gullible in a desperate way.

"Sub-Zero fridge. Antique walnut travertine bath. Turkish steam room. European touches. Garage capacity is four luxury-size cars. Or three Hummers . . ."

I glanced over at the cowboy to see if I had piqued his curiosity, but he was staring out the window at the dreary landscape of Australian pines and melaleucas and ALLIGATOR WRESTLING signs. In the southern distance, the skies had begun to darken into that deadly shade of charcoal silver that is the default backdrop of summer afternoons in South Florida, and I knew I'd better step on the gas if I wanted to outrun the tempest.

I amped up the pitch, too.

"The place has history, you know. I hear they busted Al Capone out there once," I said to him, but he didn't respond. "How about that for cocktail trivia?"

The cowboy was unfazed. He seemed perplexed by our approach into the western fringes of the county. He seemed lost in serious thought, something I couldn't afford as we headed for Glades Terrace. No, thinking is definitely not allowed when purchasing property at the precipitous edge of the Florida Everglades.

"It's also where they filmed parts of *The Specialist*. Stallone flick. Great sound track," I said, catching his eye at last.

He gave me a half smile but said nothing. Instead, his eyes traced the pearly buttons of my blouse like a slow bead of sweat, sending an unexpected shiver along the back of my arm. I tried to hide my uneasiness by smiling back, then glancing away as if I were trying to read the road signs. Sly devil, this one. I knew this sale—if there was to be a sale—would be no slam dunk. But it wasn't until I turned into the overgrown driveway and saw the monumental wreck that was the Glades Terrace property that I realized just how tough the sale would be. It was going to be brutal, even for me. I can sell just about anything. I once sold a 1982 Camaro Iron Duke, deemed to be one of the "50 Worst Cars of All Time" by *Time* magazine, for seven thousand bucks. I sold mangoes on eBay a few summers ago. I knocked them off the tree in my parents' back yard and gave them a sexy name: Mangoes from Paradise.

The product description went like this: "Kill the pill routine and have a mango! Would you rather choke back your daily dose of horse pills, the vitamin A, the vitamin E, the selenium, the iron, and the beta carotene? Or would you rather dig into a juicy, luscious mango from paradise? I thought so."

And just a few months ago, I sold my wedding dress. This may not seem like a big deal to anyone at first mention, but it was. This was one hideous wedding dress. It was a champagne, textured-taffeta, overly ruffled specimen handpicked by my quite misguided groom as the "something new" component of my wedding day. Now riddle me this: What kind of lunatic bride allows her fiancé to surprise her on the eve of their wedding with the Dress? The kind who deserves to wear it in front of her two hundred closest friends and relatives, as I did. But while my marriage met a crappy fate, my dress did not. It floated down the aisle at the Copacabana Banquet Hall in Hialeah Gardens on the curves of one brave Damaysi Yamisleidy Hernandez, a hairdresser newly arrived from Victoria de las Tunas, Cuba, who married the American boat captain who spirited her across the Straits of Florida. The captain was so smitten with her that he proposed on the sands of Hallandale Beach, moments after reaching dry land. Three days later he was scouring the online classifieds, hoping to find a fancy dress for his honey, and, boom, there it was, a dress that was more than fancy—it was fancy on steroids.

The "Surprise Me" Wedding Dress.

"It's not a fairy-tale wedding without a surprise," went my product description. "Fellas, this is the dress every bride will dream about. Trust me. It was the biggest surprise of my life."

I sold it for one thousand seven hundred and fifty bucks. So, like I said, I can sell anything. This was my mantra at Glades Terrace that day.

"We're here," I said in the most upbeat voice I could muster as I pulled up in the shade of a knobby cypress tree. "Home sweet home."

"Home sweet home" was an abandoned ranch-style mansion haphazardly plopped in the Florida wilds. Weeds and muck filled the grounds where a landscaper had been commissioned once to re-create an island paradise in that extravagant, over-the-top style of the cocaine-era nouveau riche. To reach the front door, I had to step along a weed-choked path in Christian Louboutin high heels, past an algae-infested artificial pond, a rusty yacht trailer, armies of screeching crickets, and the carcass of a burned-out sports car of some indistinguishable make. I turned around to check on the cowboy—the disturbed look on his face said it all.

"We'll clean it all up, plant a couple dozen royal palms. It'll be beautiful," I told him as I climbed the steps to the front door.

I braced for the worst, imagining the place crawling with swampland creatures. If that was the case, I fully deserved it for being so friggin' overeager. I had cajoled the listing from another agent, a sad sack named Brian, who had confided that he was taking a mental health day to go handle a domestic crisis. Word was he caught his wife in bed with their son's wrestling coach. I offered to help in any way I could—like maybe show the Glades Terrace property. Brian puckered his face and thought about it for a long time.

"The place is a gold mine," he finally said.

"I don't know about that," I said. "But I'm glad to help out."

What I meant was this: "Go home to your slutty wife and let me make this sale already."

Brian gave my shoulder a brotherly squeeze.

"You are a good woman, Mary Guevara," he said. "I hope you sell the heck out of that place."

So there I was at the front door of the Glades Terrace property, trying to erase the Brian tangent from my head. Truth is I was haunted by this vision of him busting his PTA wife with some paunchy, middle-aged wrestler. I found the image more unsettling than the fact that I had swiped a sales lead from him. I have to confess I felt no guilt whatsoever about taking the lead. I couldn't afford to feel guilt. I knew this sale could hoist me over the three-mil mark, land me on the top-seller map, and bring me closer to the life I had visualized on those evening workouts at home, on nights when I lost count of levels climbed on the ellipti-cal machine. I could taste it. I had worked so hard to shake off the debris of a bad divorce, make a decent home for myself and my son, and hit my stride in a brand-new career at a time when business was in the dumps. I mean, what kind of fool takes up real estate when everybody else is hanging it up? Only the queen of bad timing.

I gave the front door a good shove, hoping to scare off what-ever lurked on the other side. But the door flung open with ease to reveal a stunning sight: a late-'70s nightmare. Chrome glinted off every angle of the place. In a sepia haze of rising dust, the sunken living room seemed an ocean of browns, oranges, and burnt siennas. The glass shelves above the wet bar displayed a set of gold-leafed highball glasses and matching decanters. And, to boot, there was a disco ball. Let me put it this way: If those mirrored walls could talk, the stories would most likely involve powder-dusted hundred-dollar bills, a cache of automatic weap-ons, and a guy named El Gallo. Why Brian didn't stage this place, I'll never know. But who was I to tell any of this to a Texas mil-lionaire scavenging the spoils of a trashed market?

"Note the hurricane-proof windows. Closed-circuit alarm sys-tem. Bullet-resistant doors all around. And there's a phenomenal media-slash-entertainment room just down the hall," is what I told him as I took command of the sordid mess. The client seemed to be taking in every detail of the tour: the trompe l'oeiled-out kitchen, the gold-plated bathrooms, the hall of mirrors.

The bedroom proved to be another time-warp scene. A huge, round bed dominated the circular suite. The red, velvety bed-spread seemed to spill over into a lounge area of floor pillows, also red. Too much red. I had to glance out the window to refresh my eyes. But there was no view, only a tangle of branches through which I could barely see the daylight. It felt as if we were not in a room of a sprawling house but in some kind of pit, buried deep in the woods. I gasped to myself. Maybe it was the fear that this deal would be a bust, that this loss would send me into a free fall. My mind raced through a progression of extreme scenarios: bankruptcy. Poverty. Homelessness. How on earth would I support Max? I leaned into the window, straining for a glimpse of sunlight. But instead I saw a dove. It was pressing through the brush, methodically weaving its body between the branches. It was clearly stuck, but it didn't seem to know it. There was no panic, just the weaving in and weaving out, twig to twig. Then, in a startling instant, the dove found a clearing and flew away, into the darkening skies. The sight of this filled me with a strange defiance.

I turned to face the cowboy. He was sitting at the edge of the bed.

"You should know there was a gentleman here this morning who said this was his 'dream come true,' " I said to him.

The cowboy reclined into an overstuffed scarlet pillow and let out a rumbling sigh.

"Well, I can certainly relate to that sentiment," he said without a smile.

"You don't find places like this anymore for under four," I said. "It'll be gone in . . ."

I snapped my fingers to make the point.

"I'll give you a little time," I said, turning to leave.

I was nearly at the bedroom door when I heard the cowboy whistle.

"Darlin'," he said in an almost murmured way, "would you do something for me?"

"Sure. What's that?"

"Will you go stand over there?" he asked, signaling with his chin to some vague corner of the room.

"Where?"

"Right over there," he said, waving a hand toward the lounge area.

I made my way toward the mound of floor pillows, but I stopped abruptly when I realized what he was pointing to, something I hadn't noticed before. It was a stripper's pole, smack in the center of this musky little den area. A stripper's pole, as if the *Scarface* decor cheese hadn't been enough. And here was this man, this ungodly pile of polyester, asking me to step up to it—a stripper's pole. What did he take me for? Did I have some kind of flaming-heart tramp stamp tattooed to my lower regions? No. Was my name Precious or Peaches or Porsché? No. Did I smell of Angel eau de parfum by Thierry Mugler? Heck, no. I'm no kind of treacle-scented girl. I'm a nice, properly fragranced Cuban girl.

I fired a look at him, but he wasn't paying attention. He was checking his watch, as if to say, "Get on the pole, bitch, I haven't got all day."

Here's what irked me about the cowboy's request: In a way, I was already up there on that pole. In just about every real estate deal there comes that critical moment when you've got to do the dance. It's that do-or-die moment when the client is holding all the cards—and both of you know it. In the rarest of circumstances, the property sells itself and the sales agent is just there to breeze the buyer through it. But most of the time you do the dance, some kind of dance. You delete a clause or two. You reduce the price a notch or two. You compromise. Thanks to ol' Brian, the Glades Terrace contract was already egregiously pro-buyer—there was nothing left to compromise on. There was only the reality that this multimillion-dollar sale dangled by a thread, a buyer's whim. And there was the pole.

I needed this commission. It meant I could afford the down payment on the new house I wanted, the Spanish-style house with the enormous landscaped yard and the free-form lagoon pool and the gourmet kitchen, near the best school in the county.

I gathered myself and walked over to the bed.

"I'm not sure I heard you, sir. But if I heard you correctly, you'd like me to go stand by that pole over there."

"I would."

"Where exactly on the pole, sir?"

"Anywhere you'd like is fine with me."

"Anywhere?"

"Yup."

"Fine."

I turned and walked toward the pole, shoulders rolled back, no hurry, as if to say, "I think I'll go check out what's going on over there." And when I got to the pole, I just leaned on it politely, and I said, "You mean like this?"

"Exactly like that," the customer said in a barely audible tone. "I like them legs . . ."

"Come again?" I said.

"I said I like them sun-kissed legs, darlin' . . . longer than July."

"Thank you, sir," I said, rattled a bit but doing my best not to show it.

For the first time that day, I locked into his stare and held it for a long moment. The cowboy reddened, then he laughed out loud. And he kept on laughing in that doubled-over, knee-slapping, short-of-breath way. So pathetic. He was having a grand time at my expense. I could just imagine what the ride back to Miami would be like with McCackles riding shotgun. So, on the spot at the base of that pole, I decided to shut him up for good.

Before the customer could catch his breath, he lost it again when he saw me kick off my sandals and roll up my sleeves. He stopped chortling for a second, intrigued. I grabbed the pole with one arm and swung myself around. That's right: I swung on the damn pole. One round for the big new yard. Another round for Max's new playroom. Another round for my dream kitchen.

I gripped the pole with both hands and hoisted myself up, as if I were climbing the old coconut tree in the backyard of my child-hood house in Hialeah. I used to go up that tree when I was nine years old, on bizarre double-dares from my best friend, Gina.

"Dare ya to take your shorts off and climb that tree," she'd say.

"Fine."

I'd peel off my gym shorts and clamber up the curved trunk until I reached the top. With one hand, I'd swat at the coconuts until one of them came loose and tumbled to the ground. Then, while Gina rolled on the grass, laughing wildly, I'd stop for a minute to catch the view from up top: the fruit trees and random clutter, the non sequitur of items on clotheslines, the frayed divisions of backyard fences unable to contain the ruckus of Cuban-exile factory-class families.

So this was a tree, not a stripper's pole. This is what I told myself that day as I tucked the hem of my skirt between my thighs to prevent a peep show and I tightened my legs around the pole. I slid my way up to the top and when I got there, I could see the cowboy was no longer laughing. No, he looked like he was about to have a *patatún,* as my mother would say. I pushed off with my hands, slowly arching my back, until I was upside down. The room actually looked better that way, like a giant cherry-topped sundae. I slowly curled myself back up, wrapped my arms around the pole, and leaped off, landing nicely on my feet. I adjusted my skirt, slipped on my sandals, and casually walked back to the astounded cowboy.

I leaned down toward the bed.

"Let's make a deal, you and me," I said.

"You name it," he came back.

"If you go to that pole and do what I just did . . ."

"Yeah, what?"

"You don't have to buy this place."

The cowboy looked at me, bewildered, for a long moment. Then I heard him utter the words that would pole-vault me into a new tax bracket:

"I'll take it," he said. "I'll take it, Sweet Mary."

Two

WHEN I GOT back to the office, I found Gina in her usual afternoon spot—the second-floor terrace. She sat hunched over a patio table, reading the paper, sipping on a café cubano and smoking her three o'clock cigarette, that particular hint of street beneath her Dolce suit.

"I found myself a bachelor," she said, eyes fixed on the newspaper. "Retired plastic surgeon, avid yachtsman, wine collector. Waterfront mansion. Ski loft in Aspen. Not too shabby."

She scrawled a big red star on the newspaper with her Sharpie.

"Except he's a hundred and two years old," I said, taking a seat next to her. I could see she had red-marked several prospects already.

"No, he's eighty-seven," she came back.

"Ex-wife, kids?"

"Just a nephew."

"We know what that means."

"Quick sale, baby."

Gina's ambitions never ceased to amaze me. She's my oldest friend, the most loyal person I know, but she will stop at nothing to make a sale. I know I'm not one to talk after my gymnastics display at Glades Terrace. But, trust me, if it had been Gina, she would have given the cowboy a real heart attack. She's got a thing about rich men—preferably dead rich men. Which is why she brings the obituary section along on her cigarette breaks. And when she's done with that, she devours the local news pages for any sign of available, sellable property. Big tennis star dumps his wife? Gina Torres is on the case. Corrupt doctor busted for Medicare fraud and headed to Foreclosure Land? Gina somehow finagles the listing. If this dead plastic surgeon was as alone in the world as the wealthy, gay astrologer Gina had zeroed in on a few weeks earlier, I could guarantee that we'd be rummaging through the poor guy's china cabinet before too long.

"How much you want to bet the nephew's selling the old man's wine collection?" she said. "At bargain basement prices."

"There are rap songs about women like you," I said.

"Business is business, ma," she said. "Sometimes, business requires a girl to blur the lines just a bit. Catch me?"

Gina jammed her cigarette butt into the empty demitasse. She gave a little swagger, like she always does when she thinks she's made some ballsy pronouncement, uttered the perfect female bumper-sticker line, nailed it. I love it when she does this because it makes it all the more satisfying to knock her off her throne.

"Yeah," I said, waving my cell phone. "By the way, Mario's on line three."

Gina shot a sly look my way.

"You're a bitch on wheels, you know that? Mario?" she said. "Who the hell's talking about Mario?"

She threw her head back, amused that I'd whip out our code word on such an unworthy occasion. I usually reserved it for girls' nights when Gina's wild side hijacked her most ladylike intentions. "Mario's on three" is all I have to say. And, like magic, my girl stops dancing on the tabletop.

Mario Alvarez, pharmaceutical company exec, is the macho prick who is Gina's fiancé. He's on her like the paparazzi on a pseudo-celeb. He doesn't let her take a step without the barrage of questions, the innuendo, the color commentary. He snoops on her, reads her e-mail and text messages, digs through her gym bag. And the worst part of the repressive scenario? His captive couldn't care less about his oppressive ways. Gina just shrugs it off as the peculiarities of a man in love. I don't get it. I don't understand why a smart, hot girl like Gina would dumb herself down at the mere touch of a man, this man. Every ounce of intelligence and independence drains from her being and she morphs into one of those fembot chicas on Spanish TV with acting chops to match the skimpy outfits they wore on their themed bikini calendars.

"Speaking of Mah-rio," Gina said, because she just couldn't resist the segue opportunity, "he did the sweetest thing last night."

"I thought he was on a business trip."

"He is. He called the minute his flight landed in Brazil to ask if I had gotten home okay from the gym. Isn't that sweet?"

"You've been getting home okay for twenty years—how is that sweet?"

"Don't be harsh—"

"And let's say you didn't get home okay last night. What the hell was he going to do about it . . . *in Brazil*?"

"That's cold, ma."

"I tell you. Watch out for guys like Mario," I said. "They're all about the empty gesture. I know this from experience."

"You just forgot what it's like to be in love," said Gina.

"Guess so."

Gina folded her newspaper and got up. She tossed an arm around my shoulders and squeezed hard.

"Come on, moneybags, we've got a celebration to go to," she said.

"For what?"

"For you."

That's Gina, Mouth of the South. I had barely wiped the Everglades muck off my heels and she had told the entire office about the big Glades Terrace sale.

We went downstairs and joined the Grand Realty crew in the boss's office. Like the rest of our boutique firm, Ida Miller's office was more like a large parlor appointed with antiques, orchids, and botanical prints. Its Old Florida elegance reflected Ida's personal style. A Southern belle in her early sixties, she had distinguished herself among her overdesirous peers with her gracious, disarming way. That's not to say she was demure. No, Ida Miller may have been a warm, generous woman, but she was as plucky as they come. She was the woman who missed an important business meeting when she found her husband's beloved chocolate lab, Sadie, nearly passed out atop her own vomit one morning last year, an odd-shaped bulge protruding from the side of her belly. Ida, in her favorite pink crepe suit, scooped the dog up, gently placed her on the cream leather seat of her Lexus, and rushed her to the veterinarian's office. There, she waited while the vet performed emergency surgery to remove a foreign object from Sadie's bowels. When he was done, the stern-faced veterinarian summoned Ida into the surgical room to show her what he had retrieved.

"You really need to be more careful about what you leave in a dog's reach," said the doctor, holding up the mangled remains of a red lace bra, size 36DD. "Just a couple more hours and the poor girl might have been dead."

Ida's eyes narrowed on the bra. No amount of dog slime could erase its original color, a ghastly shade of pickled-egg red, a shade she'd never wear on a bra she'd never own, a bra three cup sizes larger than any in her collection of neutral-toned, damask brassieres. It was a bra better suited for a younger woman in need of attention, a giggly, gum-smacking tart like her husband's new "apprentice." Ida silently calculated how many times in the past week her husband had telephoned to ask if she would be going home for lunch, knowing full well she rarely, if ever, went home for lunch—three times he had called.

"Dead is right, Doctor," Ida said.

With that, she paid the $5,245 bill with her husband's platinum card and, later that day, informed him she was leaving him—and taking Sadie.

It was Ida who introduced me to the Gary Zarkan Method, the power sales techniques that made her the most successful woman in the business year after year. But here's why I went to work for her: At the end of the day, Ida was a lady, and I had a good feeling about her. I could trust her.

"The first million is like the first olive out of the jar," she told me as she pinned a gold TOP SELLER emblem on the collar of my blouse that day. "After that, they tumble right out."

"Thanks, Ida," I replied, humbled, as the room swelled in applause.

I glanced around at my coworkers, a nattily dressed bunch, and caught sight of sad-sack Brian's empty desk, his wedding picture still propped in one corner, next to his favorite mug. WORLD'S BEST REALTOR, it read.

Thirty minutes later, Gina and I were sitting side by side at Nail Fever Deluxe, sipping on mango sours. While a nail tech polished my toes in Pistol-Packin' Red—hey, I had earned it—I let Gina do what she did best: inflict her happiness on the world.

"What would go better with a yellow diamond engagement ring—coral or hot pink?" she asked the young Korean nail tech before answering her own question: "Coral, I think. Go with the coral."

"But you don't have a yellow diamond engagement ring," I said.

"Yet," said Gina.

She tossed back the rest of her mango sour. She held up her empty glass and signaled to the nail tech to go fetch her another.

"We need a girls' night out tonight," she said.

"No, I need a hot bath."

"But I'm single tonight," Gina said. "In fact, I'm single for a whole month."

"Exactly. We can do it another night."

"Come on."

"Can't. Gotta go pick up Max," I told her.

"I thought Dickhead had him tonight."

"No, he's at my folks' house."

"Ladies and gentlemen," she said, offering her trademark roll of the air drums, "The Addams Family of Hialeah."

I hate to say this, but Gina's description of my folks is not too far off. Lilia and Herminio Guevara make a feisty pair. Don't get me wrong. I would throw myself into a fire for them, but the truth is they drive me to the brink. I've often wondered if I was adopted, snatched from the arms of some unsuspecting woman, a perfectly sane, law-abiding woman, on a normal street in Miami circa 1976. Maybe I wasn't meant to live my life as Mary Guevara. Maybe I was meant to live it as Alicia Fernandez, some random little girl whose parents never haggled down the meter reader, never gave her presents with the plastic security tags still attached, never tried to pass off drunk Uncle Lazaro as Santa Claus. Such a child never had to explain to her friends why her Santa never brought any real presents to her house. He brought things like dead pigs and he sang slurred tangos, never Christmas carols, while her mom egged him on with shots of Johnnie Walker Red.

It's not easy being the daughter of Lilia Guevara, queen of labyrinths and double standards. She wants to be the boss but never shoulders the blame. But my biggest peeve about my mother was the fact that during my marriage she always sided with my ex. Tony could do no wrong in her eyes. It didn't matter that he was an arrogant, overbearing tool who just wanted a trophy wife. He was rich. He was French. He sang Aznavour. That was enough for her.

That night as I drove to her house, I imagined my mother was exactly where she was every night, watching the evening soap. There was probably some forlorn farm girl on-screen, posed against a stately chateau in some unspecified Latin American country, sobbing about the baby that was taken from her by the evil governess. I bet my mother was crying, too. But not for the farm girl. She was crying because that stately chateau might have been her own destiny if not for her spineless husband and inopportune offspring. I exaggerate, but you get the point.

While the *telenovela* plays, she ignores everything—Max, the dirty dishes, even the relentless hollering that comes from the next room.

"Ma!" it goes. "*Ma!*"

She doesn't respond to anyone or anything, not until the stroke of nine o'clock. That means my father is in charge of watching Max, and that involves a whole other can of peas. Daddy likes to show Max his prizefighter photo albums, flipping through his treasured portraits and saying things like, "That was Bartolo, best fighter I ever had. Undefeated. He had the power of Joe Louis and the speed of Kid Gavilan."

The unfortunate thing is he's not talking about a champion boxer. He's talking about a gamecock. Think barrel-chested rooster with a Brazilian wax. Daddy's eyes well up each time he cracks open those albums, and seven-year-old Max has to console him:

"Don't cry again, Grandpa," Max tells him. "Maybe he flew back to Cuba."

The flash of horror in Daddy's eyes forces the kid to backtrack.

"Or maybe he went to live with his mom."

Daddy used to be a pig farmer in Cuba until Castro came and took the family's only possession, a small plot of land on the northeastern tip of the island. This was the thanks he got after he supported the rebels, giving them food and supplies and even a couple of horses for their treks into the mountains. He and my mother fled to Miami, where they fell into the exile trance of factory jobs and weekend nostalgia.

About ten years ago, Daddy suffered an accident at the aluminum factory where he worked twelve-hour days as a machine operator. The rolling mill he was on, a rumbling monster of a machine that cranks out three thousand feet of aluminum foil per minute, hit a snag and threw him off. Daddy hit the floor, shattered his hip, and sprained his lumbar vertebrae, forcing him to retire and endure years of physical therapy. At seventy years of age, he has little material proof of his thirty-plus years in a factory, just a small, boxy house on a blue-collar street in Hialeah. But he still has dreams. They tell him what numbers to play.

Daddy has a wonderful heart but not much backbone. He's scared of life, and he's scared of his wife. He's even scared of his best friend. Then again, his best friend is a guy nicknamed Puddle Morales. (That's Puddle as in "Puddle of Blood," if you're translating from the Cuban vernacular.) Back in Cuba, they used to play ball together, chase the ladies, and bet on gamecocks. But here, Daddy hides in the bathroom whenever he catches sight of Puddle's limousine. Frankly, I don't blame him. I never liked the guy.

I pulled into the driveway to find Daddy and Max poking around the garage, scavenging for something. Daddy's garage is a *Sanford and Son* reprise of machine parts, busted radios, long-discarded appliances. I stepped into the clutter just as Daddy found what he was looking for: a boy's bicycle.

"Nice, huh?" he said, rolling the bike toward Max. "For you."

"Rock on, Herman!" Max said.

He high-fived his grandfather as if this bike, the one with the flat tire and the faded comic book stickers and the peeling nameplate that read BILLY, was the bike of his dreams. Max stooped down to read the nameplate.

"Grandpa, who's Billy?"

Daddy didn't answer him. Instead, he drew me aside with a troubled gesture.

"What's wrong?" I asked.

"The two hundred dollars I owe you . . ."

"Don't worry about it."

"I want to pay you back, but I can't right now. It's your mother's fault again," he said. "I had a dream last night that I caught her in bed with another man. Father Lorenzo."

"Mami?"

"So this morning I played number fifty-eight. Adultery. And number seventy-eight. Bishop. And I lost all the money."

Daddy was heartsick about this, I could tell.

"Go on inside—she wants to see you," he said with a smirk. "Sometimes I wish she would leave me already."

"Not before the cruise, Daddy."

"Even in my dreams she brings bad luck," he said.

I suspected there was something wrong in the House of Guevara when I entered through the kitchen door and found the stack of aluminum take-out containers on the stove. The label taped on top read ARROZ CON POLLO. That was the first hint. Arroz con pollo is my mother's specialty. She'd never be caught dead with the take-out variety.

"You're not cooking these days?" I called out to the living room, where I expected my mother to be, as she was every night, fanning herself against the heat, her backside stuck to a green pleather recliner. I could hear her favorite *telenovela* was playing on the tube, but when I poked my head into the living room, I saw her chair was empty. That was the second hint.

"Over here!" she hollered from one of the back rooms of the house. I followed her voice, an earthy mezzo-soprano-of-the-barrio voice, to the bedroom she shares with Daddy, an immaculately kept room anchored by a large, framed image of the Virgin of Charity suspended over a collection of Lladró figurines—a Spanish maiden, a ballerina, a girl in a pink dress, a pair of young lovers, and an angel playing the flute—arranged upon a sturdy walnut bedroom ensemble purchased the year before I was born and polished daily ever since. My mother stood at the edge of the bed, staring into a large, open suitcase.

"You're not cooking these days?" I said again.

She shot me an irked look as I went to sit on the bed. She held up her arthritic hands with an overdramatic gesture that meant to her both defiance and surrender.

"Don't you think these hands of mine have done enough cooking? Don't you think I've reached the point of *that's it*? What's the use in working so hard when your father is going to squander every penny on his numbers?" she said, picking up a stack of neatly folded, blue nylon underwear and placing it in the suitcase.

"You know that's not true," I said, but then she gave me one of those looks that usually precedes a lecture in which she casts herself—in the third person, no doubt—as the victim of a reckless, incorrigible man. "Come on, lighten up. Daddy's taking you on a cruise for your anniversary."

"He's not 'taking' me anywhere," she said, packing an assortment of matching leisure outfits into the suitcase. "This is the trip we won at the church raffle. With my winning ticket. Paid for with my two dollars. And I'm only going because Father Lorenzo's rosary group is going, not because it's my anniversary."

"They'll have Baked Alaska—you love Baked Alaska," I said, trying to coax a smile out of her, to no avail.

"How can I enjoy myself, considering the great problem I have?" she said, slipping a pair of Naturalizers into one of the suitcase pockets.

"What problem, Mami? Talk to me."

Lilia pouted in silence for a long while. Then came her prologue:

"You know Max is very special to me. But I have four other grandchildren who are not so blessed," she said as she rolled up a pair of knee-high hose.

She didn't have to say much more. I knew exactly where the riff was going. Still, I let her go there anyway.

"Your brother has made some mistakes," she said, tucking the knee-highs into a plastic bag, "but I want you to understand he's in a tough situation."

Ah, yes. This was going to be *that* conversation again, the one where she pleads with me to bail out my brother from some kind of mess—for the hundredth time.

"Whatever it is this time, it isn't my problem," I said, picking at my cuticles, as I tend to do when I'm annoyed. "And it isn't yours, either."

"He is my son—"

"He is twenty-eight years old. This is between him and his ex-girlfriends—every last one of them."

"Do you know what kind of mothers they are?"

"I do. Maybe Fatty should have gotten to know them a little better before knocking two of them up in less than a year— "

"He's gullible—"

"Or, radical thought: condoms."

"Dulce Maria, watch your tongue."

"Maybe he shouldn't be so gullible."

Lilia slammed the suitcase shut.

"Forget it. Go."

I hate it when she does this. I hate it because I always fall for it.

"What do you need?"

Lilia sniffed to herself. She patted the sides of her short, fringy do, freshly tinted in her favorite Nice 'n Easy shade—Natural Medium Ash Blonde—and styled to frame her face in slimming, forward-swept wisps.

"Did you sell that house today?" she said.

"Yes."

"Could I borrow five thousand dollars?"

"Five thousand dollars? You mean, for the cruise?"

"For child support."

She looked at me defiantly, as if I was not hers. I should have been ready for that, but I wasn't. I should have come to expect that no matter how hard I work, how much I achieve, how generous I try to be, I will always be the outsider in this house, the one mocked for her goody-two-shoes sense of honesty and civility, the one snubbed as some kind of hall monitor. Oh, but when crunch time is near, mine is the one name they all remember. In times like that, my initials might as well be ATM.

In Fatty and his woes, my mother found her favorite lamentation, an interminable, off-key ballad to a poor, luckless, misunderstood slob who couldn't seem to catch an even break. It had been this way since the day he was born, for even Fatty's birth was a near tragedy. He came into the world on a feeble cot in our garage, between hurled insults and heaps of rusted machine parts, during a late-season tropical storm. The storm had gusted in from the Bahamas without much warning as my mother neared her eighth month of pregnancy. Against the advice of her obstetrician, Lilia not only refused to go to the hospital, she insisted on getting the house hurricane-ready. She dragged in the potted plants, the Don Quixote and Sancho Panza lawn ornaments, the white-vinyl-strap patio furniture, and the parakeet cage. She secured the windows with those big, unsightly masking-tape Xs, the ultimately futile ones that are impossible to scrape off. Then she whipped up a steaming pot of stew, red beans, potatoes, chorizo, and chunks of calabaza, because it wouldn't be a hurricane at the Guevara residence without a steaming pot of some Last Supper–worthy creation.

Despite a rare scolding from Daddy, Lilia worked herself to the point of exhaustion. Her ankles swelled up like jellyfish and her cheeks grew cold and pale. I was barely five, but I remember the exact moment when my mother cried out:

"Call 411! Call 411! The baby's coming!"

I picked up the telephone beside her green recliner and dialed 911. But nobody came on the other end of the line. I didn't know it at the time, but the storm had knocked out our phone service. My father, intent on braving the wind and rain to drive her to the hospital seven miles away, coaxed Lilia into the car, only to find out the usually trustworthy vehicle, a faded burgundy Chevy Impala, would not start. The battery was dead, thanks to the storm's low-pressure system. Gripping the dashboard in desperation, my mother called out the names of every saint she could think of, pleading for their divine intercession. Help finally came from a most unexpected source: Perica Jimenez, the hateful woman who lived across the street. Perica was the neighborhood gossip who once told my father that she had seen my mother at Les Violins Cabaret canoodling with Father Lorenzo—hence Daddy's paranoia. Of course it wasn't true. It turned out Perica was merely deflecting her own guilt, for it was she who had snuck out with Father Lorenzo. But thanks to her obsessive snooping, Perica was watching that stormy day between the taped Xs of her kitchen window as my mother waddled out of the stranded car and nearly collapsed at the door of the Impala. A former nurse's assistant, Perica scrubbed her hands, grabbed her first aid kit, and sprang into action. She bolted across East Forty-fifth Street in the blinding rain and ducked into our garage as my mother howled in pain. There was no time to help Lilia up the garage steps into the house, so Perica grabbed a cot from a nearby pile of garage clutter and set it up. My mother wanted none of her help, but she had no choice. She pushed when Perica told her to push and spat insults at the detested midwife between contractions. It went like this:

"Push harder, Lilita, push!"

"I'm pushing, you imbecile whore!"

Then, in a miraculous instant, my mother pushed out a baby boy. She cried and cried at the sight of him.

"My poor little angel, born in a junk pile. My poor little son, brought into this world by an imbecile whore," she cried. "I will spend my life making this up to you."

And that's exactly how she raised Fatty, with a stifling amount of pity. This is why I was so tough on her that night as she asked me to bail him out.

"No," I said, getting up to leave. "Fatty needs to pay his own damn child support."

"Dulce Maria, please . . ."

"Please what? You could have at least congratulated me first."

Before I reached the bedroom door I heard a tiny voice coming from the hallway.

"Aunt Mary!"

There, barely visible in the darkened corridor, was a sleepy-eyed three-year-old boy, Fatty's oldest son. Jaz wore a giant, raggedy shirt and torn socks. I scooped him into a hug.

"Where were you hiding?" I said.

"Daddy's room. I was sleeping."

"You must be hungry—"

But Lilia shattered the moment with a clap of her hands.

"*Ven acá mi chiquitico,*" she said, summoning the boy. He rushed into her arms.

She sat on the bed and rocked him like a baby as she gave me the evil eye. Years of living bitterly, always on the defensive, had etched a scowl on her otherwise graceful face. But now, as she cradled the boy, she softened, all the hard angles relaxed, offering a glimpse of the striking beauty who once starred in a national soap commercial in Havana. That was years before a forced exile, before she was torn from her parents and her twin sister, years before she'd realize her displacement was permanent and that she would have to make her life as a garment factory worker on foreign soil and stand by, powerless, as telegrams drifted in from eastern Cuba with the news of her father's political imprisonment, his mysterious death in confinement, her mother's emotional collapse, and her twin's rebirth as a militant of the revolution. The portrait of my mother, an island of a woman, cradling that boy was more than I could tolerate.

"Have a nice time on the cruise. At least try," I said, feeling my eyes turn misty in frustration. I left the room to avoid saying anything I might regret, but I couldn't shake the image of my mother and the boy.

As I reached the front door of the house I took my checkbook out of my purse and wrote a check for $5,000. I ripped it out and left it on top of the TV, which still droned with the endless blue skies and farm-girl fantasies of my mother's *telenovela*.

The scene at my parents' house nearly derailed me. Writing that check tore a chunk out of my spirit. It wasn't about the money—it was about this realization: Just as I was moving along at a nice clip, inevitably something dragged me back into the sinkhole, the emotional pit of my childhood in Hialeah. Whatever municipal poet nicknamed Hialeah the "City of Progress" should have informed the Guevaras—they missed the bulletin. They live in no such place. Their city is defined not by progress, but by a plague of inertia.

For my own survival, I had tried my best to gain a healthy level of detachment. And I have to confess that if not for Mr. Motivation I might have succumbed to the burn of self-pity that night. After Max settled into bed at nine o'clock, I hit the elliptical machine and the play button on the iPod, and I let Gary Zarkan's sports anchor voice carry me off:

"Get in the game, people. You can get anything you want if you just get in the game . . ."

I notched up the volume on the audio and resistance control on the elliptical.

"Let's talk about the Porcupine. That's when you throw the buyers' questions back at 'em. Buyer says, 'Do you have it in green?' You answer, 'Would green best suit you?' People, this is huge. Some of you have lost major deals just because you forgot the Porcupine. You forgot to appropriate your buyers' questions and hurl them right back!"

Okay, admittedly, some of the Zarkan methods have that shark-tank, early-'90s, *The Firm* vibe to them. But that's only when they are utilized by sweaty sales guys who wear double-breasted jackets over tight T-shirts and a lot of product in their hair. You expect the shtick—the Porcupine, the Tie Down, and the "mirror your client" techniques—from them. You don't expect it from Ida Miller or any other classy woman.

"Why do we settle? Think about it, people. We settle because we are conditioned to believe that we have only one or two options for any given situation. Well, this isn't true. Life is not a multiple-choice question. Life is an open-ended essay question and we never, ever have to settle."

I climbed to levels unknown in my Zen blue bedroom as I stared out the window at the twinkle of suburban normalcy on Hibiscus Lane below. Tiny garden lights flickered on the Dixon family's gazebo across the street, catching the unmistakable silhouette of Dale Dixon, the pudgy, semiretired accountant who heads the local orchid club. Buster, the neighbor girl's American bulldog, scampered across my lawn on his nightly walk, dragging her along as he does. He stopped to sniff the mailbox, then suddenly lunged toward the curb as if he had spotted a cat or maybe a squirrel. The girl tried her best to pull him back, but Buster puffed up his chest in that bulldog stance and ferociously barked toward some parked vehicle on the curb. He barked so relentlessly that several porch lights clicked on. He didn't stop until a white van, the object of his alarm, pulled away from the curb and sped off.

I finished my workout and soaked myself in a warm, gardenia-scented bath. I checked on Max, preset my coffee pot, and nestled into bed, feeling renewed.

THREE

THE NEXT MORNING, I woke up to the aroma of Bustelo Supremo brewing in my kitchen, just as I had programmed it to the night before. I woke up Max and hustled downstairs in my sweats. Through the window, in a slant of sunlight, I saw Sam, the gardener, hauling a sack of soil in the yard. His small, wiry frame possessed unusual strength for a man of sixty-five. I had asked him to come by and spruce up the hedges of the front lawn to help me boost the curb-appeal factor, as I was hoping to put the house on the market in the following days.

I waved hello to him as I walked outside to pick up the newspaper. But just as I stooped down to grab the paper from the lawn, I noticed something curious: a white Windstar van. It was the same van I had seen parked on the curb the night before. Now the hood was propped up and two men—young and muscular types, both white—chatted beside it. One of the men, a seemingly handsome dude with close-cropped hair, leaned into the open hood, but he didn't seem to be checking the engine—he was checking me. Nice-looking mechanic, I thought. I might have been more intrigued if I hadn't been distracted by the frightful sight of hefty Dale Dixon in his too-tight robe, watering his yellow oncidium orchids.

I shook off the vision and went back inside for a cup of coffee at the kitchen counter, where I packed up a FedEx box filled with real estate brochures destined for an out-of-town client. I sealed it with a label that read MARY GUEVARA, BROKER/ASSOCIATE, GRAND REALTY and stopped for a minute to look at the tiny mug shot of me on the logo. Not so bad. I was smiling my business smile, my long, brown hair partly pulled back with a demure clip to reveal understated gold earrings. A light tan glowed on my cheeks, a remnant of a serene Sunday spent afloat in the waters off Boca Chica Key.

My reverie was interrupted by the doorbell. FedEx guy, I was sure. I grabbed the box, rushed to open the front door, and there he was, caramel god of my morning. He gave me a wink and took off, and as I watched him walk away I noticed the gardener was driving off, having left the hedges nicely trimmed and replenished with new soil. I headed upstairs to get dressed for work. As I slipped into my new gray skirt, I could hear Max slamming pantry doors in the kitchen. And just as I fastened my strappy summer sandals, I heard the doorbell again. I must have messed up the FedEx label, I thought—just what I needed when I was running late. I bolted downstairs.

"I'll get it!" I said.

I could hear Max fussing in the kitchen.

"Two minutes! Grab your lunch!" I yelled out to him as I reached the front door.

But just as I cracked the door open, something pushed it open from the other side with a *THWACK*. In a blinding instant, three men in black jackets stormed into my house, guns pointed. They tore through the living room at hurricane speed, firing orders I could not decipher. Chairs and cushions went flying. Books cascaded off the shelves.

"Take what you want and get out of my house!" I pleaded.

Two of the invaders barreled upstairs to the bedrooms. The third one sped toward me, pointing his gun at my chest. I was afraid to call my son's name. I didn't want to tip off the invaders to the presence of a child in the house. I wanted to make a run for the kitchen to grab Max, but instead I prayed he had gone out the back door and headed to the car to wait for me, as he does on some mornings. Even if I had wanted to run to him, I couldn't have gotten very far. The third invader spun me around and shoved me against the wall.

"Hands up! Don't move!" he ordered, pressing the barrel of his gun into my back.

I heard a thunder of boots and a crash of glass coming from one of the rooms upstairs.

"*Jesus God,* what do you want?"

"Are you Maria?" the third invader demanded.

"What do you want?" I snapped back in a booming voice I didn't recognize, the voice of a woman who has nothing to lose. I wasn't that woman. I was petrified that the invaders would find my son and shoot us both right then and there.

The third invader shoved the gun barrel toward my head. I was trembling but managed to glance back and take a good look at him. Trim, athletic build, late thirties, meticulously pressed black jeans. I was determined to remember him in case I had to pick him out of a lineup.

"Hands on the wall!" He shoved me again.

But then I noticed something else about him, something glinting on his belt, and I realized this was no ordinary home invasion.

The third intruder wore a badge.

"Are you Maria?"

"Yes, I'm Maria. What do you want from me?"

"Maria Portilla?"

"No, no—"

"Maria Guevara Portilla, we're—"

"That's not my name—"

Just then I heard Max at the kitchen door.

"Mommy!" he screamed, and immediately one of the invaders darted down the stairs and dove for the kitchen door, blocking him off.

"Don't touch my son!" I demanded in that unrecognizable voice.

The third invader pinned me to the wall to shut me up.

"Maria Guevara Portilla, we have a warrant for your arrest," he said.

"This is a mistake!" I said.

I heard Max cry out for me again.

"Stay back, baby!" I called out to him.

But his screams got louder.

"Why is my son screaming? Leave him alone!"

I turned around to see one of the men carry my crying boy out of the house. I bolted after him, but the third invader tripped me to the floor.

"Leave my son! Please, take me instead!"

"We're taking you, all right," the third invader said. "Don't worry about your son. He's with child services out there. We'll need names of his next of kin, anybody they should call."

"What are you talking about? I'm his next of kin. He's staying with me."

"No, you need to come with us."

"Who the hell are you?"

"You don't listen, do you?" he said. "DEA."

"I don't believe you. Show me your badge. Up close," I said.

He took off the badge and held it in front of my eyes.

"Special Agent Dan Green, DEA," he said, irked.

I studied the shield—for what, I don't know. For all I knew, it could have been a fake.

"I'm not going anywhere with you," I told him. "I want a real cop in a real cop uniform to tell me what this is about. And I want to see my son."

But Agent Dan Green slapped handcuffs on me. One of the other agent invaders, who had ducked out the front door moments earlier, returned with shackles and a chain. He fastened the chain around my waist and the shackles on my feet and helped me up off the floor.

"I have a warrant for your arrest. And let me suggest you come peacefully," Agent Green said.

"Arrest for what?"

"Can't tell you. It's a sealed indictment," he said.

"What the hell does that mean?" I demanded to know as the agents led me out of my house. But they didn't answer.

Frantic, I searched for a sign of Max. I saw him in the back of an unmarked sedan, crying, as a middle-aged woman in a floral-print blouse tried to console him and another, younger woman stood by the car, holding a clipboard. When she saw me, the younger woman rushed over to introduce herself as Tiffany Wells of the Florida Department of Children and Families.

"Your son is gonna be okay. Is there a family member he can stay with?" said the young woman, a wavy-haired girl dressed in chinos and a peasant-style shirt.

"Yeah. Me," I said.

"You'll be with him real soon," she said, "but I need someone else for right now."

I stumbled on the thought. My parents were headed for their

cruise—were they still home? And as for Max's father, I hadn't spoken to him in a couple of weeks. Tony and I had agreed that I would have Max for an extended period in the summer, while he traveled overseas on vacation. But I was pretty sure he was back home. I thought about Fatty but then quickly dismissed the thought—a wannabe rapper on parole was not an option.

So I gave the social worker every number I could think of for my parents and Tony.

"You have to call them right now. If you can't reach them, I have a close friend you can call," I said, but she cut me off before I could give her Gina's information.

"Has to be a relative, sorry. Let me call your folks right now," she said, racing off with her clipboard, then turning to call out, "Your son's in good hands."

I held it together for Max's sake. This couldn't be happening, not to me. I closed my eyes and tried to retrace the sequences of that morning. Where did my life veer into chaos? I tried to grasp the image of my home as it was just moments earlier, the easy order of cream-toned furnishings, everything in its place, my plans tucked neatly into a leather-bound agenda, the clay-colored dishes stacked clean in the cabinets, the mound of perfect pears in the blue Murano bowl, my baby boy nestled beneath his Spider-Man sheets. But in the wreckage of my home, it all eluded me. A cruel geometry of objects now defined my landscape—sofas slashed, books strewn, my favorite kitchen plaque, the one that says HELP KEEP THE KITCHEN CLEAN—EAT OUT smashed on the floor.

The home invaders took me out of 416 Hibiscus Lane in handcuffs and shackles. They took me out in front of my screaming son, my bathrobed neighbor, the school bus driver, and even the FedEx guy, who was now two doors away. Everybody was too stunned to speak. Only Buster, the bulldog, seemed lucid enough to express the appropriate rage. He barked and growled through the fence of his yard as the agents led me to their vehicle. The white Windstar van. The dog knew—he had tried to warn us all the previous night.

The back seat of the van smelled of egg sandwiches and stale coffee. The agents had chained my shackles to a metal bar on the floor to make sure I didn't escape. One of the invaders took the wheel. Another took the seat behind me. So-called Agent Green rode shotgun. I still had a hard time believing they were feds. Morbid thoughts raced through my mind: They're going to kill me and then they're going to dump my body. I craned for a look at the file folder open on Agent Green's lap. I squinted to read the bold-lettered name on the inside label. Someone had scrawled it in a black marker: MARIA GUEVARA PORTILLA/AKA LA REINA.

There was an enlarged driver's license photo depicting a rough-looking woman, late thirties, reddish brown hair, hideous collagen job. Bingo. There it was, proof they had the wrong woman.

"That's not me," I blurted from the back seat. "That picture— I don't know who that is. But if that's who you're looking for, then you're arresting the wrong person."

Agent Green adjusted the rearview mirror and fired a look that ricocheted back to me.

"Are you talking?"

"Yes, I'm talking," I said, defiant. "Why shouldn't I talk? I've got nothing to hide. I'm going to tell you everything—my name, my birthday, my Social Security number. Everything. Dulce Maria Guevara de los Santos. People call me Mary. *Dulce*—that means "sweet" in Spanish. I don't think there's a Dulce in there, am I right?"

Agent Green glanced down at the file.

"Born seven sixteen sixty-nine?"

"No, sir, I was born seven four seventy-six."

He thought about it for a second, then said, "Right."

"You think I'm lying? Unbelievable. My Social is two six four eight two zero zero zero six. I was born at Mercy Hospital. I went to Immaculate Conception Catholic grade school in Hialeah. Then Monsignor Pace High. Then FIU. Psych major. I'm a Realtor. I am a mother. I'm divorced. My ex-husband is a banker. I've lived in this house for three years. I moved here after the divorce. Before that I lived at 1025 Eagle Court in South Miami. Before that I lived at 1001 East Forty-fifth Street in Hialeah. That's where I grew up. I learned to swim at Walker Park. I was on the gymnastics team at the youth center. That's it. That's my life. That's it."

But Agent Green said nothing and there was nothing but silence between us as we wove through Miami's seamy back streets. I looked out the window at a blur of urban scenes that grew more desolate as we came to a red light. A couple of thug types ambled by. A crack addict jabbered to herself under a tree. A very old woman stared at me from a chair on her porch. Her empty gaze reflected my own isolation.

Moments later, I stood alone in a gray corridor at the federal detention center, still in my business clothes. Although they had removed the shackles from my feet, my hands were still cuffed and linked to the chain around my waist. I heard a steel door slam shut behind me, then a man's amplified voice.

"Walk to the end of the hall," it said.

When I reached the end of the corridor, another steel door opened to a clamor of raw voices.

"Walk to the end," the voice said again.

But I hesitated. I realized I had to walk a gauntlet of male inmates in their cells.

"Proceed to the end of the hall," the voice repeated, now adamant.

In my business attire, I walked amid hoots and catcalls and only brief patches of silence.

"Who'd you kill, baby?" yelled one inmate.

I kept walking. The next thing I remember is a searing flash of light. It is the flash that captured my pale, startled look in a federal mug shot.

That flash would mark the very instant my soul sprang free of my body and became chief witness in the life of federal inmate number 12618.

INTERROGATION ROOM—DAY 1

Industrial, high-gloss walls. Spartan table. Mary, her handcuffs now removed, sits alone.

I stared at the darkened, telltale double mirror, trying to detect a sign of life on the other side. After a long while, the door opened and in walked Agent Green. In the jarring fluorescent light of the interrogation room, he appeared more cocky than ever. He now wore a crisp, sage cotton shirt with the sleeves rolled halfway up his forearms. Strong forearms. Clean nails. No wedding band. Spy Le Baron sunglasses clipped casually to the front of his shirt. Dan Green was central casting's answer to a federal agent at the top of his game—not a hair out of place. I could just imagine he had run eight miles that morning, then hit the weights as ESPN droned on in the background. He probably did a few extra reps because he had allowed himself that glass or two of wine, undoubtedly chardonnay, the previous night at dinner with his girlfriend, a nice-looking but dry girl most likely named Brooke or Lindsay.

"Maria Portilla . . ." Agent Green began, eyes fixed on an open file on the table before him.

The name grated on me, but I sucked it up.

"That's not my name. But I'll be happy to wait here while you go check my driver's license records or whatever other records you need to check. Once and for all, I want to clarify these issues you seem to be having with my identity," I said in a tone I tried to keep low and level.

When he didn't answer, I went on.

"Listen, I know everybody makes mistakes. Even the feds make mistakes. Fine. As big of a mistake as this one is, I'm willing to let it go for a handshake and a brief apology."

Agent Green gave a half smile.

"You think I'm some kind of moron," he said.

In another time and place, I might have found him handsome, intriguing, dateable. But not that day. That day I did think he was some kind of moron.

"I don't know what you want from me, but this is getting old," I said. "I need to know where my son is. Now."

"What do I want from you? The truth," he said.

"I have told you more than you'll ever need to know about me," I said. "If this isn't a mistake, then it's got to be some kind of joke."

"Nobody's laughing here," Agent Green said in a smug manner that set me off.

I slapped a hand on the table and stood up to tower over him.

"Get your facts right and stop wasting my time," I said.

He leaped up in my face.

"Sit the hell down," he said. He was angry but impeccably composed.

I obliged. Rattled, I glanced up at the wall. I could see faint silhouettes moving in the mirrored glass. Agent Green tapped once on the table to pull me back in.

"Let's talk about New Mexico," he said, terse.

"I've never been there."

"You haven't?"

He took a photograph out of the open file and slid it across the table. It was a black and white picture of a Red Roof Inn motel, snapped at night from the side of a road.

"What does this have to do with me?" I asked.

He didn't answer. Instead, he peeled off another photo. This one featured a tall, lanky man smoking what appeared to be a joint in a budget motel room. Agent Green nodded at the image, then looked at me as if waiting for an explanation.

"I don't know that guy."

"Right. And you were born on the Fourth of July in the year of the Bicentennial."

"So what about it?" I said.

He shoved the picture closer to me.

"Where's El Flaco?"

"El Flaco who?"

He shoved another photo at me—a poor snapshot of a woman counting a wad of bills in the same motel room. On a table next to her there was a mound of small bags filled with what looked like a white powder substance. Then came another photo—a grainy picture of the same woman talking to the lanky man.

"Still don't know him?"

I studied the woman in the photo. She had thick, wavy hair. Her face was a catalog of cosmetic surgery—the trout mouth; the suspiciously large, perfectly arranged boobs.

"No. And I don't know her, either. Who is she?"

Agent Green narrowed his eyes on me.

"Conspiracy to distribute cocaine. Possession with intent to distribute. Large amounts, Maria. Unfathomable amounts."

Just then I realized he wasn't talking about the woman in the photo—he was talking about me. In his mind, I was the woman in the photo. I picked up the photo and took a closer look at the woman in question. The reddish hair, the oddly plumped mouth, the mammoth boobs. How dare he?

I gave the woman's photo back to Agent Green and met his stare.

"Mine are real."

Agent Green got up, placed his hands on the table, and took a deep breath.

"On November four, 2002, you made a bank deposit in the amount of one hundred seventeen thousand five hundred ninety dollars," he said.

"I don't know if that was exactly the day or exactly the amount, but that could be right. It could have been from the sale of the house after my divorce."

"So, where's the rest of the money?"

"There is no rest of the money."

"Where's the drug money?"

"I don't sell cocaine. I sell condominiums."

Agent Green stormed out. But it wasn't long before the door swung open again. This time, it was a different agent, a bookish, forty-something guy in tan Dockers, notepad in hand.

He introduced himself as Agent Gonzalez.

"I need to ask you a few more questions. Is that okay?" he asked in an almost delicate tone.

I nodded.

"Can someone account for your daily whereabouts in early 1999?"

"Daily whereabouts?"

"Where you lived, where you worked, where you shopped, banked, dined, all that."

"My family. Friends. My ex-husband. Take your pick."

"Ex-husband?" he said, intrigued. "You mean Juan Cardenal?"

"No, his name is Tony. Antoine Ramonet. And I'd like to call him now. I need to find out where my son is," I said.

"They're checking with child services as we speak," Agent Gonzalez said, nodding to the mirrored glass. "Ramonet? Is that a Colombian name?"

"No. French. His number is seven six zero nine eight zero one."

"Okay. I'll give him a call."

So this was the good cop, I concluded as the mild-mannered Agent Gonzalez directed my attention to a nearby TV monitor.

"I want you to look closely," he said, clicking a remote. "There's no sound on this, but it should be self-explanatory."

On the TV screen, the woman in the photo came to motion in a dark, grainy video. She wore large, black aviator sunglasses and a clingy, mauve-toned blouse, her hair falling on her shoulders in soft waves. She seemed far less rough around the edges than she had in the still pictures. She gestured with her hands as she spoke, but not in the trashy way you might expect from a brassy redhead with cheek implants. Her hands drew graceful swirls that mirrored the smoke of her cigarette.

I have to say that for a few moments I was riveted. I had never seen a real-life drug trafficker—not that I knew of anyway. I would have imagined her to be some jagged-haired female with the angular mannerisms of a low-rent thug. But there she was, La Reina, a mysterious woman with almost feline movements. There she was in some roadside motel, captured on surveillance tape. She was all over the place—in the case files, in stakeout photographs, on video. Everywhere except where she needed to be: facing the feds in a hot northwest Miami interrogation room. No, I was there instead.

"You had her," I said.

"Pardon me?" said Agent Gonzalez.

"You had this woman. You had her and you didn't take her down. You had her on at least two different occasions, from what I can see. You had everything you needed to make your case: the suspect, the accomplice, the money, the drugs. You had it all. You had her," I said.

Agent Gonzalez glanced off.

"Tell me something," I said, "what crack investigator did you assign to this stakeout?"

He didn't answer.

"Play the video again," I said. "I want to see it one more time, frame by frame."

The agent gave me a "go ahead" nod. I took the TV remote from the table and stood up to get a better look at the monitor. I cued up the video and began to watch it again, freezing it every few seconds to study the details. A round pendant dangled on a chain around the woman's neck. It looked like a coin of some sort, but I couldn't be sure. A cigarette box sat on the nightstand—but what brand was it? I couldn't tell. An overstuffed camouflage duffel bag lay on the bed. The lanky man entered the frame, grabbed the duffel, and scolded La Reina. She got up and screamed something back. Whatever she said, it was enough to make him drop the duffel. Clearly, she was the alpha bitch of the operation.

In a strange way, I was engrossed by the silent story playing out in that roadside motel. I would have kept watching if Agent Green hadn't come in and yanked the remote from my hand.

"You're done," he said, clicking off the video. "Go sit down."

He pulled Agent Gonzalez aside and engaged him in a hushed but heated argument. Agent Gonzalez left the interrogation room. Agent Green leaned across the table and zeroed in on me.

"How long have you been running drugs for the Cardenal organization?"

"I won't even dignify that question."

"You're wasting my time, Maria," he said.

"And you're wasting mine. I've told you everything about my life already."

"If you're gonna lie, then do me a favor: Don't talk."

"Where is my son?"

"He's with DCF," he said.

"Didn't they reach my parents?" I said. "What about his father?"

"I have no idea."

"I want to make a phone call."

"When I say so."

"Then I have nothing else to say."

This triggered a standoff, a long one. In that time, Agent Green scribbled notes, copious notes. It was as if he was taking down a ten-page confession. I have to say I was more than a little perplexed. Every so often he'd look up, knot his brow, then scribble more notes. I tried to read what he was writing. Great penmanship he had, even upside down.

Finally, I made out one line: "FOCUS! FOCUS!"

A strange realization hit me—he was writing affirmations, giving himself a little pep talk on paper. I winced at the discovery: Agent Green was Mr. Motivation's clone.

"Can I borrow a pen?" I asked.

He seemed slightly hopeful that he might get a real confession out of me. He tore some pages out of his notebook and tossed me a pen.

Concealing my handwriting, I scribbled a couple of words of my own on the page. I stopped to contemplate them, their message, their proven power:

THE PORCUPINE.

I looked up from my notes and deep into Agent Green's eyes.

"All right. What do you want to know?" I asked.

"Maria Portilla. It's January eight, 1999. You are leaving the Red Roof Inn in Albuquerque, New Mexico. You are in a crappy rental car on Route 64. Where do you go?"

"Where would you like me to go?"

"You stop at La Casa del Gavilan in Cimarron," he said, pressing on. "They give you a single room. No one knows you are there, except for American Express. Where is El Flaco?"

"Where would you like El Flaco to be?"

Agent Green slammed a fist on the table. I kept my cool, even though he clearly wanted me to lose it.

"You're in deep-shit trouble. You are one very faint heartbeat away from going to jail for an extremely long time. Why don't you let that percolate for a while?"

Red-faced and livid, he motioned to the mirrored glass. Interrogation over.

The silhouettes in the mirror seemed to blur into a solitary figure, my own, moving in a damp, cavernous passageway. I was shackled again and tethered to a dozen inmates, led by one female guard and trailed by two other guards.

"We will check you at eleven, at two, and at five," the lead guard called out as we, the prisoners, shuffled in the near darkness, her words echoing through the bowels of the federal compound. "You must stand up for each check. We like to make sure you are still with us."

The human chain of inmates then disappeared through a large doorway into a processing area.

Four

PROCESSING AREA—DAY 1
A row of dressing "rooms" separated by dingy curtains. In one of them, Mary undresses.

As instructed by a female guard, I took off my nice gray skirt and seafoam top for an inspection. I could hear the grousing of the other women detainees coming from the stalls adjacent to mine.

"Two steps forward!" the guard commanded.

I stepped out of my stall into a common area, taking my place in a motley lineup of naked women. I was the only one still wearing a bra and panties, a fact that got me an irate look from the female guard.

"Get back in there," she ordered.

I ducked into the dressing area and returned naked. I tried to cover what I could with my hands. I did my best to avoid eye contact, looking down instead at those Pistol-Packin' Red toes. What a bad idea that was.

I sized up the young woman to my left: blond, all-American, probably nice girl gone astray. She had scraped knees and an ugly wound on her right thigh.

"I hear she's the touchy-touchy guard," the girl said.

Several feet away, the guard patted down an inmate, a leathery woman in her forties who seemed to know the drill: arms out. Feet apart. Bend over.

"Your clothes and valuables will be stored and given back to you upon your release," the guard announced by rote.

Soon enough, I felt the guard clasp my shoulder. My turn. Eyes closed, I followed her orders with the same detached sense of compliance I afforded my doctors. My body felt nothing. My thoughts traveled elsewhere, escaping the federal compound into the streets of Miami. And it was along those streets that Gina Torres raced through a yellow light in her red Benz convertible, on a mission to save me. She was headed to the Star Island home of Elliot Casey, criminal defense lawyer.

I didn't know this at the time, of course. I had no news about Max, my parents, Tony, or anyone else, and I was sick with worry. But thanks to Gina and her quick thinking, help was on the way. She had gone to look for me at home when I didn't show up to work or answer my phone. It was my neighbor, Dale, who told her what he had seen.

"The feds took huh," he told her in a Jersey undertone. "Drugs, I hoid."

Gina didn't believe him. She let herself into my house with her key, only to find the wreckage inside. She called the metro police, the FBI, the DEA, the U.S. marshals, the DCF, everyone she could think of, but nobody knew anything—or they weren't saying. So she telephoned Elliot Casey, the megawatt lawyer she had befriended a year earlier when she sold him a house.

"Elliot," she said, "I need a favor."

CELL BLOCK BRAVO—DAY 1
Bare walls. Bunk beds. Mary lies awake on the top bunk.

I could hear my cellmate, the girl with the nasty thigh wound, stretch out in the bunk below. Throughout the evening she had made several futile stabs at conversation. Her name was Crystal. She grew up in Jacksonville. She was allergic to peanuts. She hated cold weather. She feared the dark. She needed a shot of Jack.

I wanted no part of it.

"Hope you don't mind sleeping up there," she said in a baby-ish voice, as if she were addressing someone she was close to. "I have to sleep here 'cause of my injury."

I rolled over toward the wall and sobbed for the first time that day.

"Hey. I'm here if you wanna talk," the girl said. Her voice had the opaque tone of an alcoholic's, a low-pitched, almost drab timbre. She dragged out the ends of her sentences like those vapid girls on reality TV.

"They busted me at Tampa International," the girl went on. "It would've never happened if I was nonstop Bogotá to Miami. But my boyfriend booked me through Panama. Genius that he is. I'm the only mule he's got and he detours me through Panama. Panama! Such a loser. Glad I don't ever have to go back. If you wanna know the truth, I'd rather take a five-year plea than go back."

The girl's monotone lulled me into a calmer state.

"How old are you?" I asked her after a while.

"Twenty-one."

Moments later the guard came for me. I could make a phone call, the one I was dreading for so many reasons. She led me to a bank of phones in a hallway smudged with hand-scrawled messages and, after giving it considerable thought, I dialed my parents' number. I couldn't hear who answered the phone but the ear-piercing blast of Miami-style rap gave me a clue.

"Fatty, turn the music down," I said. "I need to talk to you."

I could imagine the scene on the other end, inside Fatty's psychedelic room. Worn satin sheets. Gold chains dangling from the bedpost along with the black beret that transformed an obese convenience store clerk named Rosendo into Fatty Guevara, flagship voice of Sin Verguenza Records. Fatty was probably sprawled on the bed, the parolee-monitoring device tight around his massive ankle, listening to his latest joint, which surely sounded like every other one of his not-very-creative rantings. My little brother, Fatty, was Miami's answer to Ol' Dirty Bastard, the late rapper who went to live at his momma's house after racking up one parole violation too many. That's Fatty, sponging off the folks so he can go lead some fictional revolution. That's his thing, the "revolutionary" fetish. That's why he wears the single-star beret and strikes a Che pose on his YouTube video, wielding the family name as if we were related to any such simpleton. But, then again, I guess it takes one poseur to inspire another.

"Listen to me. This is important," I said.

But it was too late. Fatty had dropped the phone and belted out his greatest hit: *"Ma!"*

That cry. That cry bolted down the hallway across a wall of papal memorabilia and flamenco-themed art, and it found only empty chairs and empty rooms in a virtually empty house.

Fatty picked up the phone again.

"Oh. I forgot," he said. "They're on some cruise."

"What about Max?"

"Haven't seen him."

"Listen to me. There's been a horrible mistake. I don't know what's happened, but—"

"You're in jail," he said, unfazed.

"How do you know? Never mind," I said. "I need you to get ahold of Gina."

"Gina called a little while ago," he said.

"What?" I said. I could barely hear him over the noise in his room.

"She's the one who told me you're in jail," said Fatty.

For the first time in hours, I felt the tiniest bit connected to my world.

"Good. I need you to track down Tony. His number's on the fridge. Tell him where I am. Tell him I need to see him right away," I said. "Max is with child services. Tony needs to go pick him up."

"Got it."

"This is urgent, Fatty."

"Duh."

A long, irritating blast of simulated gunfire rattled across the telephone line.

"Turn the damn music off," I said. A half second later there was silence.

"I'll call Tony. Don't worry. I got you, sis."

"What do I do about Mom and Dad?" I said, mostly to myself.

"Call 'em. They got phones on the ship. They got everything on those ships," he said.

"No, I'll wait for them to get back."

"They'll call when they get to Jamaica, or wherever they're going," said Fatty. The thought hadn't occurred to me.

"If they call, don't say anything. It's better that they don't know."

"They'll be pissed."

"They'll have a heart attack," I said. "Don't say a word."

"All right. But let me ask you something," Fatty said. He lowered his voice to a conspiratorial tone.

"Go ahead."

"What'd you do?"

"Nothing," I said. I was stunned that he would even ask. "I did nothing."

"Okay, let me help you out here. When you say that, try to sound a little more convincing."

"You think I'm guilty?"

"Nah, I'm just saying . . ."

"You think I'm a drug dealer?"

"I don't know. I mean, how many people can write a check for five grand on the spot?"

"People who work."

"Yeah. So stick with that, only don't try so hard. It makes you sound more guilty."

"Good night, Fatty," I said, hanging up the phone.

As I lay in my bunk that night, Max's voice rang in my head. In the sleepless night, it was the one thing that reminded me who I was. I tried to imagine myself in my own bed, safe in the knowledge that my son was sleeping just a few feet down the hall. I closed my eyes and pictured his bedroom. I tried to remember the titles on his bookshelf and the faces on the basketball posters hanging on his bedroom wall, and I strained to hear the soft patterns of his breathing as he slept. This is how I finally lulled myself to sleep.

But the next morning, I heard that jarring name again when the guard came around for me.

"Portilla! Visitor."

I ran a brush through my hair, smoothed the creases of my green prison jumpsuit, and went to meet my visitor. He was a distinguished man in his early sixties, salt-and-pepper hair, strong jaw, warm eyes. Elliot Casey clasped my hand in a sturdy handshake. He was the rock star defense lawyer I had seen on cable news programs, the silver fox among the overamped pundits, certainly out of my price range. If not for Gina, he might not have been there that morning. She sold him the mansion of his dreams on Star Island, and he was forever grateful. Now I was grateful to see him.

He listened intently as I recounted the details of the raid and the interrogation. He asked no questions.

"I'll do my best to get you out on bond," he said after I was done.

"Bond? I'm innocent."

"We don't have a lot of time."

"When do we go to court?"

He glanced at his watch.

"Ten minutes."

Casey must have read my exhaustion.

"Look on the bright side," he said. "At least they moved the case to your home turf, where you have a community and a standing."

"They think I'm a drug dealer from New Mexico."

Casey leafed through some of his documents.

"From Colombia, via New Mexico, via the Florida Keys. If that makes sense."

"Where do you see that?"

"Don't get too excited—it's only seven pages. Six of them are devoted to your illustrious co-conspirators."

I had no idea what he was talking about, but there was no time to ask. Casey signaled for a guard and gave my shoulder a reassuring tap.

"Come on, let's get you out of here."

* * *

There's only so much you can say in a letter to a seven-year-old boy. How do you explain that life has turned upside down, that people are accusing you of things you didn't do, that not even a judge believes you—he denied you bail and sent you back to cell block Bravo, back to the cell with a girl whose tweaker boyfriend blew a hole in her leg with a .357 Magnum? What do you say?

"Dear Max," you say, "Today I learned about codes. A code is like a hidden message that not everybody understands. It takes good eyes and a smart mind to read a code.

"Here is one for you: I love you more than anything on this earth, more than all the starfish in the sea.

"Love, Mommy."

In the blur of days that followed, I raced for my life. I hit the law library and scoured drug cases, determined to find cases similar to my own. I pestered Casey for updates. I left repeated—and unanswered—messages for Agent Green. I brainstormed with Gina in twice-daily phone sessions. But I was simply treading water. Five days had passed since my arrest and nothing seemed to change my situation. Tony was still AWOL. According to his secretary, he was on a yacht, sailing around the Greek Isles, and was last known to be docked off the beaches of Corfu, where he would spend the last few days of his vacation blissfully disconnected. My parents were still away, as their one-week cruise was drawing to a close.

But it was I who felt as if I were adrift on a boat in the middle of nowhere, cut off from the world and, most flagrantly, from Max. Casey had been able to verify that my son had been placed in a temporary foster home until his father or grandparents returned. Casey had been permitted to deliver two of my letters to Max via the young social worker, Tiffany. But Max had not been allowed to write me back. Although I heard only assurances that my boy was holding up okay—"like a little champ," the social worker told Casey—I didn't buy it. I knew my son too well. I knew he wasn't "holding up" in any way that would be considered cooperative. He was giving them hell. He was making noise. He was making demands, just like his mother would be doing in his place.

One week after my arrest, my parents returned from their cruise. Gina had waited for them at the dock when they disembarked from the *Illusion of the Seas*, and she had broken the news. Incensed, Daddy jumped into high gear.

"I need to get home. *Rapidamente*," he commanded, tossing the luggage in Gina's car. Once back home, he darted toward his bedroom closet and retrieved from the top shelf a faded pink box bearing a half-peeled beige label inscribed in a spidery hand.

DULCE MARIA, it read.

Box in hand, Daddy asked Gina to drive him to the detention center. In a rare show of machismo, he ordered my mother to stay home.

"Don't worry, I'm bringing her back home with me. In this box is all the proof they need," he told her.

Gina didn't have the heart to tell him he wouldn't be allowed to bring anything inside the visiting area, that he would be searched on his way in to see me. So when they arrived at the jail and Daddy held up the box, demanding to see the person in charge, he triggered a security alert that brought a stampede of armed guards to the reception area.

"Put the box down, sir," ordered the chief guard.

"No!" said Daddy. "This box doesn't leave my hands. It belongs to my daughter."

Gina tried to intervene, explaining to the guard that Daddy was harmless and that there was nothing illegal or explosive in the box—even though she had no idea what was actually in it—but it was too late for rational explanations. Two guards wrestled Daddy to the floor, sending the pink box flying and causing its contents to scatter all over the floor. There, atop the filthy, government-issue linoleum, lay precious relics of my childhood, all the mementos Daddy had saved since my birth. As Daddy wept, crumpled in a chair, the guards inspected each item as if they were examining a cache of stolen goods: my birth certificate, my baptismal certificate, my first baby tooth, my first pair of white knit booties, a wallet-sized photo of my first Holy Communion, all my report cards from the first through sixth grades, and a curled lock of hair tied with a yellow satin bow.

When the guards placed the final item in the box and returned the box to Daddy, he took it with a sense of vindication.

"You see, my daughter is innocent," he said.

But neither the mementos nor Daddy's good intentions would make a difference that day. By the time the security alert was canceled, visiting hours were over. Gina took Daddy back home, but she promised to deliver the box to my lawyer as evidence. Satisfied with that, he set his focus on the next mission: bringing Max home.

"I'll have him home first thing tomorrow morning," Daddy said when I spoke to him that night. My heart leaped at the thought. But I wondered why neither Casey nor Gina had mentioned it when I spoke to them earlier.

"Is there news? Did you talk to the social worker?" I asked.

"No, I left her a message. I'm going to call her again in the morning," he said with a flat confidence, a level tone that had made me feel safe as a child.

"I love you, Daddy."

"Sweet dreams, my girl."

I went back to my cot that night feeling hopeful.

But the next day, just as morning began to dissolve into afternoon, I had no news from my father. According to my mother, he had left the house early and had not returned or called. I did, however, receive a visitor. Under normal circumstances, I might have run in the opposite direction at the sight of him, for we had ended our relationship on bitter terms. But on this day, I welcomed my ex-husband as if he were some long-lost friend.

Tony, his coiffed brown curls tousled across his forehead, greeted me with what seemed to be genuine concern.

"Are you feeling okay?" he asked, pressing a manicured hand on the Plexiglas division between us. His crisp denim shirt brought out the blue of his eyes—eyes like Max's—and he seemed almost kind.

"When did you get back?" I said.

"Two days ago," he said. "I came back as soon as I heard."

"But I called your office two days ago and they said you were in Greece," I said.

"They were confused. That's not important. What's important is that Max is doing quite well," he said. "Fantastically well."

"You saw Max?"

"I picked him up yesterday," he said. "I wanted to reassure you that you don't have to worry anymore about Max. He's with me."

I wasn't too sure how I felt about the news. On one hand, I was thrilled Max was out of the foster home. On the other, I felt stung by the fact that no one had bothered to contact me, not Tony, not the social worker, and certainly not Agent Green. Besides, I didn't trust Tony. But, considering where I was at the moment, I had no choice. I had to trust him.

"Make sure he visits my parents," I said.

"Of course," said Tony.

"And, please, don't tell him where I am. Tell him what I told him in a letter: I'm working with the police on a special kind of job. I don't think he'll buy it, but it's better than telling him I'm in jail. Are you with me on this?"

"Of course, *chérie*. It's for his own good that he doesn't know. In fact, just to ensure his safety—until you are back home, of course—I'm going to the family court today."

"What do you mean you're going to family court?" I said, alarmed at the news.

"It's a very normal thing. I just filed a motion asking the family court to give me temporary custody of Max. No big worries. They will decide very soon."

I knew exactly what Tony meant by "no big worries." In that serpentine language of his it meant "Why don't you just look the other way, *chérie,* so I can do what I want?" I should have known he was up to something the minute I heard him tell the guard in the visitors' area that he would like to spend some alone time with his "lovely wife, Maria"—meaning, of course, me. It was just like him to try to schmooze and confuse his opponent before delivering the knockout punch.

"That is entirely unnecessary," I said. "You already have custody—joint custody. What is there to ask the court about?"

"I want to protect our son."

"Protect our son? From whom, Tony? Who would take him away from you?"

Tony glanced off in that way he does when he's about to say something really horrible.

"I don't know what kind of problems you're involved in," he said.

That passive-aggressive metro prick. I rapped on the glass to force him to look at me.

"The charges are bogus. You can't possibly believe this is real," I said.

"I just want to make sure," he said.

"This is basic, Tony: I'm stuck in here; you take care of Max. That's always been the deal. If one of us is somehow incapacitated, the other steps up. Basic. But here you go turning a nonissue into a damn federal case."

"I'm not the one in jail. On a federal case."

Sooner or later, without fail, Tony reveals his darker motives. And there it was. He had me where he wanted me, confined. With me out of the way, he could speed ahead to his goal, to take full custody of Max and complete his new family. His new wife, Victoria, a shrill, highly ambitious woman who favored garish pantsuits and apricot lipstick, could not have children of her own. At age forty-five, she was three years older than Tony but didn't look it at all—she looked a good twelve years older. She was the rebound love he turned to after I left him, a woman who was my opposite in every possible way. (I guess that was the point.) I was the woman he wanted to mold into his ideal Cocoplum socialite wife. She was already there, a regular on the gala circuit Tony so desperately wanted to access. She became his Svengali and her whims became his honey-do list. And, somehow, that list grew to include a ready-made family. Now the two of them were barreling ahead with their instant-family plans at my son's expense, and at mine.

"Guard," I called out, because I couldn't look at Tony another minute.

As I got up to leave, I leaned into the glass partition and narrowed my eyes on him. He shifted in his seat, coward that he was.

"Watch yourself," I said to him. "I won't be in here forever."

* * *

I called Casey as soon as I could get to a pay phone. I told him about Tony and his custody plans.

"He can't do this. We have to stop him," I said.

"I'll check in on family court. But that's secondary right now," Casey said. "We need to keep your head clear for federal court. I want you to be one hundred percent at your court appearance. Got it? There will be plenty of time to deal with everything else."

I wasn't so sure, but I decided I needed to trust my lawyer and put Tony and his schemes on the back burner. Of course that didn't mean I could not obsess over Max. My son was all I could think of as I walked the dingy courtyard during exercise hour or when I sat alone at mealtime, barely touching the food, those sandwiches of stale white bread and processed yellow cheese slices. I didn't eat because I wanted to think about Max. I didn't sleep because I wanted to think about Max. I avoided conversation because I wanted to think about Max. In the next two weeks, I came to believe that if I thought about him hard enough, he would not only know it—he would be able to hear it. I would drift into a deeply meditative state and try to send him messages in sharp telepathic bursts.

"Mommy loves you."

"Mommy will be home soon."

"Mommy sends you butterflies each time you are sad."

If Max was doing the same, I knew he must have been thinking some pretty horrendous thoughts. All I kept seeing was my son, a waif of a boy, cooped up in that Grove Isle penthouse, in a home where he was not allowed to run or scatter his toys on the mahogany floors or eat Frosted S'Mores Pop-Tarts for breakfast. I could see him peering down from the second-floor railing at that floral chintz living room, where every object had its aesthetic purpose and its place. How Max would have loved to spread out his action figures on the soft blue rug, engineer his battles and quixotic matchups from behind those perfectly fluffed sofa pillows. But instead I'm sure he stood behind that railing and watched as Victoria spent hours each night with the ladies of her politically connected coffee klatch, plotting her campaign for a seat on the county commission.

"Vote Victoria Ramonet," went her election slogan. "For leadership and family values."

FEDERAL COURTROOM—DAY 21
Mary, in her green prison jumpsuit, sits at the defendant's table beside Casey.

The judge assigned to my case had a sterling reputation. Judge Darius Rolle, veteran of the bench, was a respected civil rights pioneer, a man of few words with a keen bullshit detector. That's what I had heard about him anyway.

"In the matter of *The United States of America versus Maria G. Portilla . . .*" he began, then interrupted himself: "This is a Texas case?"

The prosecutor, a fortyish woman named Anita Butler, rose to respond. She wore a navy suit, her golden tresses tucked into a bun.

"New Mexico, Your Honor. And good morning," she said. "Assistant U.S. Attorney Butler appearing on behalf of the United States and its agency, the Drug Enforcement Administration."

"Got it. Will the defendant, Maria Portilla, please rise?" said the judge.

I had warned Casey I would no longer respond to that name, so he quickly stood up instead.

"Elliot Casey, Your Honor, for Ms. Dulce Maria Guevara Santos."

But the judge didn't catch the name discrepancy. He shot me a nasty look from the bench.

"Will Ms. Portilla please rise?" he said again.

I did not. I turned around to scan the courtroom to make my point: I, too, was looking for Ms. Maria Portilla. As I looked around the courtroom I spotted Gina, who waved a discreet hello. My parents sat next to her. A few rows behind them sat Agent Green. He would not look at me.

Casey responded again on my behalf.

"Your Honor, this is a case of mistaken identity. My client is an upstanding member of her community. She's a PTA mom. She's a successful real estate agent. She's a reputable woman who has never committed a crime. Yet she was dragged out of her house in front of her young son—in shackles, mind you—and wrongfully arrested . . ."

The prosecutor raised her hand to interrupt, but Casey steamrolled over her intentions.

". . . She is not even remotely the same woman the court is seeking," he continued. "Not only was she born in a different country—*this* country—she was born on a different day in a different year. The only thing she shares with this alleged drug queenpin is the fact that she is of Latino heritage. Pardon my candor, but it seems to me the DEA has once again suffered an unfortunate case of Hispanic Panic."

"We'll dispense with the satire," said Judge Rolle, flipping through some documents. Then he looked up and directed his words at me: "When I ask you to stand up, I'm not asking you to enter a guilty plea or an innocent plea. I'm just asking you to stand up. Understand?"

"Yes, Your Honor," I said.

"In my courtroom, everybody gets a chance to be heard. But you've got to show me some respect," he said.

The judge turned toward the prosecutor with a hard look.

"Ms. Butler, if this young lady was removed from her home as a result of yet another wrong house raid, I don't want her in my courtroom one more minute. Understand?"

"Yes, Your Honor," the prosecutor said. With a certain swagger she reached into her briefcase and fished out a document.

"We have a law enforcement officer from New Mexico who can make a positive ID," she said.

"Objection," said Casey. "About this witness, judge: Why didn't we hear about him before today?"

"Overruled," said the judge. "Check the updated list, Mr. Casey."

Apparently, the prosecution had covered its behind by filing an extensive list of potential witnesses, this law enforcement officer among them. But as luck would have it, this particular witness's flight was delayed.

"Bad weather on his layover in Dallas–Fort Worth, Your Honor," explained the prosecutor. "He should be here by two o'clock."

"We'll recess until after lunch," said the judge.

As Judge Rolle left the courtroom, I leaned over to Casey with an urgent question: "Who the hell is this witness and how can he possibly make a positive ID?"

FIVE

DURING THE BREAK, Casey and I huddled in a small conference room and lunched on take-out subs. He had no information about this witness other than the fact that he was some kind of "special crimes" investigator.

"It doesn't matter who this guy is. You're innocent," Casey said.

As we returned to the courtroom, I caught a glimpse of Agent Green talking to the prosecutor. He glanced up and finally acknowledged my presence with a nod. I nodded back as the courtroom rose for Judge Rolle's return.

"Where are we on this witness?" the judge asked, back in session.

"He screeched in just in time, Your Honor. We're ready to go," said the prosecutor, sounding pleased with herself.

"Proceed."

"The people call Special Crimes Investigator Lieutenant Earl Winrock to the stand," said Butler.

I turned to catch a look as the witness made his entrance. He was a large guy, in his early seventies, bushy mustache, ruddy cheeks. His eyes appeared bloodshot, as if he had been traveling for days. As he took the stand he surveyed the courtroom, seeming rather impressed to be there.

The prosecutor smiled at him and began her interrogation.

"Lieutenant Winrock—"

"Earl."

"Earl. Please describe your involvement with Operation Colombian Snow."

"I was lead investigator on that case for the EPD."

"Sorry, can you tell the courtroom what 'the EPD' stands for?"

"That would be the Española Police Department."

"And just recently you were visited by two federal agents regarding this case. Correct?"

"Yes, miss. They said they had some kind of fresh lead."

Winrock shifted his weight in the seat and cleared his throat.

"Thing is," he continued, "at the time of the original infraction, our two principal subjects fled to parts unknown. We set up a perimeter. But it being the rugged terrain of New Mexico, well . . . the trail got cold."

"Lieutenant Winrock—"

"And, as unfortunate timing would have it, I entered into voluntary retirement soon thereafter upon—"

"Lieutenant—"

"—at which time my superiors believed it would be best to forward the findings of the investigation thus far to our colleagues at the federal level—"

"Yes, Lieutenant, but let me ask you—"

"—being that we were no longer equipped with the investigatative expertise of my presence. And, well, a few hundred gray hairs later, here I am."

Casey and I exchanged perplexed glances: What the hell did he just say?

"Lieutenant, do you see in this courtroom the perpetrator you were seeking?" asked the prosecutor.

"Yes, miss," the witness said, nodding at me. "That would be the young lady right there."

"Are you sure?" asked Butler.

"That's the defendant, isn't it?"

Casey objected.

"That's not a positive identification, Your Honor," he said.

"Mr. Casey, you'll have your shot," said the judge.

Butler asked the judge if she could approach the witness. He obliged.

She placed a photograph in front of Winrock.

"I want you to be very sure of what you are saying," the prosecutor said. "Is this the same woman you videotaped on your stakeout during Operation Colombian Snow?"

Winrock carefully studied the picture.

"Yep."

"Let the record indicate that the witness has identified the defendant's police mug shot," the prosecutor said, placing another photo in front of the witness. "Same girl, Lieutenant?"

"You bet."

"The witness has identified a still photo from the surveillance footage. No further questions. Your witness, Mr. Casey."

Casey got up from the table but didn't begin right away. He seemed lost in thought for a long moment.

"Lieutenant, maybe you can help me understand something," he began. "Your suspect was—*is* a Colombian national, correct?"

"She is."

Casey put on his reading glasses and peered at a document from his open briefcase.

"I'm looking at a list of Colombian nationals—all Maria G. Portillas, Maria Guevaras, Maria Portillas. And variations on the theme . . ."

He handed the sheet to the witness.

"Here are their alien registration numbers."

He handed Winrock another sheet.

"Here are their corresponding fingerprints."

"I see," said the witness.

"My client is not among them. You see, she has no alien number. American-born citizens aren't assigned such numbers, as you may know in your *investigatative* capacity."

"Birth certificates can be forged, counsel," said Winrock. "People run away from who they really are—they do it all the time."

Up to then I had been the courtroom's most patient observer, but I had heard enough. Against my better judgment, I stood up.

"I didn't forge my birth certificate, sir," I said directly to the witness, sending a ripple of surprise through the courtroom.

In the hum, a voice bolted out from the audience: "How can a baby forge a birth certificate?"

Daddy. He waved an old, folded document in his hand.

"I have my daughter's birth certificate. I've had it since the day she was born. It's the same one you have there. I gave it to the lawyer. Nobody forged anything."

Judge Rolle slammed his gavel.

"You, sir, sit down," he said, pointing a finger at Daddy before turning to me. "And you, Ms. Portilla, take your seat."

"With all due respect, Your Honor, may I ask you to call me by my real name?" I said.

Judge Rolle had had enough. His eyes narrowed at me as he spoke to my lawyer.

"Mr. Casey, please explain to your client what it means to be held in contempt of court. Because I'm about ready to call it if she doesn't take her seat," he said.

Casey tried to quietly calm me. As he did, I happened to look inside his open briefcase and something in it caught my attention.

"What's that photograph over there?" I whispered to Casey.

"You mean this one?" he said, reaching for the picture.

"I have an idea," I said, leaning over and whispering the thought in his ear.

When he heard my idea, Casey beamed. He got up with a new resolve and continued his cross-examination of the witness.

"Lieutenant Winrock," he said, "you'd recognize this woman from a mile away?"

"I'll never forget her," replied the witness. "I've cracked more than a few drug cases, but I'll never forget this one."

"Why's that?" said Casey.

"Because it was owned, operated, managed, and controlled by a female. Can't ever forget that," said the witness.

"Fair enough," said Casey.

He reached into his briefcase and pulled out the photo I had seen.

"Permission to approach the witness, Your Honor," said Casey.

"Go ahead," said the judge.

Casey quite casually placed the photograph before Lieutenant Winrock.

"So this is our suspect, correct?" Casey said.

"Yes, indeed," the witness replied.

"You're positive?"

"Absolutely positive."

Casey turned to the judge with a broad grin.

"Your Honor," he said, "I'd like to enter into evidence a picture of my daughter, Sara."

"Objection, Your Honor," said the prosecutor. "Is this really necessary?"

"Overruled," said the judge. "You've got my attention, Mr. Casey. Go on."

Casey handed the witness yet another document.

"Here are some mug shots of the Colombian nationals I mentioned earlier. Recognize any of them?"

Lieutenant Earl Winrock stared at the mugs, perplexed. He looked up and pointed at me.

"I recognize her," he said.

"Clearly this witness is unable to make a coherent identification, much less a positive one," said Casey. "Therefore, I ask that these charges be dropped, so my client can go on with her life."

The prosecutor jumped to her feet.

"The people request time to review the documents presented by Mr. Casey," she said. "We'd like to conduct a fingerprint analysis."

"I'll save you the trouble, Ms. Butler," said Casey, handing a stack of documents to the court clerk. "I introduce into evidence a fingerprint analysis conducted by the chief of the immigration fraud unit, at my request. That would be your colleague in the federal ranks, Barbara Dawkins."

Butler was not amused. She asked the judge for a sidebar conference. He declined.

"Let me take a look at those," Judge Rolle told the clerk.

The clerk handed him the fingerprint analysis. The judge perused the report for a minute.

"Any of these prints match the defendant's?" he asked, scanning the fingerprint diagrams.

"No, sir," said Casey.

The prosecutor wasn't buying it.

"What about the inconclusive ones?" said Butler.

"Inconclusive is right," Casey said.

"Give me a couple of minutes," said the judge.

As the lawyers fiddled at their respective tables, Judge Rolle continued to leaf through the report, comparing diagrams and notes. After what seemed a long period of silence, he cleared his throat with a quick cough.

"Will the defendant please rise?" the judge said.

This time I obeyed him.

Judge Rolle looked directly at me with a calm, confident demeanor.

"To paraphrase Lieutenant Winrock: People do run away from who they are. They do it all the time. Identity can be a murky thing," the judge said. "They leave town. They change their names. They elope. They reinvent themselves in new cities. Some of them do it for benign reasons and others do it for entirely malicious ones. But at the end of the day, these matters of identity are never clear-cut. And perhaps because of this, I don't see the kind of irrefutable evidence I demand of a case this serious, especially in respect to the identity of this woman who stands accused before me today. I find no conclusive evidence linking this young lady to any drug trafficking ring. Therefore, I find no reason to detain her any longer."

A mix of reactions hummed across the courtroom. The prosecutor tried to protest, but the judge cut her off.

"This matter is closed," said the judge; then he turned to address me. "Ms. Portilla—"

"Guevara, Your Honor," I said, invoking a deferential tone.

"Ms. Guevara," Judge Rolle said as he cracked a smile at last. "You are free to go home, Ms. Maria Guevara."

I exhaled in disbelief. I felt as if I had been teetering on the side of a cliff, then been swept back to solid ground by a powerful gust of wind. I hugged my lawyer in gratitude.

"It was the picture of Sara, you know," he said. "That's what did it."

"Please tell Sara Casey I love her forever," I said.

"Don't worry, I will," Casey said, giving me a squeeze. "It's over. You're going home."

But as thrilling as the moment was, I couldn't shake the questions that lingered in my mind: How did things get this far? What might have happened if Casey had not pulled out that ace-card photograph from his briefcase? What could have happened if he hadn't ordered that fingerprint analysis? I shuddered at the thought that I had been this close to spending another night—or God knows how much longer—on that rank cot in cell block Bravo.

At the processing area, a guard gave me back my clothes and jewelry and directed me to a proper dressing room. As I slipped on my business clothes, I felt as if they belonged to somebody else. The skirt, a silvery gray Nanette Lepore pencil skirt I had bought myself to celebrate a big sales week, seemed two sizes too big. And the keyhole detailing on the top, once my favorite seafoam-colored pullover, sagged atop my bosom. I recognized neither the fit of the clothes nor the woman who once filled out their seams. But that was fine by me. Whoever I was now, I was out of there.

On my way out of the processing area, I bumped into Agent Green. His face lit up when he saw me, as if he had been waiting for me a long while.

"Hey. I wanted to catch you before you left," he said.

I brushed past him without a word. But he hustled after me.

"Look, there's something I want to tell you," he said, touching my elbow to slow my pace.

"The judge released me, you know," I said as I hurried to the front door.

"I just want to say we do our jobs as best we can. It's not personal," he said.

"Really. Why don't you go tell that to my son?"

Agent Green glanced away for a minute.

"For what it's worth, I'm sorry," he said.

But I wasn't in the mood for apologies or explanations. I kept on walking until I was out of that airless building and into the balmy Miami afternoon, where my parents waited by the entryway. I hugged both of them in relief.

"Go on home and rest," I told them. "I'll come see you after I pick up Max."

Nearby, in the sunlight, I spotted my driver and our getaway car. Gina waved to me from inside her red convertible. As I walked to the car, I dialed Tony's number on my cell phone, but he didn't pick up. So I texted him: "Good news: Charges were dropped. Will come by later to pick up Max. See you then."

I jumped into the convertible and gave Gina a hug.

"Come on," she said, "let's blow this taco joint."

Without saying anything more, we blazed out of the parking lot. I raised my arms and let the wind race through my fingers and press me back into the passenger seat.

We passed all the familiar streets, the usual cluttered strip malls and all those gable-roofed developments with Castilian names. We wove along blocks dotted with FOR SALE signs. I noticed there were royal poinciana trees in places I had never noticed before—they were stunning. This sweltering mess of a city never felt more like home.

Gina pulled into my driveway on Hibiscus Lane. The neighbor, Dale, was outside, smoking a cigarette. I waved hello, but he turned away and walked back toward his garage.

"You think the judge believed me?" I asked Gina before I got out of the car.

"What do you care? You're home," she said.

"I'll call you later," I said, giving Gina a hug.

"What about Max?" she said.

"I'm picking him up right after I shower," I told her.

Inside, the house was still a wreck. I could tell Daddy had come by to tidy up a little because the books were now stacked on the living room floor, the cushions were back on the sofa, and three weeks' worth of mail was piled neatly on the kitchen counter.

After a hot shower, I leafed through the mail until I came across an official-looking one. The return address on the envelope sent a wave of dread through my body.

FAMILY COURT SERVICES, it read.

When I ripped it open, my worst fears were confirmed in black and white. It was notice of a custody decision in response to my ex-husband's emergency motion. It said the judge, Miami-Dade Circuit Court Judge Jane Anne Costello, had granted Tony's request for temporary custody in my absence. And it also noted that a psychiatrist would be assigned to Max, at the request of the father.

Of all the ways my sense of freedom could be cut short, this was the worst. Tony, whose callous deeds seemed to compete with one another for Worst in Show, had outdone himself.

Bravo, Tony, I thought to myself. You finally got your wish. You got my attention.

I grabbed my keys from the kitchen counter and raced out of the house. I tore out of the driveway so quickly I nearly bulldozed the neighbor's hedges.

SIX

GROVE ISLE PENTHOUSE—DAY 21

Mary, envelope clutched in hand, knocks at the front double doors of a swanky condominium. Wearing sweatpants and a thin wife-beater T, she looks out of place in the baroque splendor of the resort residence.

When he opened the front door, Tony took a step back. I suppose he was shocked to see me in civilian clothes so soon. Although my time in detention seemed like an eternity to me, I'm sure it was not nearly long enough in Tony's mind.

"*Chérie,*" he said, holding the door tightly so it wouldn't swing open all the way.

"Where's Max?" I said, forcing the door open and letting myself in.

Tony followed as I barreled forth through the living room.

"He's at the tennis camp today," he said.

"I'd like to see him," I said. "I'd like to see him right away."

"He'll be back in a few hours. Come, let's visit for a minute or two," Tony said, clearly jangled.

He coaxed me into his office den and offered me a seat on a hard beechwood chair of Italian minimalist design. He took a seat on the far more spacious and comfortable leather sofa across from me, making sure we were separated by a safe distance and a large, round glass table with a dramatic, sculpted glass base.

"Why don't you take some time off?" he said, crossing his legs like women do.

"I'm fine. I just want to see my son," I said, trying to keep my tone level.

"So we will visit you tomorrow," he said.

"No, Tony, you won't visit me tomorrow. This little game is over now. I'm in the clear. I'm here to pick up my son and take him home. Didn't you get my message?" I said, tracking his eyes as they shifted.

"I hate to break it to you," he said smugly, "but you're not exactly in the clear."

"Really. Why don't you go ask the federal prosecutor who dropped the charges against me and the judge who released me with his deepest apologies?" I told him.

"From what I understand, that judge had his doubts," Tony came back.

"How do you know if you weren't there?" I said.

"I have my sources," he said.

Tony was clinging to whatever shred of power he had amassed on the day of our jailhouse visit. He wasn't about to let it go without a fight. And, believe me, I was ready for it.

"Do you have doubts?" I said.

"I don't know," he said.

"You can't be serious about this custody thing," I said. "The deal was, everything would go back to normal when I got out. That's what you said. And now you bring in a damn shrink?"

"Legally, I am in the right," he said. "The judge said I have custody for now. That means you have to request visitation if you want to see him."

"I expected something better from you. I expected you to show more respect for your son," I said.

But before I could say anything more, I glanced up to see Victoria had appeared at the doorway. She was wearing one of her neon-colored pantsuits and her fixed campaign smile, and she gusted into the room leaving a trail of L'Air du Temps. She made her way to the leather sofa, where she took a seat next to her husband. From there, she blew a diplomatic kiss my way.

Tony seemed newly invigorated by her presence. He took her bejeweled hand and gave it a grateful smooch.

"You see, Mary, I am thinking about Max. He has suffered a serious trauma," he said, now appearing to speak for a force greater than himself.

I tried to block out Victoria's presence and focus all my attention on Tony.

"I'll explain everything to him in due time," I said.

"Yes, but this is a process," he said, using an almost militant tone.

"The process is done. Max needs to go back to his normal life, to the way things were—"

Before I could finish my thought, I was cut off by a swift, unexpected protest.

"He doesn't want to go home," said Victoria, in a voice I can only describe as grating.

I gave her a long, cold look, but I directed my response to Tony.

"Why don't you tell the family values candidate to stay out of this?" I said.

Victoria got up and left the room without another word. Tony reddened.

"You don't come to my house, uninvited, and insult my wife," he said to me. "I want you to leave now."

Tony motioned toward the door, but I ignored him. I got up and made my way around the glass table to the sofa, until I was hovering over him, within inches of his face.

"I'll give you till tomorrow morning to bring Max to my house," I said without raising my voice.

This time, Tony didn't look away. He lifted his chin in defiance.

"Oh, my *chérie*," he said, "you'll have to ask Judge Costello about that."

Out of Tony's sight, I collapsed against the wall in the ornate corridor outside the penthouse and wept for a good twenty minutes. It had been three full weeks since I had seen my son, and I couldn't help but feel responsible for our separation. I'm the one who had agreed to our original joint custody despite my fragile relationship with Tony. I knew it could all fall apart at any moment, yet I gave Tony the power he didn't deserve. I did it because I believe a boy needs his father. But now Max was trapped, and it was my fault.

I left Grove Isle and sped off to see the one man I believed could help return my son to me.

LAW OFFICE OF ELLIOT CASEY—DAY 21
Mary enters an elegant suite overlooking the Miami River, the stately den of Miami's premier defense attorney.

I found Casey at work behind a massive antique desk piled with files. Behind him, an enormous window framed the hourly streaming of local fishing boats, feisty tugs, and Haitian freighters along the five-mile river route. I once found the river so comforting, a vigorous sign of life in full motion. But now I wondered how many of those vessels were carrying contraband, felonious merchandise hidden beneath a colorful façade of used appliances, children's bicycles, and ice chests of "fresh fish." And how many of those crusty, prototypical boat captains were in truth drug-smuggling crooks? In light of my new reality, all scenarios were possible.

"The son of a bitch got his way," I said, taking a seat across from Casey.

He looked up from his work and lifted a hand to stop me from speaking any further.

"Relax," he said. "You've been out of jail for, what—two whole hours?"

"Two and a half," I said, tossing the letter from family court on his desk. "And I came home to this."

Casey skimmed the letter and handed it back to me.

"He's just trying to rile you," he said.

"At the expense of his son," I said. "What kind of man would do that?"

"I don't know," Casey said, mulling the question for a moment. "What kind of a man is he? Tell me."

He said this with a sly lift of his voice. By his tone, I knew what kind of information he was asking for and I relished the opportunity to spill it all to him. Casey didn't want to know about Tony Ramonet's Neiman Marcus–catalog looks or the fact that he had season tickets to the Florida Opera, a favorite table at Café Abracci, a fuzzy mole just above his left nipple, and an armoire full of tennis shorts he wears too tight. He wanted ammo.

"Have I ever told you how Tony made his fortune?" I began.

Casey reached for a legal pad.

"Go for it," he said, jotting some notes. "Don't leave anything out."

I scraped together every fragment of knowledge and memory I had stored and I delivered to him the dossier of Antoine Maximilien Ramonet. I told him how Tony fancied himself a stellar financier and often told clients he had an MBA from Wharton. He liked to tell a story of how he moved to Pennsylvania with his wealthy grandfather, a French diplomat of some relevance, but fell out of favor with the Ramonet clan when he announced he wanted to stay in the United States. Disowned by his family, Tony forged ahead on his own, working odd jobs until he landed an entry-level position at a financial firm—and the rest was history, he'd say.

The story would be true except for the fact that Tony never went to Wharton, never lived in Pennsylvania, never met his diplomat grandfather, and never came from money. The truth is his parents ran a small grocery store in a suburb of Lyon, where Tony excelled at soccer, card tricks, and bookkeeping for the family store.

His "big break" came in his late twenties when his best friend asked Tony to manage his mother's finances. The woman, a dressmaker, had inherited a chunk of money from a relative but needed advice on how to invest it. She trusted Tony more than she trusted her own son, so she bought into his idea to form a business partnership. Long story short: The woman lost her business, her money, and her son's best friend. Tony fled to Miami a wealthy man.

"I found the woman's letters and confronted him," I told Casey. "That's why I left him and that's why I've never taken a penny in alimony from him."

"Can you prove any of this?" Casey asked.

"I have everything—the bank records, the financial statements, and the letters," I said.

"Did you make any of this public during your divorce?"

"No," I said. "I wanted to keep it clean for Max."

A wicked smile crossed Casey's lips.

"Well, well," he said. "It's a whole new deck of cards now."

As much as I wanted to believe him, I wasn't about to relax, not just yet. I needed to make sure Casey understood that.

"I'm determined to make this happen one way or another," I told him as I got up to leave.

But Casey had a warning for me, and he minced no words.

"I know you want to see your son," he said, "but be smart about this. Don't jump into the gutter with Tony. Don't rile him up. And that means don't go showing up at Max's school to stir things around. We'll go through the proper channels, and we will be civilized."

PALM SHORES ELEMENTARY—DAY 22

An Art Deco–style grade school on a leafy residential street. It buzzes with students in blue-and-green striped polo shirts who shuffle beneath a sign that reads SUMMER SCHOOL'S IN SESSION. *Mary sits in her parked car, observing the children.*

I couldn't wait any longer to see Max. Against Casey's advice, I drove to Max's school and waited until Tony's Lexus pulled up to the driveway. And there he was, my boy with his lopsided walk and morning hair, carrying an enormous backpack. I ran after him as soon as I saw the Lexus pull away, but I lost sight of him and had to go straight to his classroom.

At the classroom door, Max's teacher, a twenty-four-year-old woman with porcelain skin and Goth black nail polish, lit up when she saw me.

"Hey, Mary," she said. "I'll go get him."

I peered into the classroom and spotted Max settling into his desk. The teacher whispered in his ear and he jumped up to look for me. He ran into my arms and buried his head in my chest. We hugged for a long, tearful time.

"I want to go home with you, Mommy. Please take me home."

"Okay, baby, but first I want you to go back in there and have a great day at school. Will you do that for me?"

"I will for sure."

I gave him a good-bye squeeze and he ran back to his desk. Before leaving, I called the teacher over.

"How's he doing?" I asked her.

"Okay. I do my best to keep him busy," she said. "Sorry about what happened to you. We're so glad you're back."

"Listen . . . you know you can call me if anything comes up I should know about."

"Will do," she said. "By the way, that guardian's a little creepy, don't you think? Kinda reminds me of Janet Reno."

"What guardian?"

"The one appointed by the court. She's intense, like she's looking for another Elián to save."

It was a jarring piece of news for me, but I didn't want her to know it.

"How many times has she been here?"

"Twice this week. Kinda disruptive."

"I'll talk to Max's father."

I tried to hide my indignation as I blew a kiss to Max and headed back to the car. I took quick, angry steps, replaying the teacher's words in my head. A perfect stranger was stalking my child—how could that be? Thanks to Tony's request for a child psychiatrist, he had opened the door to greater scrutiny. He didn't realize that by hyping Max's "trauma" over the federal raid—and blaming me for it—he had stirred up questions in the judge's mind. She wondered why I was in jail. She noted Tony's hostility toward me predated my arrest. She wondered if his request for a child psychiatrist was a sign of Munchausen syndrome by proxy, the mental disorder that causes a parent to inflict harm on a child as a way of attracting attention. So she decided to take a closer look, and once she did, she sent the case into a bureaucratic holding pattern. Sometimes in family court, all it takes is a fleeting suspicion to lock a case into the cumbersome system. And although I didn't know it at the time, this is exactly what happened in Tony's wholly unnecessary foray into family court. He raised such a ruckus that the judge not only ordered a shrink for Max, she also appointed a guardian *ad litem* to speak for the boy. An otherwise simple custody issue had entered a *Night of the Living Dead* dimension, and it was lumbering ahead on its own phantom limbs, no longer responding to fact or reason.

As I walked to the parking lot, I dialed Casey's number, but there was no answer. So I called Gina. She was already at the office. I filled her in on what the teacher had told me. Gina was outraged.

"That's what assholes like Tony do," she said. "They have to go and piss in the kiddie pool."

"Exactly."

While I was on the phone, I passed a trio of school moms I knew from the PTA. I smiled and nodded hello. But they just sniffed at me like stuck-up sophomores. They traded looks of disgust as if someone had just stepped in dog crap.

I groaned. Gina picked up on it.

"Who'd you see?"

"Some ice-cold PTA moms."

"Say no more."

"To think I've made banana cupcakes for those witches."

"Let it go," Gina said. "By the way, Ida wants to talk to you."

"Okay. Patch me through to her," I said.

"Not on the phone," said Gina. "I think she wants to see you in person."

I drove home to change out of my sweats. I slipped into my most upbeat summer outfit, a bright green eyelet dress I hoped would mask my wretched mood. I wanted to present a cheerful, knock-'em-dead disposition at the meeting with the boss. I wanted to assure her every ounce of legal drama was now behind me, even though I knew it wasn't true. Ironically, I was about to put an Ida Miller affirmation into practice, right in her office.

"Fake it," went her favorite saying, "fake it until you can make it."

GRAND REALTY OFFICE—DAY 22
Ida Miller chats on the telephone in the exquisitely trimmed parlor that is her office. Sunlight streams in through bamboo wood slats, finding green orchids arching in robust clay pots. When she spots Mary, she hangs up and waves her in.

It was good to see Ida, strong, wonderful, optimistic Ida, the woman I credit wholeheartedly for my transformation from lost divorcée to confident businesswoman. Just stepping into her serene office brought back a cascade of dreams I had allowed myself to dream before the raid. It was a good thing I had come to see her in person, I thought, for it reinforced my identity and the gut feeling that told me this job would keep my life on track and my sanity in check.

"I'm just over-the-moon glad you're okay," Ida said, sweeping me into her arms.

"I am, too, believe me," I said as she led me through a set of French doors and into her jasmine-scented courtyard abloom with bougainvillea, bromeliads, and verdant ferns. We took seats on wrought iron patio chairs beneath a large canvas buttercream umbrella.

"What was it like?" she said. "Must've felt like hell and back."

"I'll put it this way: I'd rather sell a double-wide in Goulds than go through that again," I said.

"You poor darlin'."

"But that's history now. I'm here and I'm ready to get back to work," I said. "I've got so much to catch up on. I'm way behind on all my listings."

"I don't want you to worry about a thing. We've done our best to keep all your clients happy for you," she said, wrinkling her nose.

"I appreciate it," I said. "I'll follow up with all of them right away."

Ida's smile faded a bit as she seemed to turn a solemn thought in her head for a moment.

"There's no need to rush back, Mary," she said.

"I know. But I want to pick up where I left off. It's important that I do," I said.

Ida grew serious. She leaned over and took my hand as a mother might do.

"You've been through so much already. I would hate for you to be harassed in any way," she said. "Maybe it's better for you if you just stay off the radar for a while."

I let her words sink in. For a moment I wondered if her concern was real or merely selfish. Was *she* faking it?

"I've been off the radar for more than a month, Ida," I said.

She pulled her hand away and stiffened a bit.

"We've gotten some press calls about you," she said.

"What kind of press calls?" I said.

She hesitated, then stood up.

"Come," she said, extending an arm toward the French doors, "I'll show you."

Back inside her office, Ida picked up a manila folder from her desk and handed it to me. Inside, I found a copy of that morning's *Daily Press.*

"It's the first story below the fold," she said.

When I flipped the paper over and read the headline, I was floored. It read REALTOR RELEASED, BUT EVIDENCE MURKY, FEDS SAY.

The story went on to suggest I had been released on a mere technicality and that—I'm paraphrasing here—no one in their right mind believed I was innocent. Supporting this slanderous implication were quotes from unnamed federal sources, a PTA mom—anonymous, mind you—and, of course, my son's father.

"The well-respected financier Antoine Ramonet, who shares a young son with Guevara, said he was concerned by what he described as erratic changes in his ex-wife's behavior," read the story.

Who spoke for me? According to the story, "neither Guevara's lawyer nor her family could be reached for comment." They did manage to interview my neighbor, Dale, who said, "I didn't know her very well. She always kept to herself."

I looked at Ida for a sign of indignation at the sensationalistic piece, but instead I got a most gentle, blank stare.

"There's nothing murky about my situation," I said, the anger in my voice rising. "You have to believe that."

Ida shook her head and took a step back toward her desk.

"I think you should stay off the radar a little while. It's just better for everyone involved," she said, giving my forearm a pat.

I got it. Her gracious delivery aside, Ida's words meant those lovely, carved-wood antique doors of hers were closing ever so graciously in my face.

"I understand," I said. "I'll make sure to thank everyone on my way out for picking up my slack."

"Oh, yes," Ida said, her smile clicking on once again. "Do thank Brian. He's been picking up most of your old leads."

Karma came wrapped in the scent of jasmine that day, I realized. Would things have played out differently if I had resisted the Glades Terrace lead, if I had displayed a tad more humility, if I had not trivialized Brian in my head as some pathetic cuckold? I would never know that. But I did know this: No matter how overconfident or even zealous I might have been in my days as a revved-up real estate agent, I had never sold cocaine, never trafficked cocaine, never touched cocaine. I had never been to New Mexico, never met a guy named El Flaco, and never had a stitch of plastic surgery. And my name was never, *never* Maria Portilla. So if indeed karma had boomeranged into my life to make some thunderous declaration, it needed to pick up line three and listen to this message from me: Take a number, karma. And while you're at it, there's a French poseur in Grove Isle you ought to visit.

When I left Ida's office, I stopped at my desk to gather my things. I packed my most important files, my contact lists, and my personal photographs into a crate, and without a word to anyone, I walked out of Grand Realty.

Gina, alarmed, raced after me.

"What the hell's going on?" she said, catching me as I headed for the parking lot. "What happened in there?"

I couldn't stop, not even for Gina. If I stopped, I would break down. I knew this about myself. So when I reached my car, I dumped the crate into the back seat and fumbled for my keys in angry silence.

"Will you wait for one second, please?" Gina said, swiping the keys out of my hand and giving me a good shake. "What's going on with you?"

"Did you see the paper today?" I said.

"Yeah. Obits sucked today," she said.

"Not the obits, the front page. Did you see the front-page story?"

"You mean the one about your case? Yeah. What about it?" said Gina, as if I had asked her if she had read Walter Mercado's prediction for Scorpios that day.

"It was full of lies," I said.

"So, who cares?" she said.

"What do you mean, 'Who cares?' "

"Nobody believes that newspaper anyway," she said.

But Gina, who knew me better than anyone else, realized it would take more than that to settle me down. She knew I wasn't about to take a smear of this magnitude without a fight. She knew I would accept nothing less than full-on clarity. She grabbed her cell phone and made a call: "Can you meet us in the Grove?"

CLUB HAVANA—DAY 22

A bustling outdoor café beneath cream-white umbrellas. Mary and Gina are seated at a table, sipping espressos. Casey joins them.

Casey, perhaps the most widely quoted legal eagle in Miami, rarely read the newspaper. He preferred to spend the time biking across the MacArthur Causeway into South Beach for a daily run along the ocean or stretching out his sore limbs in the eucalyptus-scented mist of his steam room. His morning headlines, research, and need-to-know bulletins were meticulously gathered, printed out, and delivered promptly at seven A.M. each day by his long-time assistant, Joy Ellen.

That morning, for reasons that weren't immediately clear, she had omitted the front-page story about our hearing. So Casey got his first look at the hatchet job when I unfolded the paper on the café table and read the headline aloud to him.

" 'Realtor released, but evidence murky, feds say.' Can you believe this load of crap?" I said.

Casey glanced at the story and folded up the paper again with a tepid gesture. He called over a waitress and ordered an iced green tea.

"So that's what she's so worked up about?" he asked Gina with a wink.

"Why shouldn't I be worked up about it?" I said.

"Because it's just a story, a badly reported story by one of the hack stragglers left over at the *Daily Press*. Big deal. It doesn't change the most important fact—that you are a free woman," he said.

"It is a big deal to me. 'Murky' is not good enough to bring back my life. 'Murky' is the reason my son is living away from me. 'Murky' got me canned this morning. 'Murky' is too damn murky for me," I said.

"You got canned this morning?" Gina said, dropping a spoon into her demitasse.

"Pretty much, yes," I said. "But it all goes to a larger point: Where does all the murk end?"

Casey listened as I complained about the child psychiatrist and the court-appointed guardian shadowing Max.

"How do we get rid of them?" I asked him.

"Relax. We've got a hearing at the end of the week. We're asking the judge to close this case and reinstate the original custody agreement," he said.

"Somehow I'm not encouraged," I said.

"You should be. You've done nothing wrong," he said.

"Yet there's a 'murky' cloud above my head," I said.

Casey laughed and took a swig of his iced tea.

"The hell with that. You're innocent and you're home. That alone has changed the scenario," he said. "Matter of fact, I wouldn't be surprised if the judge opens a can of whup-ass on your ex for adding to the hoopla."

Casey's projections eased my mind. For about five minutes, that is. My peace of mind shattered when Gina let out a blood-curdling shriek.

"Look at the picture on that bus!" she said.

I turned around in time to see the Metrobus come to a labored stop at the red light, its entire side emblazoned with the Picture. At first I saw it in disjointed, Picasso-like sections: frightful face. Huge teeth. Bejeweled hands. Put it all together and it was a patriotic-themed family portrait with one Victoria Ramonet smack in the middle of it. There she was with her husband and son, all in matching red, white, and blue outfits. Except the boy in the picture wasn't her son—he was my son. There was Max, campaign prop. And there was that slogan: "Victoria Ramonet. For the good of our children."

"That woman must have a penis," said Gina.

I grabbed my phone.

"It ends right now," I said, dialing Tony's number.

Casey nudged my arm.

"Put it away," he said.

"She has to steal my child to get votes?" I said. "How can Tony allow this?"

"Because he can," Casey said. "Tony is your son's father, bio-logical and custodial. You know what that means? It means he can put his son on the side of the Goodyear blimp if he wants to."

"But I'm Max's mother. Don't I have a say?"

"Yes, but that doesn't mean you rumble in the street over a sign on a damn bus. Mary, think. You're not just dealing with your ex-husband; you're dealing with a clunky, highly subjective system. The system doesn't care about campaign signs. You have to be smart about this. If you jump into the gutter with Tony, he wins. You prove him right. And you'll never get Max out of family court."

I let Casey's advice sink in with a swig of cold coffee. The midday sun glinted off the passing cars and lit up the sidewalk and all its passing stories. How many of them were true? I wondered. In a few hours, the entire block would be awash in patches of shadows. But now there was only searing sun.

Perhaps it was the relentless light that brought me to the dizzying realization that would change my quest for justice in the most radical way.

"It's all because of her," I said.

"Who?" said Gina. "Dickhead's wife?"

"No. The other Maria," I said. "Maria Portilla."

"What do you mean?" said Casey.

"Thanks to her, there will always be a cloud of suspicion over me," I said. "People will always think I'm a criminal."

"Does it matter what people think?" he said.

"Yes, it absolutely does," I said.

Gina leaned over and pinched the tip of my chin.

"You have a great life. You have an amazing son, a good house, a nutty but lovable family. You've got kick-ass real estate skills," she said. "Forget everything else. Just go home and handle your business."

"Home? There is no home anymore," I said. "I know more about that other Mary than I do about myself right now. As long as she's out there on the run, there always will be doubt about me. Tell me I'm wrong."

Casey took a deep breath and abruptly exhaled. In his eyes I saw a look, a flash of frustration, I had not seen before.

"No," he said, "you're not wrong."

* * *

Three days later, I faced Tony in family court. I walked into the courtroom feeling confident that I had enough reason and evidence to bring Max home. I was mistaken.

I had given Casey everything I had—Tony's financial records, the letters from France, even a fax from Wharton admissions officers certifying that no one named Antoine Ramonet had ever attended their school. Casey also had managed to get a rare statement from the feds in the form of the following memorandum:

TO: Dulce Maria Guevara, fed. ID-12618
FROM: Spec. Agt. Daniel Green, DEA
SUBJECT: Clearance

A review has been made in the case involving you, Dulce Maria Guevara. Based on an investigation of the facts, no evidence can be found to sustain the charges of conspiracy to distribute cocaine and possession with intent to distribute cocaine. You are cleared of any wrongdoing in this matter. This case is closed as it pertains to you.

But we never got the chance to present any of our evidence.

The guardian *ad litem* delivered a rambling report about how Max was beginning to "thrive" in his new environment. He had developed a formidable backhand in tennis and had expanded his French vocabulary, she said. It was too soon to subject the boy to another abrupt change, she said.

Despite repeated objections from my lawyer, the judge, a fellow traveler in the extreme wing of the child welfare system, agreed with the guardian. And when the court-appointed psychiatrist reported that Max was having nightmares about the federal raid, Judge Jane Anne Costello decided the boy should not be placed in a situation where he could relive the trauma. In other words, he could not come home, at least not until the psychiatrist said it was okay. Even worse, the judge decided it was best that I limit my visits with Max to once a week and that our visits would be supervised closely by the guardian *ad litem.*

"We'll monitor this case for a few more weeks, and we'll see where we go from there," the judge concluded as she set another hearing for thirty days later. She then scheduled my first visit with Max in ten days.

"This is preposterous, Your Honor. My client expected to see her son today," Casey objected.

"She'll have to be patient," said the judge, turning to speak directly to me. "He's having nightmares, Ms. Guevara. Let's give him a chance to work things out with his therapist."

"Max doesn't need a therapist," I said, rising to my feet. "He needs his mom. He needs his bed and his toys. He needs to be home."

"He does," said the judge, putting on an air of gravitas. "But let's do this the right way."

"You mean, let's do this your way," I said, prompting Casey, who was standing at my side, to give my arm a nudge.

"She doesn't mean that, Your Honor," he said, although I could tell he agreed with me.

Judge Costello fired an icy look at me. The particular setting of Miami's family court, somewhat more relaxed than its federal counterpart, allowed for more casual banter. In this spirit, Judge Costello bypassed formalities and spoke directly to me.

"According to his psychiatrist, the boy is afraid there will be another incident in your home. He's afraid you—and, by proxy, he—may be in some kind of danger. He doesn't fully understand what it is you do for a living, so he's dealing with a lot of mystery and fuzziness in his life. I'm sure you can understand this," said the judge.

"With all due respect, my son knows exactly what I do for a living. There is no mystery between us. You are way out of line in suggesting otherwise," I said, my voice rising in anger.

"He's afraid. He doesn't feel safe with you at home. And, quite frankly, I don't blame him," said the judge.

"Well, Your Honor, had you seen fit to examine the evidence we brought today, you might have known his fears are unfounded. Now that I've been cleared of any wrongdoing, there is neither danger nor fuzziness in my life. I'm sure you can understand this," I said.

"I'll make sure to note your tone, Ms. Guevara," said the judge with a slam of the gavel. "This hearing has concluded."

I didn't say a word. I didn't cry. I stared into a distance that held a disturbing, unacceptable scenario, one of protracted warfare with Tony and labyrinths yet to be traveled in family court. At the root of it all was the lingering doubt over my true identity. The judge herself inferred so in her babblings from the bench. "I don't blame him," she said of my son's supposed fear of my "mysterious" life and "fuzzy" alliances. Euphemisms. I knew what she meant to say—she meant to say I was unreliable and possibly corrupt. The way I saw it, I had only two options:

One, I could blackmail Tony with the proof of his theft and deceit. The ethics charges could derail his wife's political ambitions. He would be forced to return Max to me. But that scenario had its risks. Tony could drum up competing evidence from his shady financier sources and kick up enough dust to keep himself in the game. Such a scenario could drag on much longer than our case in family court.

Two, I could attack the disease at its root and be done with it once and for all. I could go find Maria Portilla.

SEVEN

I WENT BACK to Casey's office and photocopied the entire case file, including transcripts and pictures. I went across the street to the clerk of the court's division and researched all cases involving Portilla's coconspirators. As I found document after document, I felt something long dormant awaken inside me, an old streak of curiosity I once considered to be my greatest childhood asset. I was the girl who wanted to grow up to be a detective. I had questions about everything: Why can't chickens fly? What makes air conditioners cool? If the Easter Bunny really exists, why don't the Cubans in my family even know about him? As years passed, that curious streak faded as something else, something far more pragmatic, took its place, a blind drive to succeed. I came to think success—in school, in business, in relationships—was about well-tested formulas and proven models, not far-flung questions. Too many questions, I came to believe, were nothing but deflections and excuses in disguise, the last resort of the unprepared and of quintessential procrastinators. If you had to ask, it meant you didn't do your homework. So I sharpened my life's focus into that one brilliant Nike slogan. No questions. No curiosity. No nonsense. *Just do it*. But that day, as I stood at the counter in the clerk of the court's office, I let the questions stream into my head, first as a trickle, then a torrent. I paid $137.50 in copying fees and lugged the box of documents back to Casey's office.

I got there as he was winding down from a long day. He poured a couple of glasses of Bacardi 8. The amber liquid mirrored the sunset outside his window.

"Got what you needed?" he said, swirling the rum in his glass.

"Probably not. I'll know when I read all this crap," I said, glancing out the window just as an overloaded freighter churned across the Miami River with its mysteries. "But I know what's not in here, and I'm hoping there's still a way I can get it today."

"Can I help?" said Casey.

"As a matter of fact, yes," I said, pulling a handwritten list from my paper stack. "My wish list. Don't worry, it's short."

Casey scanned the five items on the list, checking them off aloud: "Yes on the first, third, and fifth—I've got some background on those in my files. No on the second item—I've got nothing on that. And about number four, tell me you're kidding."

"I know it may require a small favor or two, but I figure, you know, you're a connected guy. Doesn't hurt to ask," I said.

Casey cocked his head in disbelief and thought about my request for a long minute.

"You'll owe me big after this," he said, only half joking.

He clicked a few keys on his laptop and scrolled through his contact logs before picking up the telephone and making a call, all the while shaking his head at me.

"Elaine, my love," he said into the telephone receiver as he reached for his monogrammed notepad, "I need a very strange favor."

When I got home, I found my parents had descended on my house. It was their first real visit since my release from jail. Daddy was outside, sweeping the driveway. My mother was in the kitchen, cooking up a storm. She had roasted a perfect tenderloin of lime-marinated pork, steamed and fluffed a pot of white rice, boiled and mashed some green plantains, then drizzled them with a warm mojo of olive oil and smashed garlic. She sliced ripe tomatoes she had bought at the U-Pick field and put them atop a bed of thinly shaved white onions. And for dessert, cream cheese flan in a guava reduction.

I had not seen such a feast in years, since the days when Puddle Morales, Daddy's childhood friend, took up the habit of spending Sunday afternoons at my parents' house and bringing with him a collection of sing-along-worthy records—Armando Manzanero, Ñico Membiela, and, of course, Aznavour.

"What's the occasion, Mami?" I said, dropping the box of documents on the kitchen counter.

"You're anorexic. That's the occasion," she said.

"That skinny, huh?"

"You're a broomstick. But give me a week—you'll be back to life," she said.

My mother seemed uncharacteristically energized and, I must note, profoundly concerned about my health and emotional well-being. She had purchased candles bearing the likeness of the Virgin of Charity and placed them in strategic places, the way one places roach motels in the darkest, most vulnerable corners of the house. She had tidied up Max's room, washed all his clothes, and set his pajamas atop the bed as if he would be coming home to sleep that very night. She gazed at me in a way she hadn't done in a long time, not since I suffered a two-month bout with anemia at age thirteen. In that gaze was a mix of love and pity, my mother's purest state. It dawned on me that she was at her best in rescue mode. And in retrospect, it made perfect sense. She and my father had survived a harrowing sea voyage from Cuba during which their boat, a thirty-five-foot shrimper packed with forty-one refugees, ran out of fuel and drifted for nearly a week. My mother watched two women die of dehydration. She tried to save them by dragging them into a shady spot on the deck, but it was no use. The youngest one died in her arms. The incident turned my mother into a breathless rescuer. She gravitated toward needy strays and vulnerable people and kept a cool distance from strong, independent types, like me. But now that I had fallen, I was worthy of my mother's most precious gift, her empathy. I would be lying if I said I didn't welcome the maternal affection or the Cuban calories. All the questions? I could have done without those. No sooner had Lilia carved the pork than she started the interrogation.

"What did they do to you in jail?" she said.

"Nothing," I said. "What do you mean?"

"I mean, did the guards bother you?" said Lilia.

"Not really. They left me in the cell most of the time. They called me whenever I had a visitor or when it was time to go exercise. It was fine, really," I said. I smiled at her, hoping to redirect the conversation. I glanced over at Daddy—he was wolfing down his pork, paying no mind to our chatter. "What about the cruise? Did you guys have a great time?"

Lilia watched as I served myself an extra-large scoop of rice, another big helping of plantains, a chunk of pork, and some tomatoes.

"They starved you, didn't they?" she said.

"Nobody starved me. They had food. Not great food, but not horrible, either. Like the kind of food they serve at the cafeteria on Forty-ninth Street," I said. "So. Did you go dancing?"

"I like the hot turkey at the cafeteria," she said. She seemed to drift off for a minute. "Did you have to shower in front of everybody?"

"No, of course not. I had a private shower in my cell," I said. I wondered if she believed me. I wasn't about to tell her bathroom privacy was as scarce as a good, hot turkey meal in jail. "Did they have blackjack at the casino?"

Daddy looked up from his plate at the mention of blackjack. He gave me a sly wink before digging into his dinner again. Lilia didn't notice. She seemed preoccupied with her next question.

"Did they give you drugs?" she said.

"Drugs?"

"To make you talk. Did they give you drugs?" she said.

"No drugs, Mami."

It took a little coaxing, but I did get her to talk about the cruise. She described the floor shows as the grandest she had seen in decades. She admitted she had indulged in a few piña coladas at the cruise line's private beach. She even copped to skipping out on the post-prayer coffee-and-pastries hour to meet Daddy at the casino. And when she said this, Daddy lit up.

"I think your mother has a new addiction," he said.

I thanked my parents for their company and support and sent them home with a bag of key limes from my backyard tree. After dinner, I spread the box of documents on the living room floor, and I got to work.

I read all about La Reina and her lethal crew, agents of the notorious Cardenal drug cartel. Their rap sheets appeared to be intertwining rosaries of escalating charges: drug smuggling, grand theft, racketeering, aggravated assault, attempted kidnapping, and even homicide.

Maria Portilla herself was a puzzle. The files gave me little more than what I had learned about her during my DEA interrogation and court appearances. Of her four coconspirators listed in the documents, three were dead and the fourth one, a cocaine dealer named Francisco Jose Cardenal, still roamed at large. But the file on him was thin. It revealed nothing about his background, his criminal history, or his blood ties to the Cardenal clan. It simply listed his approximate age—about thirty-eight—and the drug trafficking, sale, and distribution charges against him. Who was this guy? I knew he couldn't be the kingpin.

In my courthouse research and online archive search, I learned the family kingpin, Juan Cardenal, had been missing for more than a decade and was presumed dead. I could find no information about his life, death, or unresolved charges, for it was sealed inside classified federal files. If Juan Cardenal was alive, he would be seventy-three years old, some thirty to thirty-five years older than Francisco Jose Cardenal.

I reread the charge sheet on the younger Cardenal twice, searching for some kind of clue, but it was thinner than the one on La Reina. And I was too tired to read it again. I gathered the documents from the floor and as I dumped them back in the box, a scrap of paper fluttered out of the pile. It was the information Casey had jotted for me on his monogrammed notepad. I picked it up and tucked it into my handbag.

Exhausted, I went upstairs to shower and get ready for bed. But as I passed Max's room, I felt a sad tug in my belly. After hours of research, I felt no closer to our reunification and I felt it was partly my fault. All my probing had yielded more questions than answers. I had failed my boy. I couldn't go to bed on that feeling.

I took a shower and foraged through my closet, searching

for a particular kind of outfit. I found it tucked behind my work
suits, my evening dresses, and my PTA jeans: a black, clingy slit
skirt and a black, low-cut silk top. I slipped on my strappy, black
satin, red-soled, 4 7/8-inch Christian Louboutin heels and brushed
my hair to a shiny, straight finish, letting it tumble loose around
my shoulders.

Then I called Gina with an offer.

"Are you up for a drive?"

MIAMI STREETS—DAY 25
Mary and Gina, all dressed up, speed along in Gina's
convertible.

We trailed Yellow Cab no. 0524 from the Flamingo Motel through
a patch of Little Havana and into the derelict fringes of the city.
We came to a stop outside a nightclub where the taxi dropped off
its passenger. We waited for him to disappear through the black
doors of the club, beneath a violet flash of neon:

CLUB IMAGINATION.

I glanced over at Gina, who was brushing on some mascara.

"Please remind me why I'm here," I said.

"You're not," she said. "Someone far more adventurous, daring, and slutty than you is here. You're off the radar, remember?"

I slicked on some ruby lipstick and followed Gina into the
scarlet haze of the club. Across waves of thumping bass, I spotted
the object of our pursuit. He stood, whiskey in hand, near the
stage, watching a raven-haired beauty in a G-string and seven-
inch Lucite heels shimmy out of a red satin bustier. He tossed
fistfuls of dollar bills at her feet. More than two thousand miles
from his desert home, Earl Winrock was making it rain at Club
Imagination. He had stayed in town, hoping to make the most of

his first trip to Florida, and there he was, clearly off the beaten path, watching the natives go buck wild. This wasn't one of those fancy strip joints with marquee dancers, pay-per-view boxing, and muscle-bound security. It was a dump.

The stripper, a strikingly lovely Latina, finished her number, scooped up her loot, and gave the big spender a come-hither look. When he bellied up to the foot of the stage, she whispered something into his ear.

"What foul thoughts do you suppose she's conjuring?" I asked Gina.

"A private dance for the big guy?" she said.

"Nice visual, G."

"He likes her. Then again, he gets his girls mixed up," she said.

A thought flashed between us as we watched the girl disappear through the curtains leading backstage.

"Let's go get him thoroughly confused," I said.

We staked out the side stage door until the girl reappeared, refreshed and ready for a romp in the back room. I stopped her before she headed back to Winrock.

"You know that gentleman you were just dancing for . . . ," I said to her. "He's a friend of ours. We'd love to buy him a special birthday dance."

The girl was intrigued and more than willing to take requests for $200 an hour. So I told her exactly what I wanted her to do.

Moments later, she slithered around in a private room as Winrock watched from a velour sofa. Gina and I watched, too, from the hallway, through a slit in the curtains.

"I'll be right back," the girl said to her customer.

"Where you going, pumpkin?" he said.

She blew him a kiss and disappeared through the curtains. The next thing he saw was a tanned, shapely leg peeking through.

"That's right, baby," he said, squirming in his seat. "Come on in."

And she did. The dancer slinked in wearing a red strapless dress and skinny heels. But it wasn't the girl—it was Gina.

"Let me have that pretty dress," said the customer.

"Not yet. This is a special kind of dance. You go first," Gina said.

Winrock seemed confused but eager to play along. He unbuttoned his shirt and dropped his pants.

"Come on, dance with me," Gina said.

"I'm not much of a dancer," he said.

"It doesn't matter. Nobody else is here," she said. "Just me and my girlfriends."

"Where the heck are they?"

Gina called out to the hallway and the stripper came back inside. I followed.

Winrock looked straight at me and didn't recognize me. But I didn't feel invisible, not the way I had in the courtroom as I listened to his testimony. This time, I was in control of the situation.

"Come on, big guy, boogie down," Gina said to him.

And the good lieutenant danced with abandon as we formed a merry circle around him. Gina shimmied down to the floor and scooped up his clothes. Out of his sight, she shoved them behind the curtain.

"Nice moves, Lieutenant," I said.

"Thank you, doll," he said, perplexed. He looked at me as if trying to place my face. "How'd you know I was a lieutenant?"

"Wild guess," I said.

"Wild is right. Why don't you and I get wild together?" he said.

"I think not," I said, nudging him onto the sofa. "Sit down. Party's over."

"Do I know you?"

"I look a little different in my prison jumpsuit," I said.

"You. Are you stalking me?"

"No, just here to have a conversation," I said, giving Gina a nod. She motioned the stripper to follow her to a corner loveseat, where they would cool their heels for a while. "I have some questions about the case."

"Right now?" said Winrock as he tried clumsily to get up from the sofa.

"Who is Francisco Cardenal?" I said, pushing him back down.

"I have no idea. Where'd my dancer go?" he said, searching the musky darkness.

"I'm the only dancer you have right now, so settle down," I said.

"What do you want from me?" he said.

"I want names, places, every detail you remember. I've reserved this room for as long as it takes. I have all night," I said. "And you have no clothes."

Fast-forward to one hour later and there was Gina, lounging in the corner, trading beauty tips with the stripper. (Stripper: "They call it J.Lo in a bottle 'cause it gives you this bronzy glow.") And I was finally getting somewhere with Winrock. He had remembered the feds had shared with him some Colombian police audiotapes of conversations between La Reina and one of the Cardenals. According to a DEA interpreter, they were heard discussing contacts, drop locations, and delivery dates. But when one of their key associates was arrested on a traffic violation in New Mexico, the associate, a Florida resident mentioned in the conversation, swore to police interrogators that his friends were discussing the sale of soccer merchandise, not cocaine.

"You remember the guy's name?" I asked Winrock.

"Nope. But he had a crap-load of money on him. About a hundred and twenty K," he said, swigging his whiskey.

"What was his name—try to remember," I said.

"It's on the tip of my tongue, but I can't recall."

"Think."

"Jimmy what's-his-face," he said.

"Come on . . ."

"Jimmy Paz. That's it. Jimmy Paz," he said, surprising himself.

Jimmy Paz was a notorious name in Miami. But I hadn't heard it in years, and I didn't see him mentioned anywhere in the documents.

"So why wasn't he in the indictment?" I said.

"He got a deal, I think," said Winrock.

"What kind of a deal? What do you remember?" I said.

"Don't remember anything more," he said. "Now can you please leave me alone?"

With that, Gina and I left Winrock in the company of his sultry Latina, who still had a good twenty minutes left on her dance card, more than that bungling lump ever deserved.

At the end of the night, Gina and I shared a bottle of wine on the beach, just like we used to when we were in college. We lounged on wooden chaises at the edge of an inky, luminous ocean, recounting the events of the past few hours.

"Jimmy Paz. Everybody's favorite gangster," Gina said.

"Never had the pleasure—too many degrees of separation," I said.

"Maybe not," said Gina. "You know someone who knows him."

I had no idea what she was talking about, but I was sure she was wrong. I bet not even my delinquent brother knew him. Jimmy Paz existed in a realm apart from your average delinquent.

"Who are you talking about?" I said.

But then I knew. It was something we no longer talked about, something I had tried to bury years earlier.

"I'm not going there," I said.

"That's who you need to talk to."

"I can't. The world can't be this upside down."

"Isn't it worth a try?" said Gina, grabbing her purse from the sand and putting it on the chaise. It was bursting at the seams. "It's okay to look back sometimes. For clarity, you know."

"What the hell's in that purse?"

Gina opened the bag and pulled out a crumpled pair of John Henry gabardines. She balled them up and ran barefoot toward the water. I watched her splash along the shore and throw Winrock's pants into the ocean, an offering to the gods of fresh beginnings.

RAPTURE LOUNGE—DAY 26
A dive bar in an industrial corner of town.

I heard the song before I reached the front door. It wafted through the parking lot in front of the place I had vowed never to enter again.

"I'm an ever-rolling wheel/without a destination real . . ."

I should have taken it as an omen to turn around and drive away. But instead I followed it inside, where on a small stage a not-very-convincing drag queen sang in a stunning, crystalline voice:

"You got me going in circles/oh, around and around I go . . ."

I took the only seat I could find at the bar, next to a middle-aged couple locked in a graphic kiss. A group of young toughs played a rowdy game of pool as their overly primped girlfriends drank pink wine. As I watched them, I felt a tap on my shoulder. It was Eddie, the bartender, leaning across the bar for a hello kiss.

"Hey, beautiful," he said. "Seen Joe yet?"

"Is he around?"

"Give me a minute," he said as a cocktail girl approached with an empty tray.

The girl ordered two Chivases on the rocks. Eddie filled her order, sending her back to the employees-only area in the rear of the building. I should have left then.

"He'll be out in a minute," said the bartender. "What'cha drinking these days?"

"I'll take a mango sour," I said.

"The Dulce Maria special," he said with a wink. "Coming right up."

The reference took me back to a time I hadn't thought about in years. I tried not to dwell on the memories as I watched Eddie squeeze a couple of key limes into a glass; sprinkle the juice with three spoonfuls of sugar; add a good splash of vodka, ice, and a little bit of mango juice; and give it all a good shake.

"Here you go," said Eddie, placing a chilled, sugar-rimmed tumbler before me with flair and pouring into it the sheer mango-lime cocktail.

"Thanks, honey," I said, taking a sip.

I waited through a stream of hopeless love songs. After a while, the cocktail girl reappeared, empty glasses on the tray, her blouse slightly askew.

"You can go on back," the bartender said.

At the end of a narrow hallway, I found Joe Pratts in a Cohiba haze, tallying the day's numbers in his cramped back office. I almost didn't recognize him because he seemed haggard and unkempt, nothing like the boy once voted "Most Handsome" at

Hialeah High. Then he glanced up and I remembered his eyes, soulful, deep café eyes.

"So what brings you around?" he said in a hardened tone I didn't recognize. He was annoyed to see me, I could tell.

"Been a long time," I said.

"Has it?"

His words hung in an awkward silence. I sat down across from him. He put aside his work.

"I read about what happened to you," he said. "They picked up the wrong Maria, huh?"

"I need to find the right one."

"Why are you here?"

"I thought maybe you'd know some people," I said. I pulled out a list of names from my purse.

"I don't know anybody."

He leaned back into the torn leather cushion of his swivel chair and laced his fingers behind his neck in an uneasy stretch. He seemed exhausted, like a man who hadn't slept in days. The angled light of his desk lamp revealed a thin, faded scar just above his left eyebrow, remnant of a time I wanted to forget. He volunteered nothing else, not even a shrug of feigned concern. He left it to me to break the silence.

"You're the last person in the world I want to ask for help," I said. "But I don't know where else to go."

He thought about it for a minute.

"Some people go to church. Why don't you go to church?" he said.

"I have some names," I said. I handed him the list. "I don't know what that'll get me, but I have to try."

"Why?" he said.

"Because I need to get my life back," I said.

"Which life, Mary?" he said.

I walked right into that one, but I ignored the innuendo.

"I've lost custody of my son," I said.

Joe hated me for being there. He hated it because even now, ten years after we split up, he still couldn't say no to me.

"I'm sorry to hear that," he said. He hunched forward to rest his elbows on the desk. He glanced at the names on the list and seemed to stop at one. "Why don't you leave this with me. I'll call you."

I didn't stick around long enough to make real conversation. Part of me hoped he'd toss those names in the trash and forget he ever saw me.

EIGHT

THE MINUTE I got home, I realized I had made a terrible mistake. There, surrounded by the tangible evidence of my life with Max, my life as a single mother, a businesswoman with a solid plan, I knew I had done something potentially lethal. I had looked back.

I had always believed that one day I could do such a thing. I would be deep into a new life, a sound and successful life, and it would be okay to take a glance. It would be like peering at a brushfire from atop a plateau, where I could safely contemplate the flames with appropriate curiosity. But it only took one glance at Joe to let me know that day had not yet come. Why had I gone there? It was the last thing I needed as I struggled to recognize myself, the person I had worked diligently to become. It was hard enough to recognize myself without Max in the house, without my work routine, without all those well-made plans that once filled the pages of my agenda. Who needed the phantom of a chaotic love?

I spent the next two days burrowed in the Spider-Man sheets of Max's bed. I kept myself locked in a Benadryl-induced slumber. If I slept, I didn't have to think. I existed in a kind of holding pattern, vaguely aware of the life that marched on without me, the shift of sunlight, the flow of traffic, the drone of the cellular on the nightstand. I felt paralyzed before it all, and I came to understand what it must feel like to be in a state of profound mourning. It is a state of being that transcends ordinary sadness, one that comes with the cruel realization that you will never be whole again.

Strangely enough, what roused me from sleep was an explicit vision: Joe gasping for breath on my body, grinding himself into me. The scar above his eye was fresh, jagged red.

The vision was so real it sent a shudder across the top of my camisole. I gathered myself at the edge of the bed, and I went to take a bath. Scrubbed fresh and newly alert, I dove into a cleaning frenzy—I stripped down the beds and tossed the sheets into the washer, vacuumed the carpets, yanked open all the blinds. Enough with the self-pity, I thought. Enough with the deadly visions. I was determined to steel myself against useless emotions, regret, and attempted manipulations.

When the phone buzzed again, I picked it up, ready to handle my business.

It was Joe.

"I may have something for you," he said.

"What do you know?" I said in a tone that bordered on sharp.

"I'd rather talk in person," he said.

"Say when," I said, keeping my voice distant.

"Tomorrow," he said.

The next day, I drove deep into the industrial core of Hialeah, past rows of boxy factories abuzz with workers on their morning break. They swarmed around lunch trucks for greasy steak sandwiches and hits of Cuban caffeine. I turned onto a residential block lined with flat-roof homes and oversized driveways of painted cement, a few of them displaying elaborate shrines to saints. Anywhere else, a real estate agent might take one look at the woeful expressions on the faces of those saints and deem the houses not sellable. Who would buy a house with a friggin' statue of San Lazaro on crutches, bleeding from a chest wound? But you have to be from Hialeah to understand the saint code. Those shrines symbolize promises fulfilled. They symbolize the direct opposite of FOR SALE signs. A saint on the lawn means "Not for sale—*never* for sale." That house, it says, is a miracle granted. It is home forever.

The very thought made me claustrophobic. Why would anyone—anyone besides dead-end types like Joe Pratts—want to stay there forever?

Farther up the road I came to a four-way stop at a familiar corner. Yet, in the hyper glare of daylight, I couldn't read the street numbers. It took me a moment to realize I had driven to the edge of Walker Park. I stopped for a minute to glance in at the swimming pool, the same pool where I learned to swim. A group of kids splashed around as their swim instructor patiently waded between them. The instructor, a balding man in his early seventies, demonstrated the basic freestyle technique, slicing the water with slow, steady strokes. The sight of him sent a wave of sadness over me. There he was, Mr. Bennett, bronzed as ever, his strong shoulders now slightly hunched. I remembered how calm and confident I felt just watching him glide across the water with strokes so precise they barely made a ripple. The gentle rhythm of his swimming always lulled me into a serene state. Now, in the same turquoise water, I found fragments of a memory:

I drift across the shallow end of the pool on a summer afternoon, after all the other swimmers have gone home. I feel a hand tug at my bikini bottom. I dive under to find Joe swimming away. I race to catch him at the deep end and I yank him underwater, but he's too fast for me. He swooshes upward and sweeps me to the pool's edge, his arm gripping my waist. I break loose and swat him with a hard jolt of water and a voice-cracking, adolescent shriek.

"Get away, asshole!" I say. But I don't mean it.

I'm loving the way his shoulders glisten in the pink light of the afternoon. I'm loving the sexy way he laughs at me. I'm loving the fact that Mr. Popular himself is pressing his bare chest against my back and stroking my thighs. I'm not his kind of girl—and I never aspired to be his kind. I'm studious, smart, borderline prudish. But today, July twenty-third of my seventeenth year, I swivel my body around to face him. I let him run his fingers along the sides of my breasts and lower his lips to my neck. As the water laps against our bodies, I kiss the lobe of his ear, then his cheek, then his lips. My first kiss. It is a kiss so deep it turns daylight to dusk and two unlikely souls into lovers.

But now, as I drove up to the overgrown, grassy swale outside the old yellow house on East Sixth, my swimming pool reverie was shattered by the sight of Joe on a peeling stoop, dragging on a cigarette. Pale and sunken, he nodded at me as I reached the front porch.

"The house still looks the same," I said, reaching for a little bit of small talk.

"Same as the day I was born," he said in a dull tone.

He made no move to ask me in, so I took a seat beside him.

"What do you know about those names?" I said.

"Looks like this woman's involved with some foul people," he said.

"You know them?"

Joe looked at me and let out a big laugh.

"It's something, you know," he said.

"What?"

"You've got this drug queen doing business out of a Red Roof Inn—that should've been their first clue that it wasn't you," he said, laughing himself into a coughing fit.

"Yeah, whatever," I said.

"Think about it . . ."

"Never mind. Who do you know?" I said. "Jimmy Paz?"

Joe glanced away for a minute.

"Nah," he said.

"You know someone who knows him, don't you?"

"I got a source in the Keys," he said. He glanced off again.

"I want to meet your source," I said.

"No way," he said.

"This is urgent—you know it is."

"This was a bad idea."

"Look. Just tell me where this source is and I'll go talk to him," I said.

But Joe fired a mocking look my way.

"Right."

"I'm dead serious," I said.

"Fine. I'll go with you," he said.

I wasn't ready for the offer. I said nothing for a long while. It was Joe who broke the silence. He tamped out the cigarette and stood up in a huff.

"Let's just forget it," he said, heading toward the front door.

"I can't. I need to fix this," I said.

"Not a good idea, Mary."

"Okay, *okay*," I said.

"Okay, what?"

"Okay, come with me," I said.

I blurted out the words without thinking. Joe seemed as shocked to hear them as I was to say them.

"When?" he said, daring me to repeat the invitation.

"Now," I said.

"Now?"

"Right now," I said. "Before I change my mind."

Joe held the front door open for me, and he followed me into the stifling hot confines of the house. No glimpse of the August sun shone through the shuttered windows, leaving the place a dismal still life of ripped furniture, dark wood laminates, and randomly placed Capodimonte figurines, a setting untouched since Joe's mother, Melba, died of a heart attack eight years earlier.

Joe headed into the bedroom and, for some reason, I followed him. But I stopped at the bedroom door when I saw the scene inside: A tangle of medical tubes were tethered to a manual-crank hospital bed. In it, a living ghost of a man, rail thin, seventy-eight years old, took sips from an orange juice carton as a fiftyish nurse in overly cheery scrubs adjusted the bedsheets. Once upon a time, Joe's father, Antonio Pratts, was a top-notch mechanic at the busiest service station on Forty-ninth Street, a man who rarely missed a day of work. On nights when his wife worked late at her beauty shop job, it was Antonio who would cook dinner for the family, fry palomilla steak and green plantains, still wearing that smudged uniform embroidered with his nickname, "Papo."

The sight of Papo in that bed killed me. I started to walk toward him, hoping he'd remember me. But Joe raised a hand, signaling me to stay away. I couldn't help but eavesdrop as he spoke to the nurse.

"If you need something, Danny's number is next to the phone in the kitchen," he said.

"I have it, no problem," said the nurse.

Joe leaned down, close to his father.

"How you feeling?" he asked the old man.

Papo stared ahead as if lost. His eyes flickered about.

"I have to go to work for a while, but I'll be back soon," Joe said.

He smoothed a hand across his father's forehead.

"I played your combination last night," Joe said. "We hit it on three numbers—we're rich."

The old man smiled up at Joe.

"Pssst. Jo Jo," he said.

"Yeah?"

"I've crapped my pants."

The nurse hurried over to check on Papo as Joe leaned over to give his father a kiss.

"Be nice to the nurse," he said, turning to leave.

We walked out of the house without speaking another word.

NINE

WE MADE A quick stop at my house, where I called Gina to tell her I was going away for a few days to clear my head. I couldn't bring myself to utter my real plans. I packed up my laptop and an overnight bag while Joe waited in my car. I wedged the bag between us in the car, hoping to force some distance. The scene at his house had left me feeling vulnerable, too vulnerable for my own good. It told me more than I wanted to know about Joe's life and his reasons for remaining in a dead-end existence. I had to put it all out of my mind and stay focused. So I tried to leave the mental noise behind as I drove off to catch the turnpike south, Joe riding shotgun.

"I'll put this in the back," said Joe, grabbing the bag.

"No, leave it there," I said.

Joe slouched in his seat and stared out at the traffic. The suburban landscape dissolved to a haze of mangroves as the road flowed into the northern Florida Keys. Soon we were flanked by bodies of water that shimmered in competing shades of aquamarine, the ocean to the left, Florida Bay to the right, dwarfing the narrow, two-lane highway. It is one of my favorite drives, one that rarely fails to put me at ease. And that day I might have been at ease if I hadn't been so distracted by Joe's antics. He grabbed my arm off the steering wheel and pulled it over to his side, a playful, daredevil move that irked the hell out of me. I tore it away and kept driving.

Joe leaned back into his seat with a cocky air, like a guy getting his power back. He tried to grab me again, but this time I slapped him with the back of my hand.

"What am I doing?" he said.

"Stay on your side," I said.

Joe fired up a cigarette.

"You miss me?" he said.

I shot him a blank look.

"Yeah, you miss me," he said.

"It's not going to be like that," I said.

"Like what? Are you lecturing me? I'll turn this bougie-ass car around," he said.

"You never change, do you?"

"I swear I'll do it," Joe said, eyes narrowed on me.

I jerked the car to the side of the road with a burned-rubber screech.

"Don't fuck with me. It won't work this time. I'm not the same girl," I said.

Joe's eyes lit up in a manic flash. It was the first flicker of life I had seen in him in years.

"That's right," he said. "You're someone else now. I read about it in the paper."

I fired a nasty look at him, and he looked away to avoid me. I could have said so many things to him right then. He had no right to draw conclusions about my life, no right to assume he knew the independent person I had become, the mother and business-woman. But I got back on the highway without saying another word to him. The truth is, I was beginning to wonder if, indeed, I was someone else now.

ISLAMORADA DOCKS—DAY 29
*Mary and Joe pull up into a small marina just south of
Mile Marker 82.*

Under a blazing sun, I followed Joe past a motley collection of boats. Crawling atop them were gypsy souls long ago swallowed by the tempting fringes of the Overseas Highway. They had drifted here to escape, to hide, to spend an endless summer, and they had stumbled upon a paradise of barefoot living and rum-enhanced sunsets. Everybody here has a used-to-be story, some of them jarringly different from their present-day scenario.

We walked up to an aging but sturdy thirty-foot fishing boat docked by a sign that read TARPON HUNTERS OF ISLAMORADA. On board, a leathery man in his late fifties polished the wood-grain details of his open cabin. This was Captain Nick, a reinvented menswear salesman who had lost a fortune in the market crash of 1987. He squinted in our direction and waved us over.

Moments later, he and Joe were drinking longnecks on the deck, trading fishing stories, and commiserating about financial woes. I took the opportunity to flip through the missed calls log on my cell phone—there were none that couldn't wait. I put the phone away and tuned in to the conversation just as Joe was asking Captain Nick about some guy named Gus.

"Sorry, man, I don't remember him," said the captain in a rather cautious tone.

"Of course you do—you remember Fat Gus. Big, hairy jerk from Gainesville," said Joe.

"Doesn't ring a bell. Then again, I've been out of the loop for a while," said Captain Nick. "But if you want a good deal on some hog snapper, I'm your dude."

"Screw the hog snapper, Nick. What the hell's wrong with your brain these days?" said Joe.

"My life's real simple right now, and I'd like to keep it that way," said the boat captain. He downed the rest of his beer with a bit of an attitude.

Joe walked away, frustrated. But I wasn't ready to give up on finding this Gus character, whoever he was.

"I'll take the hog snapper," I said.

"Coming right up. How much you want?" said the captain.

"Give me the smallest one you've got," I said.

Captain Nick opened up a large cooler and grabbed a thirteen-inch, reddish-coral fish. He wrapped it in a sheet of plastic and tossed it in a grocery bag for me.

"How much?" I said.

"Twelve bucks is good."

I held up a one-hundred-dollar bill. He stared at it but wouldn't take it.

"Got no change, honey."

"I don't want change," I said. "I don't want the fish, either."

"So what the hell's the money for?" the captain said.

"For you," I said. "Consider it a thank-you present for helping us find my cousin. Gus."

Captain Nick thought about it for a second before he snatched the hundred. He jammed the bill into a pocket of his shorts.

"You didn't hear this from me," he said. He glanced back as if hog snapper could eavesdrop. "He hangs out at the Dune Dog, off Duval Street."

We left the captain where we found him, one fish-smeared Benjamin richer, and we hit the highway south to Key West.

DUNE DOG TAVERN—DAY 29

A badly lit, beer-soaked hangout for locals. Classic rock and wood slab tables carved up with decades' worth of initials, dedications, and drunken shout-outs. Mary and Joe drink longnecks at a corner booth.

We had been at the bar for a good hour, but there was no sign of Gus—not that I would have recognized him anyway. In fact, I knew I could sit there for days and never recognize a soul among the rough-hewn, tattooed clientele. Joe, on the other hand, seemed to know at least one other customer, a scruffy guy at the bar. He kept his eye on the guy as we waited for Gus.

"You know him?" I said.

"Nope," he said.

The entire drive from Islamorada, Joe had kept conversation to a minimum. He seemed distant, aloof. Maybe he didn't like the fact that Captain Nick had blown him off yet had given me the lead on Gus. Or maybe he didn't like the fact that I had stopped to call Tony. Not that the call had yielded any kind of meaningful conversation—Tony, his usual prick self, hung up on me.

Maybe Joe was having second thoughts about introducing me to his sources and possibly revealing some details of his past he preferred to keep hidden from me. He had done his best to shield me from his delinquent associations throughout the years we were together. But, of course, I knew he was getting too close to some unsavory characters—how could I not know? The wads of cash, the hand-scribbled contact lists, the Saturday-night special tucked in the dresser drawer—all those things told the story Joe didn't have the guts to tell me himself. I'm sure he would have argued that those characters who drifted in and out of his life were not associates but simply friends of friends, the cousin of a guy he owed a favor to, the ex-brother-in-law of some dude he grew up with, the uncle of a kid who was like a brother. Joe had no boundaries in his life, no desire to draw lines of distinction between family and random acquaintances. Every joker who stumbled into the Rapture Lounge on nights when Joe was tending bar—years before he bought the place—found a friend in Joe. He could look a coke dealer in the eye and see not a convicted felon but a poor slob just trying to hustle a few bucks to support his kids. To Joe, the drug trade possessed a kind of gravitational pull, like a massive high tide, dragging in thugs and innocents alike. It was never the fault of these jokers—they merely were swept up by a powerful phenomenon they could not control. And I believe it was this putrid environment of nonexistent boundaries that killed Joe's life ambitions and his dreams. Once upon a time, he had dreamed of opening his own cigar shop—and this was years before the '90s cigar rage hit the retro-glam, fabulous set. There would be cigar rollers, custom-blended varieties, classes for the connoisseur, a cigar lounge streaming vintage Cuban music and Rat Pack standards, and even a midmorning cigar reader to lavish upon the old-timers, rollers and visitors alike, their favorite paperback Westerns. Joe knew his cigars. He had fallen in love with the culture as a boy, watching his maternal grandfather roll them for tourists on Calle Ocho and falling asleep at night to his stories of what life was like on the tobacco plantations of Pinar del Río. This is what he wanted, an establishment he would call Dulce Maria Cigars. This is what he wanted when he had dreams, and when he was in love with me, before he gave in to the undertow of inevitability.

But that was a lifetime ago. Now, in Key West, I had no intention of looking the other way and playing dumb. I had everything to lose if I did.

Joe had sweet-talked Darlene, the bartender, into giving up the scoop on Gus, one of her hardest- drinking regulars. In fact, she had his address and phone number tacked up beside the cash register for those nights when she had to tell the cabbie exactly where to drop off his wasted remains. Joe asked Darlene if she'd call him and let him know his favorite Cuban was waiting for him at the bar. And, amazingly, she did.

"Tell me about Gus. Is he a friend of yours?" I asked Joe.

"Was a friend of mine," said Joe.

But we were cut off when he spotted a familiar figure ambling toward our table. I turned to find an enormous man, thirty-two or so, in grungy jeans and a Grateful Dead T-shirt. Gus was a bear of a guy, and he seemed ecstatic to see Joe.

"Hey, man. I couldn't believe it when Darlene called," said Gus. He squeezed himself into the booth next to me. "I was like, 'That can't be, bro. This dude's been AWOL from my life.' Man."

"How you been?" said Joe, a little distracted.

"Outrageous. Thanks for asking," said Gus. He turned to give me an awkward pat on the shoulder. "Where are my manners, bro? Hi. I'm Gus."

"This is my wife. Janet," said Joe, nodding at me. I gave him an unflinchingly believable smile.

"Wow. She's really hot," said Gus, before taking a slurp of his beer.

"I know. She is," said Joe.

"She is. For real. Congrats, man," said Gus. "When did you get married?"

"Three months ago," Joe said.

"Big wedding, huh?" said Gus.

"Nah. We went to Vegas," said Joe.

"No shit. I never been to Vegas," said Gus, flashing a stupid grin my way, as if waiting for me to say something.

"Vegas is great," I said.

"So this is why you've been hiding, Jose," said Gus. "Can't say I blame you."

"Yeah. Been out of touch for a while," said Joe. "But I'm trying to hook up with people again. Get some business going. Except I don't know how to reach anybody anymore."

"You need a Palm Pilot, bro," said Gus.

"Exactly. Maybe I wouldn't lose Jimmy's number again," said Joe.

Gus sobered up a bit.

"You know Jimmy? I guess I had forgotten that," said Gus. "Then again, Jimmy's a celebrity, like Steven Seagal."

"Is he still working out west?" said Joe. "Arizona . . ."

"Not so much anymore," said Gus.

"Not Arizona. I'm sorry. New Mexico," said Joe, tapping his temple. "Your brain on drugs."

Gus let out a belly laugh and raised his beer in a mock toast. But Joe's mood darkened when he spotted the scruffy guy pushing back from the bar. He kept a casual eye on the derelict as he kept the conversation going.

"So why do you think Jimmy called me?" he asked Gus, bluffing.

"No idea," Gus said. He chugged his beer.

Joe tracked the scruffy man as he made his way to the bathroom. As soon as he lost sight of the guy, Joe signaled the bartender over for another round.

Ten minutes later, Gus teetered on drunk.

"I know why Jimmy was trying to reach you," he said at last. "The big man's making a comeback."

From the look on Joe's face I could tell he had no idea who this "big man" was. But he fronted well.

"I heard about that," said Joe. "Where can I see Jimmy?"

"Wanna see him tonight?" Gus blurted.

"Yeah, where—" Joe started to say. But he was interrupted when the scruffy guy from the bar appeared and gave him a shove from the back.

"Let's go have a conversation," said the derelict.

"I'm already having a conversation," said Joe. "So you need to get out of here."

"I ain't going anywhere without you, my friend," said the scruffy guy. He lifted his shirt slightly to reveal a black Glock 9 mm handgun tucked into his belt. "So let's go outside, you and me."

I reached out to grab Joe's arm, but he pulled it away with a look of caution.

"I'll be right back," he said, nudging the scruffy man out of the bar.

The exchange made Gus queasier than the beer.

"What's going on here?" I asked him.

"I don't know, but I need to get out of here," he said, scrambling out of the booth.

"Wait—you can't leave," I said, going after him.

I chased Fat Gus down a short alley but stopped when I heard screams and the crash of metal around the corner. Someone was getting his ass kicked. Joe. I was sure of it. I raced around the corner, but I stopped when I saw the bloody mess behind the Dumpster: Joe, his face cut and bruised, pointed a gun at the derelict, now crumpled up and whimpering on the pavement.

"I want to hear it again," Joe said, giving the man a shove in the rump.

"You don't owe me," the man mumbled.

"What'd you say? Say it again," Joe said.

The derelict coughed and clutched his stomach. Joe went to pistol-whip him but stopped when he saw me.

"Nothing. You don't owe me a damn thing . . . ," the derelict said.

"Yeah? So why'd you pull a gun on me in front of my wife?" said Joe, glancing back at me.

"I'm sorry, man," the derelict said.

"Sorry isn't sorry enough," said Joe. He signaled me over.

I went over, hoping to pull Joe away from there. But before I could grab him he shoved the Glock into my hand.

"Keep it on him," Joe said.

"What are you doing?" I said. My hands trembled as I gripped the gun.

"No questions. Just do what I tell you," he said.

I followed his order even though my arms trembled. I aimed the gun at the derelict's torso while Joe rifled through his pockets for cash with swift, expert moves. He found a few crumpled dollar bills and a Florida driver license, but nothing else. Joe slipped the license in his pocket and left the crumpled bills on the derelict's chest. His eyes half-open, the man didn't move, although I could tell he was still breathing. In fact, he seemed as if he had given up and was simply taking a little breather.

Done with the derelict, Joe turned and walked back toward me, his face blank of any expression.

"Let's get going," he said.

I lowered the Glock, too petrified to say anything. I slipped it into my purse and followed Joe toward the car.

Ten

SOUTHERN BREEZE MOTOR INN—DAY 29

*A '50s-era establishment of neon exteriors and worn rattan
interiors. Inside room seventeen, Mary inspects the gun up close.*

Fear is a mystifying state. Back in that alley, I had panicked at
the clammy feel of gunmetal. I was afraid I would drop the gun,
causing it to blast off and hit me in the face, or something equally
stupid. In the end, it was the fear that could have killed me. It
could have precipitated a tragic, potentially fatal sequence.

But in the quiet of my hotel room, as I examined the weapon
from every angle, I realized there was nothing to be afraid of, not
as long as the gun was in my hands and not as long as my hands
were in command. I wasn't going to fire it. I wasn't going to drop
it. I wasn't going to let it out of my sight. This realization gave me
a power I had never known. I gripped the Glock, now demystified,
with perfectly steady hands.

Joe glanced at me through the mirror, where he was cleaning

up a bloody cut at the edge of his lip. He disappeared through a door, into his adjoining room, and returned with a bottle of Bacardi. He poured a couple of shots and handed me a glass.

"Sorry about what happened back there," he said. He downed his shot of rum.

I took a sip from my glass, but I was still too riled to say anything.

"I didn't mean for you to see it," he said, taking a seat beside me on the bed.

"It's the same old bullshit with you," I said. I glared at him. "Deadbeats screaming for their money. Or their drugs. Take your pick."

"You're right. I'm just supposed to let some random freak blow my brains out in an alley," he said. He got up to pour himself another shot. "I'll keep that in mind."

"He wasn't some random freak and you know it," I said.

"Really? Who was he, then? You know his name?" he said in a smart-ass tone I had forgotten.

"How would I know his name?" I said.

"Then don't talk about shit you don't know," he said.

Had he said this a decade earlier, I might have clocked him good. But not that night. That night Joe was nothing but another fixture in my motel room, like the sea-grass lamp on the dresser. He was nothing but a middleman. This is what I tried to tell myself.

"The point is there's a right way and a wrong way to handle your problems," I said.

"There is no right way to deal with scum like that," he said.

"You mean like Gus? The scum that got away tonight? Isn't that why we came down here in the first place?" I said. "We're lucky that bartender gave up his address."

I set the gun down on the nightstand and went to sit by the window. On the street below, a couple of past-their-time frat boys on the prowl whooped it up, hoisting Big Gulp–sized cups of booze.

"You know what, Joe? You're stuck in the same exact place," I told him. "The same place I left you."

"Maybe that's where I need to be. Maybe I have obligations there," he said.

"To the junkies of Hialeah, you mean?" I said.

"To my business," he said, still hostile.

"Right."

"Among other things," he said. His tone had softened a bit.

"Right."

"What you're talking about . . . that was another time," he said.

"Yeah, well, I can't go back there," I said, pulling the drapes to expand my view of the street.

"Who's asking you to?" said Joe, pissed.

I nursed my drink, stung by the exchange.

"Tell me something, Mary. What did you think you were getting yourself into here?" he said. "You thought you'd come down, ride the conch train, applaud the sunset? Maybe pick up a lead or two from the Rotary Club?"

"And who are you to insult me?" I said. I left the window, ready to oust him from the room. I couldn't think straight anymore, not with Joe standing there, so close. I could feel his eyes on me, tracking my moves, tracing the lines of my body, my legs, my arms, the slope of my neck. "Look, I need to be by myself for a while."

But he made no move to leave. Instead, he came closer.

"Let's rewind for a second," he said, his voice dropping to a more conciliatory level. "When I heard about what happened to you . . . I mean, you, of all people, don't deserve this. I know this."

The sudden shift of emotion threw me off a bit. I wasn't ready to make nice. I sat down on the edge of the bed and let him speak his mind.

"If there's something you can believe about me, then please believe this: I'll do whatever you need me to do to help you find this Maria woman. I'll go to the end of the earth if I have to. I'll do anything for you, even if it means never seeing you again," he said. "But, honey, this business of chasing drug dealers . . . this is not your life. You need to live your life."

I looked up at him, but he glanced away and started back to his room, giving my shoulder a fleeting caress as he left.

I clicked off the light and curled up on the darkened bed, afloat on a mild rum buzz. I could hear the shower running through the half-open door between our rooms. I closed my eyes and allowed Joe's words to settle upon me, and for the first time that day I yielded to the images I had seen. I replayed the scenes at his house over and over again: Joe at his father's bedside, calm and comforting, his words so lovingly spoken. He hadn't stayed in that old yellow house on the dead-end street because he lacked courage or ambition or any of the qualities of polished, successful men. He had stayed out of devotion to his father. While some of his friends went away to school or off to find their hustle in the booming '90s, Joe took over his father's job at the mechanic shop. He worked that job for a couple of years until it was clear Papo could not return to work. Another son, one who aspired to be wealthy, might have put his own needs first. But Joe wasn't that guy. He had stayed. And yet I had seen fit to humiliate him for it, to deem him a lesser man.

The realization hit me hard that night. Maybe it was the haze of alcohol, or maybe it was the simple fact that for the first time in many hours I was standing still amid chaos, but a new awareness washed over me and with it came a flood of tears. I thought about how, in all my life, no other man had affected me the way Joe Pratts could affect me, leaving me exposed and feeling so vulnerable. He knew me too damn well. He knew things about me no other man could ever know—he knew them because he was there. He was there on that September afternoon when I came home to find out my grandfather had died in Cuba. He poured Daddy a shot of whiskey and sat with him beneath the mango tree while Daddy cried. He was there when I came home from my first job at the local fabric store, ready to talk about the tacky homecoming dresses I had enabled with my expert fabric-cutting and excellent customer-relations skills. He was there when I picked up my Outstanding Psychology Major award at FIU, when I bought my first car, when I buried my sweet old pit bull, Star. We came from the same subset of the world. The neighborhood streets that were familiar to me were also familiar to him. Our houses smelled the same and sounded the same. Our record players played the same songs. And when we fought for the first time, it took just one song—one perfect, soulful song—to bring us back together. The memory of that dance was suddenly so vivid I could hear the song:

"You got me going in circles, oh, around and around I go . . . "

No other man could make me cry at the memory of a song. Even while I was married, doing my best to forget my years with him, I'd grow sad at random memories, a fleeting aroma, a conversation casually overheard. No one else could affect me the way Joe Pratts could affect me. This is why I had left him years ago. I didn't want to love a man so profoundly, not if it meant getting stuck in a groove. I didn't want to be stuck anywhere or anyplace, to edit my dreams, confine my life to the same three square blocks. I wanted to break away from the grip of expectation, the neighborhood, the memories, and all that is implied when one marries a childhood sweetheart in that stagnant place: the same bridal registry as the chick down the block, the same outfit for New Year's Eve, the same barbecue and beer every Sunday, the same fight over the same thing, the same number on the paycheck, week after week. It wasn't a life I wanted, not even at the side of the man I most loved. And I had not once doubted my decision to leave him. Not until that night.

When I glanced up I saw Joe in the gray light of the open doorway between our rooms, so ruggedly handsome, a towel draped across the back of his neck. I lifted myself from the bed and went to him. I wrapped my arms around him and let myself melt into his body. He stroked my face gently with his lips, wiping away my tears, and he pressed close to me in a deep, sweet kiss.

"I'm sorry about your father," I said, kissing the fresh cut at the edge of his mouth.

"Hush," he said, his arms tightening around me.

I surrendered to the moment, giving myself to all those feelings I had kept shuttered in memory. And when I did, I felt liberated, not confined to a house or a street or an expectation, but truly free to love. It was as if no time had passed since the day I first fell in love with him. I knew his smell. I knew the turns of his body from memory, the width of his shoulders, the feel of his skin, the precise angle of our most intimate kiss, the unhurried dance onto the bed, where the intermittent glow of motel lights glimpsed our bodies making love.

Sometime in the middle of the night, I woke up from a stark nightmare. In my dream, someone had abducted Max. I had seen it so vividly I scrambled out of bed in a panic and went to the bathroom to slap some water on my face, hoping to shake the vision. But I couldn't. The dream intensified my sense of dread and urgency and the nausea that came with it. It felt as if all my internal organs were being suspended with forks. I couldn't catch my breath.

I returned to the room, where Joe was still asleep. Quietly, I grabbed my laptop and slipped into the adjacent room. As Joe slept, I went back to work, back to the mission that had brought me to Key West. I surfed all the real estate sites I could remember, searching property records, land deeds, and foreclosures for any shred of a clue. I typed in every name on the Maria Portilla indictment. I looked up Jimmy Paz's name in all its variations.

I tried "James Paz"—nothing.

I tried "James A. Paz"—nothing.

I tried "Jimmy Paz"—nothing.

I tried "Jaime Antonio Paz"—nothing.

I tried "Jaime A. Paz"—nothing.

I shut the laptop in frustration. Still jarred from the nightmare, I saw two difficult truths quite clearly: I hadn't come to Key West to hit a dead end in a crappy motel room. And I hadn't come to Key West to fall in love. A rekindled love affair could only weigh me down or, worse, cast me off on a pitiful tangent. I knew the passion I had felt hours earlier could derail my hunt for Maria Portilla. At the very least, it could muddy things up.

I went to check on Joe—he was still soundly asleep. The truth is I wanted to crawl in bed with him and fall asleep once again in his arms. But I knew it was an indulgence I couldn't allow myself to have. I needed to keep moving, and I needed to do so on my own, sharp, focused, unhindered by romance and its obligations.

I leaned in close to Joe and brushed my lips against his cheek, lingering to breathe in his scent one last time. He kissed me back in his sleep, then turned around and nestled into his pillow once again.

In a patch of moonlight, I tried to write him a note on a motel postcard, but all I could come up with was this: "I'm so sorry. M."

Nothing more.

I placed it on the nightstand as I grabbed the Glock, and I left Joe Pratts for the second time in my life.

KEY WEST STREETS—DAY 30
Mary's car turns off a main road and into a small thoroughfare.

Dawn was still a good three hours away as I drove through the desolate backstreets of Key West, tracing my route on a tourist map I had grabbed at the motel's front desk when I stopped to pay for our rooms.

I came to a halt outside a dilapidated apartment building and checked the number on its façade. I parked the car and found my way to apartment 26, the last door down a leaky hallway. I banged on the door, but nobody answered at first. So I banged on it harder.

"Wake up in there," I said. "Hurry up."

After a few moments, the door cracked open to reveal the elusive resident, a bleary-eyed Gus.

"Hey, what the hell are you doing here?" he said. He rubbed his eyes like a big baby.

I pushed in the door and let myself inside.

"You know why I'm here," I said. "Jimmy Paz. We still need to get ahold of him."

"Where's your husband?"

"In the car."

Gus sized me up like a muscle-head bouncer trying to decide who gets to pass the velvet ropes.

"How much is it worth to you?" he said, adopting a would-be gangster tone.

"For an address?" I said.

"Business is business," he said, thrusting his jaw out in defiance. "Five hundred."

"Like hell."

"What do you want with Jimmy?" he said.

I dug into my purse and pulled out five bills from an envelope, the "emergency" cash stash I had brought with me. I counted them out and slammed them down on a table.

"Five hundred. No questions," I said.

Gus eyed the money with diminished bravado.

"Cool," he said. He snatched the bills off the table. "I'll get his address for you."

Within minutes I was several blocks away, knocking on the door of a quaint, gingerbread-style cottage. I could see lights click on inside and hear a light rustling of steps. I glanced at the time on my cell phone: It was two a.m. After a few moments, the door was opened by a very elderly woman in a pale yellow nightgown.

"Hello there," she said, "may I help you?"

"I'm sorry to disturb you at this hour, but this is urgent," I told her.

"Are you lost, honey? Would you like to come inside?" the old woman said.

"No, that's okay—I've already been enough of a bother. I'm here because I'm looking for my friend. His name is Jimmy Paz," I said.

The woman gave me a blank look.

"I've lived here thirty years and I've never heard of him," she said.

"Maybe he's a friend of your son, or your grandson?" I said.

The old woman's eyes grew misty as a thought washed over her.

"I never had children," she said.

"I'm sorry. I didn't mean—"

"Just the cats."

"I'm so sorry, but—"

"Maybe I wouldn't be so lonely right now if I just had made different choices along the way," she said.

"No, no, I'm sure your choices were just fine," I said. "I'm sorry to have bothered you."

"You're such a nice girl, so easy to talk to. My name is Gertrude. Are you sure you don't want to come inside?" she said.

I looked at the heartbroken old woman and I had just one thought: Gus, that greasy bastard.

I apologized to the woman for interrupting her sleep and I gave her a hug good-bye.

Back at Gus's apartment I nearly tore down his front door.

When he opened it, I barreled in.

"Why are you wasting my time?" I said. This time, I lugged my computer bag into the apartment.

"You're a ball buster, ya know?"

"True," I said. "But things could always get worse."

"Yeah? And things could always get more expensive. For you," said Gus.

"I gave you five hundred dollars," I said.

"Price went up," he said, his jaw high again. "It'll cost you twenty-five hundred now."

I took a seat at the edge of his ratty sofa, and I dug into my purse. I reached past the cold metal of the Glock and grabbed an overstuffed envelope. I tossed the envelope on the floor, next to Gus's mammoth, hairy feet. It coughed out a wad of cash.

"Go ahead, count it," I said.

Greedy Gus bent down and strained to clasp the envelope, but he couldn't reach it.

"Go on," I said, inflicting upon him an empty, matter-of-fact tone, "pick it up."

He wheezed through his chest and tried again. No matter how hard he strained, he couldn't seem to reach the money. Then, in one last valiant push, he managed to grab a corner of the envelope. But just as he did, he lost his balance—and his grip on the envelope. All 358 pounds of Gus went crashing to the floor, landing a few feet away from the money.

"Shit, bro. You gotta help me up," he said, extending one of his hands. I stopped to notice how small they seemed in comparison to his beefy frame.

"Okay, stay right there," I said.

I grabbed a telephone from a nearby table and yanked off the cord.

"What the hell are you doing?" he said.

"I'm trying to get you up, moron."

"With a phone cord?"

"There's a technique. Settle down and give me both your hands. Like this," I said, demonstrating for him by clasping my hands together.

"Shit, no. I ain't falling for that."

"Fine. Stay on the floor, then," I said.

Gus flapped his arms and tried his best to sit up. He grabbed a sofa cushion in a ham-fisted attempt to balance himself. But instead, he managed to yank the cushion to the floor with him. He grimaced and groaned as he rolled on his side, then he shot me a seething look.

"Can't you see my back is killing me?" he said. The wheezing in his chest sent his voice up half an octave.

"I can see it, all right," I said, going for a tone of concern. I took a seat on the nearby sofa and leaned over toward Fat Gus as if examining an X-ray image. In truth, I did know something about back pain, for Daddy had suffered quite a bit of it after his accident at the aluminum factory. "It's a musculoligamentous injury of the lumbar spine. Painful, huh?"

"Painful as all hell."

"Feels like you just wrestled a bear," I said.

"Damn straight," he said. He glanced up at me with glassy eyes.

"It happens a lot to athletes," I said. I knew it also happened to car accident victims, overzealous weekend warriors, and fat people, but I wanted Gus to feel like the stud that he wasn't. "Are you a jock?"

"I throw the football around every once in a while," he said. He seemed suddenly lifted at the thought. "You some kind of doctor?"

"No," I said. "Physical therapist."

"No shit."

"Yeah. That's why I was trying to help you up earlier using this cord here," I said. "It looks crazy, but it works. I use this on my patients when they fall. It takes the strain off your lower back and forces you to use your abdominals and quadriceps."

"For real?"

"For real," I said. I held up the phone cord. "Give it a try?"

Gus obliged, thrusting his hands up toward me. I quickly grabbed them and tied them up with the phone cord. I pulled the cord tight so Gus couldn't break loose. Then I got up and walked away from him.

"You're gonna help me up, right?" he said.

I had to laugh as I stooped to pick up the cash from the floor. I stuffed it back into my purse. I have to confess something here— I was pumped up, having lassoed this enormous beast and rendered him powerless.

"You're a crazy bitch, you know?" he said, struggling to bust out of the cord.

"Maybe."

I retrieved the handgun from my overnight bag and aimed it at Gus—right between his eyes—with perfectly steady hands. Just outside my line of vision I could see the glint of the tiny charm dangling from my thin gold bracelet. It was a delicate starfish, picked out by Max just months earlier, on Mother's Day. I put the gun down and held it at my side.

"Let's give this another try, my friend. Where's Jimmy Paz?" I said.

Gus squirmed around but offered nothing. Still holding the gun at my side, I poked through my bag, searching for some ammo. I found it in a clear cellophane bag—leftover road food. Pork rinds. Fried, crispy, fluffy, melt-in-your-mouth buttery, decadent Mr. Piggy pork rinds.

I munched on the junk food as Gus hemmed and twisted on the floor. Each time he'd try to get up, I'd aim the gun at him and he would collapse again. I repeated this stupid little routine over and over: munch on the pork rinds. Aim gun at oaf. Watch oaf tumble back. Half-amused, I took it as a kind of drill to sharpen my reflexes.

Gus, of course, was not amused.

"Man, I'm gonna faint from hunger," he said at last.

"Sorry to hear that. Your call," I said, crunching on a pork rind.

"I'm not gonna tell you anything. I'm not trying to mess up my gig," he said.

"Your gig. Your extremely high-paying gig. What is it that you do exactly, fetch water for Jimmy Paz?"

"As a matter of fact, I do much more than that," he said. "I get a nice fat check every two weeks for my services."

"Glad to hear it. Guess that means you can give me back my five hundred bucks."

"Not exactly," he said, his eyes darting to the kitchen counter, where he had placed the bribe money I gave him earlier that night.

I walked over to the kitchen and snatched the money from the counter.

"Seriously, bro, I'm too hungry to think straight," he said.

I tucked the bills in my pocket and popped another pork rind into my mouth.

"Who's Jimmy working with these days?" I said.

"Bunch of people. I can't remember their names," he said. "Can I have one of those?"

"No."

"You want me to starve?"

"I want you to give me some names," I said.

"Okay, okay. Just one. Give me just one and I'll give you a name," he said, eyeing the bag in my hand.

I took a big, fat pork rind and held it out in front of him.

"Promise?" I said.

"Promise."

I dropped the pork rind into his mouth. Gus scarfed it down, making animal-like noises.

"That was so damn good," he said.

And that's about all it took.

"There's the Big Man," he said, opening his mouth wide so I could toss him another rind. I did.

"Who's the Big Man?" I said.

"I'll think of his name in a minute," he said. "And then there's the Big Man's son. He's some rich junior. Spoiled rotten. I'll think of the name," he said.

"Go on."

"And there's this Colombian chick," he said.

"Tell me about her," I said.

"She's the Big Man's wife. Ex-wife, I mean. Bitch took him for a ride," he said. "I heard she was hiding out at one of Jimmy's places, up near Cocoa."

"What's her name?"

"Who the hell remembers? Colombian chick—that's all I remember," he said.

I put down the bag of pork rinds and shot Gus a hard look.

"There's something you need to know before you get too cocky here. Jimmy's in trouble," I said.

"Jimmy?"

"He's in trouble. Why do you think we're trying to reach him?" I said.

Gus knotted his face as he turned over the thought. He seemed truly confounded. I was afraid I wasn't going to get much more out of him, so I slipped the gun in my waistband and went off to do a little digging. I was determined to turn his apartment upside down if I had to. I started with the kitchen. I rifled through piles of old mail on the kitchen counter, looking for a bank statement, a receipt, a phone log, whatever. I jerked open all the drawers and searched through them. They were jammed with an assortment of garbage: matchbooks, old lotto tickets, stale candies, pocket hair combs, and a couple of plastic zip bags of weed. Tucked behind one of those bags I discovered a thick batch of check stubs. Intrigued, I pulled up a chair and began to flip through them. All of them were identical, all issued in the amount of $1,200, payable to Agostino Calabrese, all from the same corporation, a Guerra Group South LLC.

I took the wad of stubs back to where Gus was sprawled on the living room floor.

"Hey, Agostino. Who are these from?" I said. I waved one of the check stubs.

Gus would not answer me.

"Really," I said. "I'll find out for myself."

I took my laptop out of the case and within minutes I was sifting through lists of limited liability companies on the Florida Department of State Division of Corporations site. I got a hit on a Guerra Group, but when I checked the page I found it had been inactive for a couple of years. The registered agent listed was not an individual but a law firm in Melbourne. When I checked the firm's website, it had been taken down.

Undaunted, I dove into all the real estate sites I knew, checking for property bought or sold by this mysterious Guerra Group.

"Guerra's an interesting name," I said, scanning the property listings on my screen. "You'd think he'd try a little harder. I mean, 'war'?"

"I know what 'guerra' means," he said.

"And the opposite of 'guerra'—that's interesting, too," I said.

"Is that a question?" said Gus.

I clicked into another search and there it was: Guerra Group South, a limited liability company with links to a dozen properties scattered across Florida, in places like Miami, Orlando, Malabar, Naples, and Sandy Key. I checked the property records on each address. All but one of them had been sold by Guerra Group to various buyers. The remaining property sat on a street called Surrey Court in Malabar.

"So what's the opposite of war?" I said.

"Peace, bro. Peace."

"*Paz* to you, too, my brother."

Jimmy Paz, the wordsmith, had purchased quite a collection of properties using his business LLC, which he had named Guerra, the opposite of Paz. I scanned the real estate agate on my screen for clues. I had found at least twelve of Jimmy Paz's past and present properties, including the one at 251 Surrey Court in Malabar. When I looked it up on the map, I found it was a tiny town about twenty-five miles south of Cocoa Beach.

"So you think she's still up around Cocoa?" I said.

"Who?"

"The Big Man's ex-wife," I said.

"Don't know," he said. "Last I heard, Jimmy was on the outs with her."

Suddenly, a flash of recognition crossed Gus's face.

"I think I remember now," he said.

"What?"

"Her name," he said.

"Spit it out."

"It's Maria—Maria Porto-something."

"Portilla?"

"How'd you know?"

With the gun still tucked into the back of my waistband, I went over to Gus and loosened the cord around his hands.

"Hey. I'm sorry I had to tie you up," I said, feigning remorse. "Especially when you did something so heroic."

I handed him the bag of pork rinds as a peace offering.

"What did I do?" he said. Once again, he tried to help himself up from the floor. Once again, he failed.

"You may not realize this, but you saved Jimmy's life," I said. I outstretched my hands to him.

Gus gripped my arms and steadied himself.

"Okay, now. Push up from your quads," I said. "Come on. You can do it."

I dug in my heels and gave him a good, sharp tug, and, astoundingly I managed to help Gus back onto his feet. He plopped himself onto the sofa as if he had just run a few miles.

"Hey, Gus."

"What's that?"

"You know this has to be our secret, right?"

He glanced up at me, still trying to catch his breath.

"If you say a word about this to Jimmy or anyone else—ever—you'll be dead," I said. "Got it?"

"One hundred percent," he said. "You can count on me, Janet."

Gus had caught a bad case of Stockholm Syndrome. He got up from the sofa and smothered me in a bear hug and then waved good-bye from his leaky hallway.

ELEVEN

OVERSEAS HIGHWAY—DAY 30

The sun rises over Big Pine Key as Mary's car tears along an empty stretch of the Overseas Highway.

I couldn't get out of Key West fast enough. For all I knew, big dumb Gus could have called his boss the moment I left the apartment. After two days of chasing Jimmy Paz, I was now speeding away in the opposite direction. The truth is I no longer needed him, not when I had the Malabar lead, a lead I considered to be pretty solid. So I raced northbound as quickly as I could, hoping to remain under the radar as I headed to a new hunting ground.

I drove fast, trying to shake from my mind the sequences of the past day and night, Captain Nick and Fat Gus, Darlene and the derelict at the bar, old Gertrude and her cats. Janet and Joe. But I couldn't shake my rekindled feelings for Joe. I knew these feelings were dangerous—they could take over my life if I let them. They could send me on a passionate detour, away from what I had to do. They could distract me. Joe was that powerful in my life. This is why I had to leave him—without a car, without a ride, without a word. If I had allowed him to step foot in my car again, particularly after our night together, I'd be in trouble. The car would go where he wanted, stop where he wanted, wind up where he wanted. I knew myself that well; I had fallen that hard. Still, I couldn't stop thinking about him. I wondered if he was still asleep. Was he dreaming? Had he woken up and read my note? Was he pissed? Did he miss me?

The sun rose over the ocean, glinting off the waves and the fishing boats, and its light streamed through my car windows in pink, iridescent layers. I glanced over at the passenger seat—it was still angled back the way Joe had set it on the ride down. I rubbed the back of the tan leather seat, believing for some reason that it would still retain his body heat, and then I reached for my phone. I dialed Joe's cell number.

He answered the phone in a sleepy, gravelly voice.

"Change your mind?" he said, sounding close enough to kiss.

"How did you know?" I said, my voice turning lighter than I had expected.

"I know you, honey," Joe said. I could hear him stretch out in bed and I imagined him there, his straight brown hair swept across his eyes, a light, sexy stubble on his unshaven face, his torso warm and rippled. "Why don't you just come back to bed?"

"We need to let it be for now, Joe. I have a pretty good lead on this woman, and I need to go for it," I said.

"Just like that?" he said.

"I'm afraid so."

"Where is she?" he said.

"Malabar," I said, expecting him to ask where Malabar was. But he didn't.

"Glad it worked out for you," he said with a soft yawn.

I fumbled a bit in awkward silence.

"So, listen," I said, "there's a flight to Miami at noon. I reserved a spot under your name, just in case."

A gloomy silence swelled between us, and, in fact, I thought for a moment that he had hung up on me or that we had been cut off.

"You there?" I said, asking a million questions with just one.

"I'm here," he said.

"Good. Thought I had lost you," I said.

"Nah. You didn't lose me," he said. "But don't worry about me—I know how to get home."

I could hear him sink back into bed, and it sounded as if he was moving farther away from me, slipping into a middle distance, a place I couldn't reach.

"I love you," I said, stunned at myself for blurting out the words.

"I love you more," he said, coming right back. I could tell he was smiling.

"I have to do this alone, you know. I need my mind to be clear," I said. "Please say you get it."

Joe thought about it for a moment.

"I get it," he said. "But do me a favor. Call me if you get in over your head."

"I won't be getting myself in over my head, don't worry," I said, although I didn't believe it for one minute.

"But promise me you'll call if you do," he said.

"I will."

As I hung up, I heard my message signal buzz, so I pulled to the side of the road to check my e-mail. Gina, who had no idea where I was—and was going a little bonkers about it—had sent me a vintage-Gina message:

*Gurrr Morrrrneeeng, Dulce Maria. I'm about to hunt you
down, yo, I'm serious. Where the hell are you at? Just
making sure you're not too depressed or passed out drunk
on a yacht in the middle of the Bahamas somewhere—
woops, sorry, that would be me I'm talking about. Anyways,
tell me—did you finally go to Joe's house that day? What did
he know? What happened? Please tell me everything's okay.
You know I worry, woman . . .*

*On another note, it looks like our favorite candidate is
in deep-shit trouble. Some funny business going on with her
campaign contributions. Anyhow, the* Daily Press *is all over
her tranny ass. I guess that rag is good for something other
than obits after all.*

Don't forget to call me!

XOXO,

G.T.

Three hours later I was back in Miami, pulling into the driveway
of Gina's swank condo building on Brickell Key. I tossed the keys
to the valet attendant and used my pass to let myself in through
the residents' entrance.

I took the elevator to the fourteenth floor, where I found Gina
in her robe, sipping coffee on her wraparound terrace and staring
groggily into the bay below.

She turned around when she heard me open the sliding glass
door. She looked seriously hungover.

"Rough night?" I said.

"Not even," she said, bringing the warm ceramic cup to her
forehead to soothe her headache. "So where did you go to clear
your head?"

"You first."

"Nothing to report here. Just a girls' night—me and my bottle of Santa Margherita 2005 pinot grigio, blue-corn chips and salsa, and a *Flavor of Love* marathon on TV," she said. "You?"

"Long story. I'll tell you in the car," I said. "Get dressed. I need you to go someplace with me."

"What's up?"

I reached in my purse and pulled out the Glock.

"I need to learn how to shoot this thing," I said.

Gina set her coffee cup down on a patio table. She picked up the gun and examined it coolly, as would a ballistics expert or a cop—or a felon.

"*Vamos,*" she said.

LITTLE RIVER GUNS AND PISTOL RANGE—DAY 30
A warehouse-type gun shop with a shooting gallery in the rear.

As I drove west from her condo, Gina pointed out the way to the pistol range. To be on the safe side, I decided to leave the Glock in the glove compartment and rent one inside instead.

Gina and I leased our weapons at the front counter and she led me to the shooting range, zipping along the warehouse corridors as if she worked there. We reached our assigned stall and slipped on a couple of headphones. In utter silence, I watched Gina raise a .40-caliber Glock and aim it at a paper target. She squeezed the trigger and pumped a bullet into the bull's-eye circle.

"You try it," she mouthed, stepping back to give me more space.

I attempted to imitate her stance, not to mention her self-assured demeanor. Gina had learned to shoot a gun some years earlier, when she dated a Hialeah cop—nice guy, though a little paranoid. He had Gina convinced that one of his perps would hunt her down and kidnap her in retaliation for an arrest. So she signed up for Tae Kwon Do classes, bought a revolver, and learned to shoot. Good thing, too. She wound up using the gun not on some vengeful perp, but on her cop boyfriend, not to shoot him but to scare him away when he showed up drunk one night. She felt such a rush watching him scramble out of her apartment that she started going to the range every week. Now, as I stood there, missing the target by a mile, I wished I had gone with her.

I tore off my headphones and pulled hers off as well.

"I went to Key West," I said, pitching my voice over the din of the pistol range.

"What?" she yelled.

"I went to Key West with Joe Pratts and we had sex," I yelled into her ear before I adjusted our headphones once more. I raised the rental Glock and took aim at the heart of the target. For a moment, it looked just like Tony. I pulled the trigger and hit it spot-on.

I turned to glance at Gina. She was speechless.

Moments later, she scurried down the corridor after me.

"I want details. But I need a cigarette first," she said. She fumbled for a pack.

"That's all there is. That's all I'm going to say about it for now," I said.

"I must be a fricking psychic, because I knew it," said Gina. She took a long drag of the cigarette. "You're in love. Boy, did I ever call it, or what?"

"We'll talk about it later. Promise," I said. "I'm headed to Cocoa today. I'm checking out a few leads up there."

"So, where's Joe?"

"Still in the Keys," I said. "I had to do this alone."

"Shit, Mary. You have to tell me what happened," she said.

"I'll tell you later. I swear. Right now I need to find an address in Malabar," I said.

"Shouldn't be too hard," she said, giving up her line of questioning with another drag of the cigarette. "It's a tiny place."

About three hours later I was in Brevard County, buying a street map and a bag of Mr. Piggy fried pork rinds at a gas station mini-mart.

As I filled up the gas tank, I leaned against the car and made two phone calls: one to my parents, and the second to Tony. I told my parents I had been called away to meet a real estate client in Cocoa Beach, and I asked them to swing by my house to pick up the mail and water the plants. They thought nothing of it and wished me a good trip. I think they were relieved that I was traveling and quietly hoping that I'd grab a vacation day or two, just to unwind.

Tony, on the other hand, was not as gracious.

"Why are you calling again?" he said in that nasally voice of his. "You know you can't speak to him."

"Who's going to know? I'm his mother. I should be able to talk to my kid," I said, not even attempting a civil tone. "Put him on the damn phone."

"Not possible," said smug Tony. "He's at tennis camp today."

Our ongoing conflict aside, Tony sounded unusually rushed and overly hostile. I couldn't help but think there was truth to those reports Gina had mentioned about trouble brewing in Victoria's campaign. But, truth be told, I didn't want to hear about Victoria or her campaign. So I didn't ask.

"Just tell me one thing: Is Max okay?" I said.

"He's more than okay. He's fantastic," said Tony.

I said nothing else and hung up.

Back in the car, I studied the map for the best route in Malabar, and I drove off to find Surrey Court. The route led me past a couple of strip malls, stretches of farmland, and several boatyards. Even though it was close to the sea, this particular stretch of Brevard County felt strangely landlocked. Despite the boats, it was a place that could have been carved out and plopped down anywhere, the middle of Kansas or western Georgia or northern Texas or southern Illinois. There was a dull sameness to the landscape of megastores and megachurches, where the weekend masses flocked to be further neutralized and sanitized. There were the usual food franchises disguised as "homey" and "original," the overpriced coffee shops fronting a bohemian-chic vibe amid their canned music and premixed frappes. This seemed not like a place where life was lived, but a place where it was rehearsed and mimicked.

Following the map, I turned into a warehouse area and traveled several blocks before finding Surrey Court, a rather desolate street in a remote corner of a sprawling but virtually empty industrial park. It didn't look like the kind of place anyone would call home, not even a drug queen on the run. And the only sign of life I found at the building marked "251" was a collapsed sign that read PROPERTY FOR SALE, INQUIRE WITHIN.

"I think I will," I told myself as I walked toward the building, which housed an abandoned warehouse of some sort. I tried to pry the front door open to no avail, so I walked around the back. I came to a door with a blackout tint on the glass window, but it also was locked.

I paced around the back lot in disbelief. I had driven six hours to arrive at a deserted warehouse. I wasn't about to get back in my car and go home empty-handed. I scoured the littered yard for some kind of heavy object. Next to a few hubcaps, I found a tire iron in some overgrown weeds. I used it to shatter the back-door window of the warehouse. I rationalized the act by telling myself that this was not simply a random warehouse but an empty warehouse, an empty warehouse that belonged to a known felon, and, not to mention, a warehouse with no surveillance cameras. Besides, no one was around for miles. Who would know?

I reached in and unlocked the deadbolt on the door. Inside, the cavernous space had been swept clean. An efficiency-style kitchen stood nearly bare in a corner. Only a roll of paper towels and a stack of red plastic cups remained. In another corner I found six empty boxes. I checked the labels on them—all were addressed to the same person.

SOFIA VILLANUEVA, 251 SURREY COURT, MALABAR, FL 32950, read the address labels.

The return addresses only intensified the mystery. Three of them had been shipped from the Home Shopping Network in St. Petersburg, Florida. The three others had come from some place called A Flair for Crafts in Murphy, North Carolina. They were stamped with signs that read: AS SEEN ON TV! But there was nothing from Colombia, New Mexico, Key West, or any other location referenced in the drug trafficking case against Maria Portilla.

I locked the door on my way out of the warehouse and walked over to a row of mailboxes. I flipped each of them open—all were jammed with junk mail addressed to the other empty warehouses. All, that is, except for the one marked "251." It was empty.

I went back to the car and drove it to a shady spot, settling in for a stakeout. If the mailbox was empty, it could only mean someone was coming by to pick up the mail. I pulled out the crossword puzzle from *Florida Today* and went to work on it.

Twelve-letter word for "hard metallic shade."

Pass.

Nine-letter word that means segments of equal length.

"Congruent," I said to myself, jotting the letters in the boxes.

I must have been there for a good hour by the time the mailman came around. I saw him stuff a bundle of mail into the box marked "251." About a half hour and a deadlocked crossword puzzle later, someone pulled up in a silver Toyota Corolla. I studied the driver as he got out of the car. He was a tall, skinny man with careless wisps of flaxen hair and Ray-Bans. He walked over to mailbox 251, flipped it open, and grabbed the wad of mail.

In belted jeans and a striped polo shirt, he cut an oddly familiar silhouette. Where had I seen him before? I thought for a minute, then reached for the Portilla case file on my passenger seat. I leafed through the file and fished out a black and white photograph. I studied the man in the photograph and then studied the man in the silver Corolla—it was the same guy. He was the lanky man from the surveillance video, back at the DEA interrogation room. The man in the silver Corolla was none other than El Flaco.

I squinted to read his license plate: NTA-114.

I scribbled the number on the case file folder as El Flaco started to drive away. I waited one prudent moment before pulling out behind him. Not that he would have known who I was anyway. The story of my "murky" release had not been picked up outside Miami. Still, to be on the safe side, I kept an ample distance from the Corolla. I meandered through the industrial zone and into the surrounding neighborhood at a somewhat breezy pace, even allowing a random car or two to cut in front of me. All the while, however, I kept my eye on the silver Corolla. The scene reminded me of the time Gina and I tailed one of her boyfriends, a mysterious dude who had claimed to be a black-belted martial arts phenomenon and a movie stuntman, most notably in *True Lies,* the Schwarzenegger film partly shot in Miami. With Gina hiding in the front seat of my car, I followed the guy's beat-up Firebird to a storefront jujitsu gym. We watched from a nearby parking lot as some skinny teenager gave Gina's boyfriend the smackdown of his life. Of course, it wasn't as bad as the ego bruising he took later from Gina over the phone. I'll give him one thing, though—he did drive like a wannabe stuntman.

And so did El Flaco. He didn't make it easy for me to keep up with him once we left the neighborhood surrounding the warehouse. He managed to confound me as he zigzagged across town on a tour of the absurd. He stopped to check out the gear at a scuba shop. He stopped to test golf clubs at Sports Authority. He swung by a fine jewelry shop to examine the Cartier watches. El Flaco, it seemed to me, was not only excessively rich—he was bored out of his flaxen mind. As he lingered over the jewelry counter, I typed his license plate number into a premium reverse directory to which I had a subscription.

The owner of the car came back with a familiar ring: Guerra Group South LLC.

I was no closer to learning El Flaco's identity. But I was learning about his impulses. In the most spectacular of his pit stops, he walked into the showroom at a luxury car dealership, strolling between Bentleys and Lamborghinis, Jaguars and Rolls-Royces. He came to stop at an electric blue Tesla Roadster, and the color triggered a non sequitur in my head.

Electric blue, I thought, mulling the phrase in my head. Twelve-letter word for "hard metallic shade."

But El Flaco moved on to the next toy. Purely on a whim, he test-drove a Ferrari F430 Scuderia. When he returned, pumped from the ride, he corralled a sales rep into a glass-enclosed cubicle, and he dove into manic shopper mode. From where I was parked just outside the showroom, I could see El Flaco was frothing up some kind of deal. His dramatic, jabbing hand gestures seemed out of place in that rarefied parking space created for the luxury vehicles of the crème de la crème. It seemed to take some haggling on his part, one very heated phone call to God knows who, and an almost comical display of angst, but El Flaco got what he wanted that day. He drove away in a canary yellow $220,000 special series Ferrari.

To celebrate his purchase, he zoomed over to Sugarlump's Burger Joint and feasted on a double-with-cheese combo. Then he headed for a nearby strip mall, where he entered a storefront salon called A Brand New You Day Spa.

Once he got inside, amid the soft jazz, silk flowers, and pink-robed, suburban tranquillity seekers, it was evident El Flaco was that guy you never want to meet at a spa. He was impatient, obnoxious, and loud. He paced between the serenity fountains, barking insults into his cell phone.

"Fuck your facial. I'm waiting two minutes, then I'm leaving," he said, the veins on his neck protruding in outrage. "What do you mean—don't you even want to see it? Then come out here. It's parked outside—where else would it be parked?"

I pretended to browse through meditation books at the spa gift shop as El Flaco continued to pace the lobby. He ignored the stares of several pink-robed ladies who sat in the lounging area sipping herbal tea and reading celeb magazines. Moments later, he was met by a woman in an oversized spa robe, her hair wrapped high in a towel, her face smeared with some kind of orange glop.

From their body language, it seemed these two were not a couple. She treated him like a servant or a wayward child. She sniffed and talked down to him. Of course I wondered if this could be the woman in the video, the object of my pursuit. Could this be La Reina herself? But she seemed so much younger, more lithe than the Maria Portilla of the DEA photographs. She carried herself with a rich-bitch arrogance and an almost regal air, like a woman who knows exactly what she wants. And, from the looks of it, she didn't want a 510-horsepower, $220,000 luxury sports car. When she caught a glimpse of the Ferrari through the storefront window, she nearly had a conniption.

"Are you insane?" she said in a loud hiss. "What are you trying to do to me?"

"I couldn't drive that piece of shit one more day," said El Flaco, turning away from her, almost sulking. "It was embarrassing."

"It wasn't embarrassing. It was a safe car. This is not safe. This is suicide," the woman said in whispered staccato.

"What's the big deal? It's not your money," said El Flaco, jabbing a finger at her robe.

"Correction: It's not your money," said the woman, lifting her orange-goop cheek in scorn. "You will take that ridiculous car back right now."

She zipped around to go back inside. As she was leaving, El Flaco called after her in a voice that was loud enough for all the lounging ladies to hear: "Hey! At least I'm not blowing my money on stupid crap from TV!"

I dropped the meditation book I was pretending to read as I watched El Flaco storm toward the front door. Stupid crap from TV? It didn't take a crack investigator to wonder if this stupid crap he was talking about had arrived at the Surrey Court warehouse in boxes stamped AS SEEN ON TV! But even if it was true that this woman had ordered gratuitous merchandise from TV shopping channels, it was a comparatively modest over-shopping sin. The supposed TV crap came in brown cardboard boxes delivered to an empty warehouse, where no one could see it. A yellow Ferrari, on the other hand, didn't simply scream conspicuous consumption, it Z-snapped it for the whole world to see.

"Check. Me. Out," said the yellow Ferrari.

The fundamental question had grated on me since I saw El Flaco in that auto showroom: Why would a wanted man like El Flaco go on a balls-out buying spree in the first place? Why would he be so obvious?

As he bolted out the door, he left me with a dilemma: If I followed him, I might lose track of this mystery woman. But if I stayed to check her out more closely, my afternoon could prove to be a bust, and I would have to stalk El Flaco at the warehouse all over again. I was convinced this woman was too young to be La Reina. Her English was too fluent—perhaps I was mistaken, but I imagined a Colombian national would still possess the lilt and syntax of her native tongue. This woman simply didn't fit the profile of an undocumented drug queen from Colombia. Besides, what were the chances the real Maria Portilla would be out in public, getting facials at random day spas?

But there was something about the woman that intrigued me just enough that day. As she headed back toward the treatment room, I walked over to the reception desk.

"I want whatever facial that woman's having. It looks exactly like what I want," I said to the young spa attendant.

"That would be the mango-papaya deluxe," she said, checking her book for availability. "And it seems I can squeeze you in for a half-hour treatment right now."

"Good deal," I said, taking a locker key and a pair of slippers from her.

Within minutes, I was dressed in a pink robe, sitting in a foamy white recliner, next to El Flaco's friend. Three aestheticians attended to her, a facialist, a manicurist, and a pedicurist. It was quite a ballet of swirling motions and lotions, and it kept me staring until I felt a tap on my cheek.

"Honey, you need to relax," said my own aesthetician, who

rested my head against a small pillow. "This is papaya enzyme. Just a little sting now," she said, as she smeared the orange paste on my forehead. "So, what's your name?"

My name.

I had no idea. I knew it couldn't be Maria or Mary. It couldn't be Janet, either—what if the Key West gang somehow put two and two together?

"Angela," I said.

"Oh—that's my sister's name," said the aesthetician, her face lighting up.

I closed my eyes in hopes this aesthetician would shut up and let me eavesdrop on my neighbor. It was hard enough to hear myself think with the Kenny G ambient noise streaming through the speaker system.

I glanced over at the next chair, where El Flaco's friend sat with her eyes closed in attempted bliss. I could tell she was a woman of medium build, although I couldn't see the shape of her body because her robe was too large. She had absurdly long nails, freshly painted by the manicurist a ginger frost shade, and her face looked hideous in that orange clay mask. Then again, who was I to talk? I could have been her twin just then, with my own face smeared in what the spa brochure described as "a deeply rejuvenating elixir made from natural botanicals and fruit enzymes."

"Relax, sweetie," her facialist told her. "Don't worry about him right now."

The glop on her face moved and cracked as the woman grimaced beneath it.

"He's an ungrateful, spoiled-rotten brat," she said.

"No, no, no—no frowning," said the facialist, starting to peel off the woman's orange mask.

The facialist placed a damp washcloth on the woman's face

to wipe off the excess product and then removed the towel from her head. El Flaco's friend shook her hair loose like the women in shampoo commercials.

"Wow. Look at the glow on you," the facialist said, handing the woman a gold-rimmed mirror.

I tried to get a look at her, but the woman had sat up with her back to my chair. I could tell she demurred a bit before taking the mirror and giving herself a slow once-over. She tilted her head coquettishly as if she were looking into a camera on the red carpet.

"Very nice," she said, leaning back into her lounge chair.

I couldn't help but glance over at her. And when I did, I gasped to myself at the sight of her face. It was a face forever burned into my memory, the same face I had seen in the surveillance video and the police photos at DEA headquarters, the face I had seen in my nightmares. It was the same face, the face that had derailed my life. It was La Reina, in the newly polished flesh.

Bad Mary.

In some ways, she looked like an entirely different woman. Her hair was no longer wavy—it hung unnaturally straight, as if she had had it ionically pressed. She was toned and slender, far less puffy than she had appeared to be. Even her mouth, collagen-pumped as it was, didn't look so botched up as it had in the photographs.

I wanted to pick up my phone and call Agent Green right then and there, and that's probably what I should have done. But the sight of La Reina sitting so close to me, a woman who had just been my mirror image in orange clay, infuriated me to no end. Now that I had her within my reach, I wasn't going to risk losing her.

"Yeah, look at the glow on you," I said in feigned admiration. "I hope I look as good under all this nonsense."

She gave me a polite smile and leaned back as her facialist applied a sweep of makeup on her forehead.

"I need a drink, Brenda," she told the facialist.

"Have you tried the coconut smoothie?" the facialist said.

"Does that come with a double shot of Bacardi?" said Bad Mary dryly.

"Sign me up for one of those," I said, settling back into my chair as my aesthetician wiped the mask off my face.

"Two virgin coconut smoothies coming up," one of the cheery attendants said, rushing off to the spa juice bar.

Bad Mary sat up and gave me a once-over look, checking out my newly treated skin.

"You've got a glow on your skin, too," she said, reclining into her chair again. "These masks are fabulous, aren't they?"

"They are," I said, trying to sound as if I was simply having a casual conversation.

"Between the masks and the Pilates, you can take ten years off," she said with an authoritative wave of her hand.

"Exactly," I said. "Just look at me—I'm sixty-five."

Bad Mary guffawed, causing her forehead to wrinkle unnaturally, revealing the edges of scar tissue at the hairline. Upon closer inspection, she seemed manufactured in a sense, not a genuine woman but a strategically arranged composition of other women's features, all designed to camouflage her in society, not distinguish her in any way. Bad Mary was a friggin' fembot.

She took her coconut smoothie from the cheery attendant and sipped it through a straw, once again demonstrating her alien nature. Her lips, numb from collagen abuse, pursed awkwardly around the straw, making her eyes bug out. She drank her smoothie much like a fish might drink a smoothie.

"This certainly hits the spot," I said, taking a sip of the shake.

But it was clear Bad Mary didn't share my taste for it. Her face puckered in disgust as she sucked on the straw. She kept taking sips and stopping to lick her lips, as if each sip was supposed to taste different from the previous one.

"They used the wrong coconuts," she said, smacking her lips again to judge the flavor. "Old coconuts."

"Old coconuts?" I said.

"Yes. There are young coconuts, which are nice and sweet, perfect for piña coladas and coconut cream flan. And there are old coconuts, which are *bleh*. These are old," she said in a decisive manner.

"Coconut cream flan sounds delicious," I said.

"It is," she said assertively.

"Do you cook much?" I said.

"A little," she said in contrived modesty. "Just enough to be considered a gourmet cook. In fact, I'm now writing my first cookbook."

"A cookbook—I'm impressed. What kind of cookbook?" I said.

"The foods of *Andalu-thia*," she said, feeling the need to add: "That's a region in the south of Spain."

"Ah. Are you Spanish?" I said.

Bad Mary turned rather chilly at the question.

"No," she said, offering nothing further, just a weak smile as she got up and disappeared toward the dressing room area.

A little while later, I bumped into her at the spa checkout desk, where she was paying her bill in cash. She looked up with a dead-behind-the-eyes smile.

"It was very nice to meet you," she said, slipping a humble beige Liz Claiborne wallet into a shoulder bag of matching jacquard-print design.

"Same here. Good luck with the cookbook," I said, my mind scrambling to keep the conversation going.

"Oh, thanks," she said, starting to walk out.

"I'd love to try that coconut cream flan sometime," I said, undaunted.

Bad Mary nodded diplomatically, as if to detach herself from the chitchat.

"You should," she said as she brushed past me on her way out to the parking lot.

I tried to follow her out without seeming too obvious, and I even managed to scribble down her license plate. But just as I turned on the ignition of my car, I saw the spa checkout attendant waving at me from the front door.

"Come back," she said, waving a scrap of paper.

I cursed to myself as I turned off the car. I went back in to see what she wanted.

"What's wrong?" I said.

"You forgot to pay," said the attendant.

"Sorry," I said, horrified at my lapse, "I guess I'm a little too relaxed."

"No prob," said the girl, handing me the check.

I paid her with a large bill, glancing back to catch sight of Bad Mary driving away in a white Volvo S70, an outdated but perfectly safe car.

"Shoot. I forgot something else," I said to the attendant. "I forgot to give that woman out there my phone number. I'm supposed to show her some houses later. Do you know how I can reach her?"

"No prob," said the attendant, sliding a notepad across the counter and handing me a pen. "Go ahead and jot your number down, and I'll have her call you."

"Will do, thanks," I said.

"I'll go get your change," she said. "Be right back."

When the attendant left the desk, I went around the counter

and pretended to use the phone at her desk. I spied the large appointment book, which was open on the desk, and I scanned it for facial appointments. And there it was—gold. I scribbled down the name, number, and address of the most pampered client at A Brand New You Day Spa: Sofia Villanueva.

"Sofia Villanueva, you sorry bitch," I thought as I slipped back to the other side of the counter, "I hope you like surprises."

TWELVE

RED ROOF INN—DAY 30
A generic, functionally appointed hotel room designed for the traveling-sales-rep set. Mary, visibly antsy, hunches over her laptop, the cell phone glued to her ear.

Sofia Villanueva didn't exist. Except, perhaps, to the good folks at the Home Shopping Network. Her name was nowhere to be found in the property and vehicle records I thoroughly searched online. Both her license plate number and the address written next to her appointment on the spa log corresponded to a different name entirely: Natalie Newhouse.

Who on earth was Natalie Newhouse?

For all intents and purposes, it didn't matter who she was. For all I cared, Bad Mary could have called herself Nancy Reagan. I knew she was Maria Portilla—I was convinced of it. Besides, contrary to what the feds may have believed, Bad Mary simply was not that smart. It took just one comparative glance at those two last names to know I was dealing with the same pathetic human being.

Villanueva.

Newhouse.

She wasn't too bright at all. Clearly, she shared Jimmy Paz's affinity for word games. Whatever. I had her cold.

I rang up Agent Dan Green's desk at DEA headquarters. My heart leaped when I heard the voice on the other end.

"Agent Green, it's Mary Guevara," I said. "I hope you're sitting down."

"I'm sitting down, but I'm not Agent Green," said the guy who answered the phone.

"Is this Agent Gonzalez?"

"Not him, either," he said. "Gonzalez is no longer based in this office. Green, I'm not too sure where he is at the moment. But I'm glad to take a message."

"Are you an agent?" I said.

"Special assistant. My name is Marcus," he said.

"Marcus, this is urgent," I said. "Please tell Agent Green this is Mary Guevara."

"Spell it," he said.

"G-U-E-V-A-R-A."

"You mean like Che?"

"No, sir, not like Che."

"What's the message?"

"Tell him I've located Maria Portilla, the fugitive drug dealer they confused me for. I found the real Maria Portilla. I know where she is. She's in Malabar—"

"Spell the name," he said, giving no indication he had recognized the tip.

"P-O-R-T-I-L-L-A . . ."

"Okay. That's your name?"

"No, my name is Guevara," I said.

"Like Che."

"Yes," I said, annoyed, "like Che. Please tell Agent Green he needs to call me. My number is six four zero two nine four eight. It's extremely important that he call me right away. I'm going to wait by my phone, okay?"

"Yep. You'll hear from him as soon as he gets this message," said the assistant, hanging up.

But when I didn't hear back within a half hour, I called Agent Green's desk again. This time, I didn't get Marcus, or any other live voice. I got Agent Green's answering machine. The outgoing message went like this: *"You have reached the desk of Special Agent Dan Green of the DEA. I will be away from the office and unavailable to receive phone calls until Monday the seventeenth. You can leave a message at this number, if you'd like, or you can dial zero to speak to an agent on duty. Thanks."*

I dialed zero, but that only bounced my call to another recorded message: *"This is the Miami office of the DEA. We are closed for the day. Our regular office hours are eight a.m. to six p.m., Mondays through Fridays. If this is a police emergency, hang up and dial 911."*

How could the office be closed? Worse still, how could Agent Green be on vacation? What gave him the right to be away for so long? The seventeenth was two days away—I couldn't wait that long. Maria Portilla could be gone by then. I had to make a decision on the spot, and in my gut I sensed it would be the wrong one, no matter what I chose to do. I could call 911 and report Maria Portilla's whereabouts. But to someone unfamiliar with the case, the tip might sound far-fetched and unreliable. I didn't want to take the chance. Nor did I want to surrender my information to someone who didn't know my story—what if the Brevard County sheriff's office turned the investigation on me?

I'd be back to where I had started. On the other hand, I couldn't just swoop in and grab La Reina on my own.

I paced the mauve confines of my room, trying to figure out what I should do next. As much as I wanted to see Bad Mary go to jail and as desperately as I wanted my old life restored, I wasn't a delinquent or some hot-dog vigilante—okay, despite that minor false-imprisonment incident back at Gus's apartment, the breaking-and-entering situation at the Surrey Court warehouse, and the illegal handgun stashed in my nightstand. The point is that, undoubtedly, I was an upstanding citizen. So, I decided to wait for someone to return my call from the DEA. For a little while, at least.

I lay on the bed as I stared at the panel on my cell phone, ready for my favorite screen saver, the goofy picture of Max I'd snapped at the beach two months ago, to light up with a ring. But I had a feeling it wouldn't light up at all. So I struck a little deal with myself: If fifteen minutes passed and the phone still had not rung, I would take it as a sign from the universe that I should proceed on my own.

To kill time, I grabbed the hotel phone and called my son at Tony's house. When I heard Tony's voice answer the phone, I could tell he was still in a bad mood.

"Hey, it's me," I said, keeping an eye on the time. "I'd like to speak to Max."

"Why do you bother to ask when you know what the answer is? Besides, he's taking a nap now," Tony said.

"Max never takes a nap, not unless he's sick—what's wrong with him?" I said, obsessively checking the cell phone to make sure it was on.

"He's tired. He's been working very hard in therapy. You know, with his pediatric psychiatrist," Tony said flatly, in the same manner another father might describe a son's visit to the dentist or the barbershop. "He's doing some very important emotional work, you know. Victoria and I are quite proud of him."

"Any therapist who would keep Max from me is a hack and you know it," I said.

"For your information, he is not a hack. He came very highly recommended," said Tony.

"Really. By whom?" I said, my eyes darting between the cell phone screen and the alarm clock.

"By someone with excellent contacts in the child welfare community," said Tony, pronouncing the word *"walfare."*

"Who's that?"

"Victoria," he said.

"What does she know about child psychiatrists?" I said, baiting him.

"Plenty. Dr. Howard is one of Victoria's closest advisers on her Children for a New Society campaign. He is an extraordinary advocate for children," he said.

Tony had stepped in it big-time. I'm sure he hadn't intended to admit that this shrink was one of Victoria's political cronies, but he did just that. For all the times Tony had tried his best to unnerve me, pushing my buttons to prove his contention that I was an unfit mother, he had finally proven to be my best ally. Unwittingly so, of course. He had buried not only the shrink and Victoria but also himself.

I didn't call attention to his gaffe, not just then. I tried to do the opposite.

"Sounds like he's pretty competent, then. Did he prescribe any medication?" I said, playing into the Ramonet pathology.

"Just a minor dosage," said Tony. "Max really needed to sleep."

"Let him rest, then," I said. As outraged as I was, I kept my tone level.

I hung up with Tony and buried my head in a pillow. Even though I now had evidence of a flagrant conflict of interest, I couldn't help but feel defeated. I was worried sick about Max.

After a few minutes, I checked the time again. The fifteen minutes were almost up. I paced by the alarm clock until thirty seconds remained on the allotted time and then I picked up the cell phone to make another call. This was a call I didn't want to make because doing so was an admission that I just might need help. I'm a woman who takes pride in handling my business, earning my salary, paying my bills, raising my child. And I was 98 percent sure I could handle the likes of Maria Portilla—singlehandedly—but there was that nagging 2 percent chance that she could get away. I couldn't take that risk.

So I made the call. The phone rang a few times before an answering machine picked up. When I heard the beep, I left this message: "Listen, I may need your help tonight. I found her. The address is Forty-seven Sunset Terrace, in Malabar. I'm headed over there now. I need you to come out and wait nearby until I call you. And one more thing . . . Bring your gun."

THE RETREAT AT MALABAR—DAY 30
A suburban development of palm-lined, winding roads and Mediterranean-style houses of nearly identical size and appearance. Mary's car weaves along a quiet street.

Even at night, I could tell the development had been aptly named for a woman of Maria Portilla's characteristics. Indeed it was a retreat from the life of a runaway drug dealer, a place to blend in, to mimic the lives of others. This was a place where your home looked like everybody else's home—from the outside, that is. Everybody's door had a wreath of dried flowers and everybody's backyard had a vine-covered pergola. Those who may value a more refined sense of individuality might stay away from such a compound, but Bad Mary was not one to, well, retreat from The Retreat. Her freedom depended on her ability to go undetected among the neighborhood joggers, the tennis club members, the Tuesday-night bridge enthusiasts.

And I have to say, it wasn't a horrible place. It was quite lovely. In fact, in some ways, The Retreat at Malabar reminded me of my own neighborhood back in Miami. The similarities had nothing to do with the houses or the community layout, mind you. It had to do with a sense of order, diligence, and calm I felt as I drove along Sunset Terrace. It was that unmistakable feeling of safety that comes from a certain level of predictability in which every routine is honored, every hedge trimmed, every newspaper collected from the lawn, every window aglow at a certain time of evening. Such quotidian rituals bring with them a sense of safety. I learned this as a child in my parents' home. I learned it in the repetition of similarly lived days, the shuffle of my father's steel-toed work boots on the kitchen linoleum at dawn, the wheeze of my brother's school bus at the corner stop, the aroma of steak and onions frying in a pan at dinner, the way the lock on the front door squeaked as my father clicked it shut each night.

And this is what I missed the most about my home, the feeling of security it engendered. I feared that feeling might be lost in me forever. If the federal raid of my home taught me anything, it taught me there is no such thing as safe.

Bad Mary was about to learn the same suburban lesson.

THIRTEEN

A RECTANGULAR HEDGE of nondescript shrubbery traced the way to Bad Mary's front door, a sturdy, hacienda-style wood door hung with an odd wreath of dried roses embedded in a tangle of dehydrated eucalyptus. As I got closer to the door, I could hear the distant strumming of a Spanish guitar in a spirited rendition of *"La Malagueña."* I wondered if she had company, although that possibility didn't stop me from ringing the doorbell.

After a few moments, the door cracked open, a chain tethering it to the frame. Bad Mary, the door concealing half of her face, peered at me with a bewildered look. I didn't stare directly at her at first as I pretended to search my bag for one of my business cards—one I had printed up just a few minutes earlier at a nearby Kinko's, mind you.

"Hi there, I'm Angela. I'm a Realtor," I said, handing her one of the cards and trying to give her the impression I did not recognize her. "I've got some clients in the area who are interested—"

The door slammed shut in my face. A few seconds later, it reopened, no longer tethered by the chain. Framed in the doorway stood Bad Mary, wearing a bizarre little apron that appeared to have been crafted while its maker was drunk. It bore the likeness of a bird—some kind of bird—and it seemed abruptly cut off by a slanted, ball-fringe hem. She dragged on a cigarette.

"Hey. It's you," I said, seemingly taken aback. "What a huge coincidence."

"You're a Realtor?" she said, flicking her cigarette ashes on the threshold, then sweeping them outside with her terry cloth slipper.

"Yeah. I work a lot in this neighborhood, too," I said, eyes bright.

"But my house isn't for sale," she said, resting a hand on her hip.

"I know. But I've got buyers champing at the bit for this particular model," I said, following my script perfectly so far. "So I decided to stop by on the off chance the owner might consider an above-appraisal bid."

"Can I ask what are they bidding?" she said, taking another drag.

"Two million seven. For a smaller house," I said, quoting a figure I decided might grab her attention.

"What would this house go for?" she said, indeed piqued by the number.

"I'm not sure," I said. "I'd have to see it."

Without another thought, she flung open the door to Sofia Villanueva's residence.

"Come on in," she said. She sounded notably underwhelmed. "What a strange surprise, no?"

"Very," I said with a chirp in my voice. "I'm sorry, I didn't get your name at the spa today."

"Sofia," she said abruptly, as if she had rehearsed it and feared forgetting it.

As the guitar music ebbed and flowed, she led me through the marbled foyer beneath a series of elliptical archways that connected the living room, a wood-paneled family room, and a small office. To say the decor in these rooms was bland would be an understatement. It was worse than your average suburban bland—it was a vile imitation of it. Lots of earth-toned sofa pillows and pea-colored throws. Leather-bound tomes—surely unread—were stacked on the occasional tables next to bouquets of silk flowers in that clear resin base otherwise known as "faux water."

There were no personal photographs or family mementos. But there was a medium-sized room that served as her crafting quarters. There, spread across two adjoining banquet-hall-type tables, were the contents of all those boxes I had seen in the warehouse. I was sure of it. There were bundles of synthetic flowers, boxes of glitter, bins filled with stringing beads, macramé projects in progress, and baskets brimming with ribbons of morose shades.

The room was a craft addict's dream, but there was one glaring omission: the scrapbooking supplies.

Even a noncrafting woman like me knows every craft addict spirals into a scrapbook-making binge every once in a while. Why would Bad Mary be any different? That's a rhetorical question, I guess. After all, what on earth would "Sofia Villanueva of The Retreat at Malabar" put in a scrapbook about her life? Her "Wanted by the DEA" mug shots? Some spent casings from her Colt .45? A couple of surplus zip bags of cocaine? Would she decorate the pages with craft store stickers or cartoon speech bubbles containing quippy expressions, like "LOL, Suckers," or "The Godfather's Little Angel," or "Caution . . . Drug Queen On Board"?

So, yes, it was a rhetorical question. But I had to go there anyway, if only to get her to talk about herself.

"Do you scrapbook?" I asked her.

"No," she quickly said. She inspected an unfinished macramé hammock, an ambitious project that might take the average hobbyist a good two weeks to complete, and set it aside for later. "I don't have the patience."

"I can relate to that," I said. "Are the bathrooms this way?"

"I'll show you," she said, directing me down the hall into the rest of the house.

Moments later, I was standing in her lemon yellow guest bathroom, surveying the grape-toned sink accessories. I ran my hand along the stiff lace border of her eggplant-colored guest towels, and I concluded they were too prickly to be functional. Besides, they were ugly as hell.

"These are lovely," I said, quietly noticing the slipshod finish on the towels. "Did you make them?"

"I did," she said, momentarily beaming.

But our chat was disrupted by the slam of the front door, then a rumble of footsteps through the house. Bad Mary must have been expecting company, because she didn't seem too alarmed at the ruckus.

"Flaco!" she called out. "Don't touch anything in the kitchen!"

"What?" a man's voice hollered back from the other side of the house. "What did you say?"

"Moron," she mumbled to herself.

"You have company," I said.

"No. He's not staying," she said, straightening the towels on the rack. "Why don't you take a look at the Roman tub and the sauna over here? I'll be right back."

But as soon as Bad Mary found El Flaco in the kitchen, all hell broke loose. I couldn't make out what they were saying, but it sounded like they were wrangling pretty good. And, more importantly for my purposes, it sounded like the brawl could go on for quite some time, carving out a precious window of opportunity for me. I snuck out of the bathroom and into the master bedroom. It was decorated in that severe Old World style, featuring a massive four-poster bed, ornate furnishings with carved scroll motifs, brocade bedding, and pillows in saturated tones. A deep green velvet-lined, Chippendale-style chair anchored one corner, adorned with an embroidered pillow of some sort. I searched the dresser and nightstands as quickly and efficiently as I could, digging through drawers filled with brand-new socks and lingerie, T-shirts in every neutral, and workout clothes that seemed to be untouched. In fact, many of the clothes still had price tags attached to them. In the walk-in closet I found a similar pattern, unworn blouses and pantsuits hung in no particular order. There were Jackie O sunglasses and Sophia Loren hats, silk scarves like the ones worn by Princess Caroline of Monaco, and smart, strapless dresses like those modeled by Isabel Preysler, Julio Iglesias's ex-wife, on the pages of ¡Hola! magazine.

I found no drugs, no weapons, no trashy dresses, no vestige of a life lived as a drug queen. It was as if Maria Portilla, La Reina, had never existed. Instead, there was evidence of a woman, ambiguous about her brand, noncommittal in her style, a woman who purchased flowing $2,000 evening gowns but never wore them. Instead, she favored mom jeans, inexpensive coordinates, and sensible shoes. So I found nothing in the closet to link her to any drug ring.

What I found atop that green velvet chair, that's another story. Intrigued by its bizarre embroidery, I picked up the pillow and studied its design pattern. It was a black feline creature of some kind with unnatural, saucer-like eyes. I turned the pillow around, tracing its uneven, shabbily finished edges. And that's when I noticed it had two zippers. What kind of pillow had two zippers? I squeezed the quilt batting near the zipper lines and heard a strange rustle inside. It wasn't the sound of foam or cotton or any other filler. It was a mix of plastic and paper. I unzipped the first opening and slid my hand into the pillow. But all I could feel was loose fiber filling. So I unzipped the second opening and reached inside once again. This time, I felt not fiber but plastic. I grabbed hold of the plastic and pulled out a zip bag containing a bundle of letters. I opened the bag for a closer look: All of the letters were addressed in neat block handwriting to a "Señor Juan, 64 Calle Luna, Cali, Colombia." Wedged between the letters were three passports. I opened only the first one, a Colombian passport, and found a photo of Bad Mary looking the same way she had in the police video. The page adjacent to the photo listed her first and last name, and there they were, the ringing words that placed this woman in a class apart from everybody else in Stepford, those words that validated all the reasons for my subterfuge: PORTILLA, MARIA.

I reached for my phone and made the call I thought I wouldn't have to make.

"You need to be here in one hour," I said when the answering machine picked up.

I grabbed the passports and the letters and slipped them into my purse. I zipped up the pillow, returned it to its chair, and ducked out of the bedroom to the hallway. There were two more rooms down the hall, but I didn't search them. I had what I needed. Besides, I could hear the fight between Bad Mary and El Flaco was still raging in the kitchen. I wandered within earshot of them. Their theatrical back-and-forth in Spanish sounded like an ill-scripted scene from my mother's *telenovela*.

Had it been a *telenovela*, these would be the subtitles:

BAD MARY: Do you know what the word "betrayal" means? Because that is exactly what you've done to me.

EL FLACO: I betrayed you? How could I? You invented the
meaning of betrayal.

BAD MARY: You crafty, wicked scoundrel. Thanks to you, I
have to live each day in fear—fear of losing everything I
have worked for.

EL FLACO: You worked for? Aren't you forgetting someone?
Didn't he work, too? What do you care—you stole
everything he had. And then you stabbed him in the heart
on your way out the door.

BAD MARY: I stole nothing from him. I took only what was
rightfully mine.

EL FLACO: Yours, was it? Well, I've got news for you. It
won't be yours much longer. I know where you're
hiding it.

BAD MARY: You have no idea.

EL FLACO: And so will he.

BAD MARY: You wouldn't dare tell him!

EL FLACO: I already placed a call to him. The message is on
its way to him as we speak. I suggest you pay him back
what you stole. If you don't, I can no longer protect you.

BAD MARY: Go to hell, you swine!

As a standoff swelled between them, the kitchen went silent,
except for the highly appropriate sounds of canned flamenco.
Clearly, El Flaco's words had rattled Bad Mary. Who knew how
she would react to his threats. She could fight them or she could
flee. I knew I had to make a move before I lost my fugitive.

I wandered into the kitchen, airhead-like, as if nothing had
happened.

"I have to say, Sofia, your house is just beautiful," I said in a
sunny tone.

"Who's this?" El Flaco asked under his breath.

Bad Mary was visibly shaken, her eyes smeared with black mascara and tears.

"Angela, meet Francisco, my business partner," she said, extending an arm in my direction. "Angela is a Realtor."

El Flaco offered me a cold, feeble handshake.

"Francisco was just leaving," she said, glaring at him. "Unfortunately, he has other commitments this evening."

El Flaco nodded a half-assed good-bye and left, slamming the front door on his way out. When he was gone, Bad Mary turned to me with a steely look.

"Where were you all that time?" she said.

"When?" I said, keeping my cool.

"When I was in the kitchen with Francisco—where were you?" she said, knotting her brow.

"In the bathroom," I said.

She shot me a cynical look.

"I had to go," I said. "Sorry."

Bad Mary seemed satisfied enough with my explanation, but I could tell she was still angry over her fight with El Flaco. She seemed preoccupied and not overly bothered by the fact that I was still standing in her kitchen. Certainly, I was not going to remind her that we hadn't finished our tour of the house. I just watched her as she, without preamble or explanation, started dinner. She took a butcher's knife from a rack and, knife in hand, she assembled some ingredients: a yellow onion and a potato from the fridge, and a can of tomato puree from the pantry. She took the onion and, without peeling it, chopped it on the counter, then scooped it into a dish. She did peel the potato, however, carving it up with her butcher's knife until only a shadow of it remained. Done with that, she put down the knife and opened up a bottle of red Spanish wine, pouring herself a full goblet.

"So what's your best guess on the house?" she said without looking at me.

"I'd say close to two point nine," I said, trying to stay focused on my original script.

She went to the fridge and pulled out a whole red snapper. I noticed her hands were trembling as she laid the fish across a chopping block.

"That much? Maybe I'll sell it after all," she said, taking a swig of the wine.

She grabbed the knife again, raised it, and brought it down with a WHACK on the chopping block, sending the fish's head tumbling off the counter. It landed on the kitchen floor with a wet thud. Bad Mary picked it up and tossed it into an empty stockpot on the stove. She didn't wash it first, or dust it off, or even check it for dirt. She just dumped it into the stockpot. Some gourmet, this one. She took the fish and scraped off its scales with a vengeance, an exercise that alternated with hard swigs of wine and cigarette puffs. I couldn't stop watching the train wreck that was Bad Mary's cooking demo, as I was both disgusted and morbidly engrossed.

"He's not well, you know," she said, the cigarette dangling on her frosted lip.

"Who?" I said, playing dumb.

"Francisco," she said with another WHACK of the knife as she pierced a jagged spout on the can of tomato sauce. "Want some rioja?"

"I'll get it," I said, helping myself to a glass of the wine.

She put down the knife for a minute—it was smeared with blood and fish scales. But it wasn't as offensive as the detail I noticed next. It was the smallest detail in her "country style" kitchen: a little plaque bearing a familiar saying.

HELP KEEP THE KITCHEN CLEAN—EAT OUT, it said.

Fourteen

I CAN'T BEGIN to describe the nauseating feeling that burned from the pit of my stomach to the base of my throat. Of all the offensive things I had seen in that house—faux water included—this was by far the most offensive. Up until that moment, I had recognized nothing of myself in the woman who had taken my life from me. We had zero in common, not a hobby, not an article of clothing, not a single style of shoe. But the plaque . . . the plaque was sacred. The plaque was mine. That plaque meant dinners shared around my kitchen counter, Max's tales from school, my mother's crispy double-fried plantains, pizza on Heat game night, mango sours on girls' nights. The plaque was sacred. The plaque was mine. Enough was enough.

I reached for the butcher knife—it glinted red in my hand. Startled, Bad Mary put down her wineglass.

"What are you doing?" she said nervously, backing into the counter.

"Let me help you," I said, taking over.

I charged in front of her and grabbed the fish by the tail, and I started to clean it the proper way, scraping its sides from tail to head, then turning it over and doing it again, then rinsing it off in the sink with bold, demonstrative moves.

"You don't have to cook for me," Bad Mary said, indignant.

"But I want to," I said, searching through the cupboards for spices and condiments.

"I know what I'm doing," she said in a convinced tone one might use if one's name was, say, Wolfgang Puck or Eric Ripert. "I'm writing a cookbook, you know."

"Which makes you an expert?" I said.

"Yes," she said, cocking her head at my question, "I believe it does."

"Okay," I said, plucking a blood-spattered recipe card from the counter, "let's see . . . *Snapper Valencia*. Your recipe, right?"

"Of course it's my recipe," she said.

"Really," I said. "So where are the capers?"

"I don't have any capers."

"Where's the garlic?"

"I don't know."

"And the dry sherry—I don't see it anywhere," I said. "All I see is fish."

Bad Mary glared at me. "Snapper *Valen-thia* is my specialty dish," she said, feeling a need to add, "And, for your information, that's how they pronounce it in Spain."

"Your specialty dish."

"Yes," she said.

"So why does this card say '*Jenny's* Snapper Valencia'?" I said.

"I have no idea."

"How is it yours?" I said, flicking the end of the card with my fingernail.

"Because it's in my recipe file, you idiot. What's your point?" she said.

"My point is you can't steal other people's recipes and call them yours," I said. "You can't steal other people's things and call them yours."

I grabbed the butcher knife and slashed the plaque off the wall. The plaque nearly sliced Bad Mary's ear as it flew across the room. She shuddered.

"You can't steal other people's kitchen slogans," I said.

"What are you talking about?" she said.

"You," I said, my accusations thundering against the flamenco sound track. "You can't steal other people's lives and call them yours."

"I don't know who you are, but you need to get out of my house," she said, slowly backing away from me. The fact that she was afraid of me gave me an unhealthy boost of confidence.

"I don't know who I am, either," I said, leaning toward her, knife at my side. "But I know who I used to be before you ruined my life."

"I'm calling the police right now," she said.

"Go ahead, do it," I said, "I dare you."

In a bold, sudden move I didn't expect, Bad Mary thrust an arm upward and knocked the knife out of my hands. She dove to the floor to grab the knife, but I kicked it out of her way. She grabbed my leg and brought me tumbling to the floor, yanking my hair and twisting it in her fists. I jabbed her thigh with my knee and managed to scramble away from her—for a minute, that is. She yanked me down once again and clobbered me with her shoe. But in one jolting move, I poked her hard in the breast and dove for my purse. I grabbed the Glock at the same time as she grabbed the knife from the floor. Her hands were trembling as if she had never brandished a knife before, something I found hard to believe. Then again, I was aiming the gun at her, right between her eyes.

"Drop the knife," I said.

"No," she said, trembling still.

"Drop it now," I said, shoving the gun closer.

"If you want it, come and get it, bitch."

And I did. I whipped the knife out of her hand with the gun, and I grabbed it off the floor. I must admit, I had a hard time believing that I was the one left standing—with a gun in one hand and a knife in the other. She, on the other hand, was slumped on the floor. But I knew I couldn't afford to be too cocky or confident. A woman like Maria Portilla always has a plan B.

"You're a psychopath idiot. I don't know what you want from me," she said. Slowly she climbed onto a chair.

"I want it all back," I said in an almost clinical way. "My job. My reputation. But most importantly, I want my son."

"I still don't know what you're talking about," she said.

She lifted her chin and said nothing, as if trying to engage me in a game of chicken. Browbeating was the only weapon she had left within her reach, for I had the Glock and I had the butcher knife and I had checked the drawers and cabinets to find no other firearms or explosives. So she was determined to browbeat both weapons out of my hands. Fine, I thought, game on.

But there came a very distinct moment in our tense little standoff when she realized she had been outplayed. It was the moment when, the Glock in hand and the knife guarded at my side, I swiped one of her cigarettes and fired it up, taking a long, slow drag. I pulled up a country-style kitchen chair and sat down, propping my feet up on the kitchen table. Truth be told, I didn't recognize the woman who took possession of my body that night. I didn't smoke. I didn't throw my feet up on tables. I didn't sit with my legs open, an elbow angled on a knee. But in a rush of adrenaline, I became a horrid imitation of what I imagined a bad chick to be.

Bad Mary straightened her shoulders and narrowed her eyes with a swagger I had not yet seen, and for the first time that day I glimpsed the thug in her.

"Get out of my house, *puta*," she said.

I swung around in my chair and aimed the gun at her again.

"No," I said, pointing it at her heart. "You get out of mine."

I kicked a country-style chair toward her.

"Sit down," I said, rising to my feet.

She obliged.

"Your name is not Sofia Villanueva," I said, pacing, stopping every so often to linger over her. "You're not a cookbook author at all. You're a drug dealer. You were born the sixteenth of July in 1969 in Cali, Colombia. You entered New Mexico on the twenty-seventh of December, in 1998. You vanished one month later. Were you in Colombia? Were you in Key West? Were you in New York? Who knows? But what the feds do know is that you've been on the run ever since. Now, aren't you tired of running, Maria Portilla?"

Bad Mary glanced off without a word.

"Thirty days ago, federal agents crashed through my front door," I said. "They ransacked my house. They took me away in shackles. They did this in front of my son. And do you know why?"

"I haven't the slightest clue," she said, glassy eyed from wine and rage.

"Because they thought I was a drug queenpin," I said.

"Well, Angela, maybe they're right," she said.

"My name isn't Angela. It's Mary. They thought I was a drug queenpin named Maria Portilla. *La Reina* of the Cardenal crime family. They thought I was you," I said.

"You're a fucking liar," she said.

"And you're La Reina."

"That's not me," she said.

"Prove it."

"That's not who I am."

"Right."

"Not anymore."

"It doesn't matter."

"I don't know what happened to you, but it's not my fault," she said.

"It doesn't matter," I said. "As long as you're out there, I have to live under a cloud of suspicion. As long as you're on the run, I have no life. People will always think of me as a lowlife drug dealer. They'll think my life, my nice, upstanding life, is just a disguise. They'll think my business is a front. They'll think my family is immoral. They'll think my son is better off with his father. So I'm sorry to tell you this, but I'm going to have to turn you in, so I can go on with my life. My original life."

She gave me a look of disbelief, then collapsed onto the kitchen table in heaving sobs.

"You think I'm running away from the feds?" she said with a snort. "The feds are nothing. The feds are easy."

"Good. So you won't have a problem when I take you in," I said, trying to detach from her hysterics.

"You don't understand. Whatever they do to me, it's nothing compared to what my ex-husband will do to me if he ever finds me. And he can find me anywhere, even in federal detention," she said.

"Ain't that the truth," I said aloud, but only to myself. "I've got one of those myself."

"But my ex is not just any ex. My ex-husband is Juan Cardenal," she said, letting the name resound in a theatrical pause. "He said he'd kill me if I ever tried to leave him."

"Yeah, well, I don't believe you," I said, although I did in fact believe her. But I wanted her to tell me more. "If that's true, why are you still alive?"

"Because I'm very good at hiding," she said, rather proud of herself.

"Hate to break it to you, but if a novice real estate agent from Miami can find you, you're not that good," I said.

"You have no idea how ruthless this man is. He is so controlling of everything," she said, undaunted by the slight. "Example: He's the kind of man who goes to your house, and he doesn't like your furniture. So he buys you new furniture. He goes into your closet and he doesn't like your clothes, so he buys you new clothes. He looks into your eyes and he doesn't like your face . . ."

She broke down again, then she flipped over a section of her hair to reveal a ghastly scar.

"So he buys you a new one," she said, heaving. "And the worst part is . . ."

But she couldn't finish the thought.

"What?" I said, growing impatient with all the sobbing and husband talk. "What already?"

"I let his son come with me. He begged me—he promised to help me. Stupidly, I believed him."

I should have connected the dots of the Cardenal crime family much sooner, but I was too busy zeroing in on Bad Mary. Her business associate was, indeed, a Cardenal. He was the one Fat Gus had referred to as "some rich junior." When I overheard the fight in the kitchen earlier that night, I had glossed over El Flaco's threats. I realized, in retrospect, he was talking about Juan Cardenal, and that Juan Cardenal was his father. If his threats were real, he had already sent a message to the kingpin, disclosing Bad Mary's whereabouts. And it all made sense now as I thought about it. With the flashy car and the shopping sprees, El Flaco was living the life of someone who wanted to get noticed, someone who didn't want to hide anymore, or, perhaps, someone working for the other side. El Flaco had flipped on her. And if this was true, her life truly was in danger.

"Francisco Jose Cardenal," I said, remembering the name from the court documents.

"Yes," she said. "El Flaco. He hates me. He knows I have his father's money, so he hounds me."

"What do you mean?"

"He hounds me for stupid things. Expensive things. Clothes, jewelry, expensive toys," she said. "He wants everybody in the world to know he's a millionaire, swine that he is. He doesn't give a shit if they find us."

"So where's the money?" I said.

"I don't care about the money," she said. "Seriously, I don't care."

She gave me a pathetic victim look that peeved me to no end. She didn't care about the money? As a woman who had walked away from a wealthy man without a dime of alimony, I found her contention to be pretty lame. She wasn't trying to make it on her own, the way I did after my divorce. She was still sponging off the old geezer's money, financing her big adventure in suburbia— the spa treatments and crafting blitzes and culinary dabbling and late-night addiction to the Home Shopping Network—with stolen riches.

If there was something in life I despised more fiercely than a liar or a poseur, it was a woman who couldn't stand on her own, a woman who refused to handle her business. A woman like that gave the rest of us a bad name.

"You don't care about the money," I said, tossing her words back in her face.

"Seriously, I don't," she said, attempting to sound earnest.

"Then why did you take it?" I said in a hardened tone.

"I had my reasons," she said, glancing away.

"Why did you take the money?" I said, narrowing my eyes on her.

She stiffened up a bit and met my stare.

"Because I wanted to take his power," she said.

"Bullshit."

"His money is his power."

"You're rationalizing."

"It is—the money is his power," she said, pounding a fist on the table.

"The cartel is his power. The drug trade is his power. The thug violence is his power. Power is his power. The money is replaceable," I said.

A look of panic flashed in Bad Mary's eyes. Her greed had not allowed her to look past the money, to consider the ramifications of her theft.

"When you took the money, you declared war. Not because it was his power or because he couldn't live without it, but because you stole from him. Plain and simple. You fired the first shot," I said. "So what happens now if he finds you?"

"I'm dead."

"Exactly. Where's the money?"

By now, Bad Mary was a sniveling mess. The truth is I didn't expect her to answer me. I was simply stalling, checking my cell phone every few moments for a sign of life from the outside. As annoying as I found her to be, I feared she could be right. What if Cardenal was, as we spoke, on his way to kill her? She may have been called La Reina once upon a time, but now she seemed to be anything but the poster girl for the drug queens of the world. She was just another woman trying to shake a hateful ex-husband.

I didn't expect her to answer me. But she did.

"It's in an offshore account," she said between sobs.

I don't think she noticed when I flinched in surprise. And, certainly, she didn't know that I had not planned for this. In the scenario of her capture I had planned, the possible retrieval of stolen funds from offshore accounts never entered the picture. But I wasn't about to tell her that.

"Where's this account?" I said.

Bad Mary couldn't answer. She wept inconsolably beneath the jarring fluorescent light of the kitchen interrogation room. As she did, the headlights from a slow-moving vehicle pierced the shrubbery outside, along Sunset Terrace. The vehicle came to a stop outside Bad Mary's house and its driver got out with a slam of the door. Moments later, the black-gloved hand of the unseen stranger reached for a pistol-grip shotgun and a munitions satchel.

I neither saw nor heard any of this. I didn't know there was anyone there until I heard someone kick the front door open. My thoughts raced through the worst possible scenarios of abduction and murder. Panicked, I threw an arm around Bad Mary's neck and pressed the revolver to her cheek.

"Walk," I said, trying to hide my nerves as I thrust her forth as my shield.

"What's going on?" she whispered, scared out of her mind.

"I don't know," I said in a similar murmur—and, unfortunately, I was telling the truth. "Walk."

We inched along the wall to the great room, turning a corner to find only vacant shadows along the corridor. Tightening my grip on her, I slid along the wall until I reached the corner just before the living room. Whoever it was, the invader was standing on the other side of that corner. I clutched Bad Mary tighter and charged around the corner into the living room with an uncharacteristic, guttural scream.

"Who's there? Identify yourself," I said, roaring the words. "I've got a gun."

I gasped as I came face to face with the barrel of a Remington short pump shotgun. TacStar rear pistol grip and a twelve-inch ported barrel. Serious heat.

"I've got a gun, too," the invader said, half-amused.

After one look, I dropped my arms and released the grip on my hostage, who gave the invader a curious once-over: the short black skirt. The black knee-high boots. The tight black gloves.

"What the hell took you so long?" I said.

"Traffic was a mother," said the invader, plopping herself on a sofa as only Gina could do in the middle of a hostage crisis.

"Who's she?" said Bad Mary.

"My business partner. Go sit over there while I talk to her," I said, motioning to an armchair in the living room. I held up the Glock to remind her I was still in charge.

Keeping an eye on the captive, I pulled Gina aside and quietly brought her up to speed. The late hour and the possibility that El Flaco or Cardenal himself could be on the way to find Bad Mary added a layer of urgency I had not planned for. I had planned to corral the woman and call the authorities, stand guard over her until they arrived to arrest her. But the fact that Agent Green had not called, coupled with my fear that no other law enforcement officer would believe me—one look at my unregistered firearm and my heat-packing accomplice and they'd haul us both in for sure—forced me to change my plans.

"We have to find a way to get her out of here," I told Gina. "I don't think she'll go voluntarily, and I don't want to drive all the way to Miami with a gun on this woman."

"Why not?" said Gina.

"Because it's a stupid idea," I said. "What happens if I get pulled over? There's got to be some other way."

"I brought Xanax," she said.

"Now you're thinking."

But I stopped Gina as she reached into her bag for the pills.

"Not yet," I said.

There was something else I needed to do while Bad Mary was still lucid: I needed to track down the money. Granted, I didn't *need* to track down the money. But it certainly would score major points with the feds. If I could deliver that kind of money, or at least some rock-solid information leading to its retrieval, I wouldn't go down in history as some random vigilante. I would be a hero. So, yes, I could have doped up Bad Mary and taken her in with minimal effort. But after she told me about the money and the offshore account, it was all I could think about. Where was it? How much was there? Ten million? Twenty million? How much was a drug kingpin worth? I came to view the situation not as a tangent I ought to ignore but as a puzzle I had to solve. I had come so far. I had cornered my suspect, broken her down, rendered her virtually harmless. Why not go all the way?

Yes, I could think of many reasons why I should walk away from the proverbial money on the table:

A) It could delay my mission.

B) It was risky.

C) It belonged to a notorious drug lord.

But I could think of one convincing reason to track down Bad Mary's stolen funds: If I recovered the money, I'd take her power. I'd take away her access to premium, highfalutin lawyers and cushy backroom deals and hired guns who might smuggle her to freedom.

In the case of Juan Cardenal, that money was replaceable. His extensive drug trafficking operation would see to it. But Maria Portilla had no such operation. Her infamous title, La Reina, was honorary at best, as I was beginning to see. In truth, I would come to learn, she was a cog in the Cardenal machine—nothing more. Without Cardenal's money, she had zilch. She had no job, no support system, no discernible skills or experience. She was a former cabaret dancer who teased and flirted and whored her way to the lap of Cali's most distinguished gangster. And once she had secured her place in his bed, she aimed for the stars: shopping in Milan. Wine tours in the Loire Valley. Concerts in Vegas. Berlitz courses in Miami. She polished her English and her table manners—somewhat, anyway—and eventually grew bored with the exquisite plateau that was life on Cardenal's tab. Soon enough, she set her sights on something greater than that plateau: his empire. She gained his professional trust by running some moderate-level drug deals at first—enter Operation Colombian Snow—and later progressed to more lucrative and brutal ventures.

I would learn days later that the nadir of her drug-running career had come just after midnight one January night some years earlier, when three of her bodyguards went missing during the Carnaval del Diablo in Riosucio, when the devil figure and his band of fallen angels spring through the town. She sent some of Cardenal's men out to investigate, but they returned with sobering news: Her bodyguards had been taken hostage by paramilitary thugs demanding a ransom of one million dollars. It was chump change for the lives of three loyal servants. But La Reina, who just days earlier had blown a half mil on a Parisian shopping spree, refused to pay. Two weeks later, a box arrived at the gates of the compound she shared with Juan Cardenal. A housekeeper opened it to find three ripped-out human hearts.

La Reina never took responsibility for precipitating those killings. She blamed the ransom messengers, the families of the bodyguards, the inclement weather, everything and everybody except herself.

Now, in her living room, she fidgeted in the armchair as she tried to eavesdrop on my conversation with Gina. I pulled up a seat in front of her.

"Where's the money?" I said.

"I told you already—offshore," she said.

"That's not good enough," I said, glancing over at Gina, who was quickly catching on. She strolled over to where Bad Mary was sitting and gave her shoulder a little tap with the barrel of the Remington.

"Come on, Reina, you can do better than that," Gina told her.

Bad Mary bristled. She hated Gina, I could tell by the way she stared at her in disgust, her tanned legs; her tiny waist; the perfect, all-natural lines of her breasts; her smooth skin, untouched by any scalpel, needle, or laser; and her hair, the flowing, lustrous, jet-black mane that swept past her shoulders as she strutted in those boots, those tight killer boots.

"Listen, bitch," she told Gina with a haughty sniff, "what I can do and what I will do are two different things."

Gina and I traded a knowing look—she would back off the captive for a while, and I would resume my line of questioning.

"So let me get this straight," I said. "You want the money after all."

"That's not what I said," Bad Mary replied.

"But it is what you want. You want him to come after you, don't you?" I said.

"That's ridiculous," she said.

"But it's true," I said. "You just can't give up that connection, can you? You say he was controlling. You say he was abusive. You say you ran for your life. But the truth is, you never had any desire to cut him off completely."

"I left him—don't you understand that?" she said, standing her ground.

"I don't," I said.

"You must be stupid, then," she said, her remark prompting a smack on the arm and a rebuke from Gina.

"Watch yourself, sister," Gina said.

"Here's my problem, Maria," I went on. "I'm trying to help you out and you're not listening."

"You're trying to send me to jail," she said, uttering the most perceptive line she had said all night.

I was, indeed. But from the looks of it, I would have to do a better job at convincing her otherwise.

"I'm trying to save your life," I said. "You know he's going to kill you. It's just a matter of hours or days. But it doesn't have to be like that. You can save yourself—and you can bring him down."

"How so?" she said, leaning forward in her seat.

At last, I had her attention, and I knew I had to use it wisely.

"The only reason the feds are after you is because they think Cardenal is dead. I saw the federal documents. They think you're the new boss. If you can lead them to Cardenal, I guarantee you they'll make a deal," I said, twisting the facts I had seen in the documents to serve the moment.

"You really think so?" she said, intrigued.

"Of course. They can probably even put you in some kind of witness protection program," I said. "They'll give you a new name, send you to a new city. You'll get to live in a new house. No Cardenal. No Flaco."

Bad Mary's eyes flickered with grand new thoughts.

"Grand Cayman International Bank. That's where the money is," she said. "I've got the documents somewhere in the house. I could go look for them."

"Let's go," I said, glancing at Gina in surprise.

We followed Bad Mary down the hall and into the midsize room where she indulged her Martha Stewart inclinations. Gina watched in astonishment as the woman floated through the craft room as if it were an enchanted place. She seemed to be a different person in there, lighter and more chipper.

For the next hour or so, we stood by as Bad Mary opened box after box, bag after bag, file after file in search of her offshore bank papers. It was only then that I could appreciate the magnitude of her Home Shopping compulsion. The woman not only needed jail time, she needed rehab.

"Think, Maria. Just visualize the bank statement on its way to you," I said, hoping to jog her memory. "The mailman arrives. He puts the envelope in your mailbox. You pick it up. You bring it inside. Where do you put it?"

"I don't remember," she said, eyes closed in compliance.

"What color is the statement?" I said.

"Green," she said, eyes still closed.

"Do you see it?" I said.

"I see it. I do," she said, her eyes popping open. "It's in the bead box."

"What's a bead box?" said Gina.

"I'll show you," said Bad Mary.

She walked over to a shelf stacked with clear plastic, snap-together storage boxes, the kind with the stackable trays and removable dividers, the kind every bead-stringing fanatic collects by the truckload and fills with beads, clasps, wire, crimping tools, glue, and string. There were eight such boxes on Bad Mary's shelf, and she began to count them, bottom to top. When she reached the fifth box from the bottom, she stopped and pulled it off the shelf. Carefully, she unfastened the snap enclosures and flipped open the box. There, amid fragments of turquoise, coral, and Swarovski glass, she spotted a batch of envelopes and some stray scraps of paper bundled together with a thick rubber band. She fished out the top envelope and unfolded the document inside.

"Here," she said, handing the document over to me. "I don't want any of it. I want a new life. I want peace. I'll sign it over, whatever I have to do to keep this money out of Juan Cardenal's hands."

When I glanced down at the bank statement, the most recent one she had received, I nearly fell back. It confirmed that she—Sofia Villanueva, that is—was the only signatory on an account containing a balance of forty-two million dollars. I let Gina glimpse the balance. She took one look at it, and out of Bad Mary's sight, she reached for the vial of Xanax.

FIFTEEN

AS TORMENTED AS she appeared to be, Bad Mary seemed as if a tremendous weight had been lifted from her shoulders. But I wasn't too sure she was any closer to jumping in the car willingly for the ride to Miami.

We hadn't discussed specific logistics. And, for some reason, she seemed to be under the impression that she didn't have to go anywhere in the immediate future. She thought some federal agent would drive up to The Retreat at Malabar and interview her in the comfort of her living room. She would offer a statement regarding Juan Cardenal and sign a few papers under oath. She would peruse brochures of potential new cities and then select the ideal place to begin her new life. Ah, yes, and she would get compensated handsomely for all the above.

Somehow, this is what she had concluded from our interrogation session. I know this because she kept talking about what her new life was going to be like as "a government informant on salary." And this was before the Xanax.

There was no way she was going to come to Miami voluntarily and turn herself in to be handcuffed and shackled and sent to cell block Bravo. No way in hell. So, on to plan B it was.

"I think this calls for a celebration," I said, nodding at Gina. She disappeared into the kitchen in search of drinks and glasses.

"You can celebrate without me," said Bad Mary. "I have a big headache. Too much drama today."

"Then you definitely need a drink," I said.

She thought about it for a minute, her face haggard from the exhaustion. Absent the anger, sneering, and self-importance, she now seemed to be a shell of a woman, a fragile being with distorted features and vacant eyes.

"Actually," she said, "I would love a drink."

Gina came back with three glasses of champagne, one of them containing a particularly tart sample. Bad Mary gulped the wine so fast she didn't notice its unusually sharp taste. And, within minutes, she was groggy.

"How much did you give her?" I whispered to Gina as I snatched Bad Mary's empty glass from her hand.

"Not enough to kill her. Don't worry," Gina said.

Outside, the sky began to take on that pale gray tone that transitions to dawn. Gina waited for Bad Mary to fully pass out on the sofa before bringing out the handcuffs she had packed in her munitions satchel. As she snapped them on her, I searched the bedroom drawers one more time to make sure I hadn't missed anything. I stuffed a few changes of clothes for her in a weekend bag, and I put them in the car, while Gina watched her sleep.

When it came time to leave, we rustled the woman so she was awake just enough to be coaxed to the car without causing a scene. Luckily, there wasn't a soul around, not even the newspaper delivery man—he had made his rounds a half hour earlier.

"Come on, sleeping beauty," Gina said as we nearly carried Bad Mary to my car.

"Where are we going?" she said, too groggy to open her eyes all the way.

"To the Magic Kingdom," said Gina, "that's where we're going."

After some maneuvering, Gina and I managed to get the woman into the back seat of my car. I propped a pillow beneath her head and covered her with a soft beige throw I had found in the living room. I closed up the house and went to huddle with Gina by my car.

"So what route are we taking back?" said Gina.

"Let's go down 95 to Indiantown, then cut over to the turnpike," I said.

"Sounds good. I'll be right behind you," she said as she buckled up for the ride home.

"We did it, G," I said, stopping to take in the moment. I reached out and gave her arm a squeeze. "Thanks."

But Gina's mood darkened when she spotted something unusual on the street. I turned to see what had distracted her, and when I saw it for myself, my heart skipped a few beats: A black sedan with tinted windows crept along Sunset Terrace at an ominous pace. There was some kind of marking on its side, but I couldn't make it out from where I was sitting. But once the black car stopped in front of Bad Mary's house, I didn't want to wait around to read its sign. Whoever it was, they had picked the wrong time to show up.

"Quick, get in your car," I told Gina, throwing my car into reverse. "Let's get out of here."

She jumped into her convertible and screeched out of the driveway, but she hit the brakes as soon she saw what I saw. What I saw was a vision that caused the world to tilt ever so slightly: A young girl, about eight years old, emerged from the sedan with a pink backpack and scampered along the manicured hedge to the front door, where she rang the doorbell a few times. Then she turned to wave good-bye to the sedan driver. For his part, the driver must have believed everything was okay, because he waved at me as he drove off. It was as if he knew me, as if he believed me to be trustworthy, as if he'd never suspect me to be a person who could drug and abduct the lady of the house.

But then I realized that this driver, like Agent Green and Lieutenant Earl Winrock before him, thought I was the lady of the house. And even more remarkable, the little girl thought I was the lady of the house.

"Mommy! Mommy!" she screamed as she spotted me in the car, her soft curls bouncing at her cheeks as she ran to me.

I turned to read the sign on the side of the sedan as it drove away.

BUTTERFLY GIRLS SUMMER CAMP, it said. The girl, it seems, was coming home from a weekend camping trip.

I got out of the car to go talk to her. But when she got a good look at me, she suddenly stopped.

"Hi there," I said, coming a little closer to her. "What's your name?"

"Natalie," said the girl, now on the verge of tears. "Do you know where my mommy is?"

"Who's your mommy?" I said.

"Sofia."

The girl, with her beautiful hair and tiny voice, a girl just a little older than Max, brought my life to a veritable standstill. I glanced over to find Gina—she had parked and walked over to my car to keep an eye on the slumbering passenger. Silently, I grappled with a thousand questions: How did I not know about this child? Why hadn't her mother peeped a word of her to me? Why hadn't

I checked those last two rooms of the house? If only I had done so, I might have discovered she existed. I might have understood the deeper reasons why Maria Portilla left her husband. Why hadn't I read those letters, the ones addressed to "Señor Juan" on Calle Luna in Cali? Surely they would have offered a clue to all of this. But now it was too late. Now the child was there, staring at me with fierce saucer eyes, asking about her mother. What was I going to do with her?

"Come on, Natalie. Let's go sit on the doorstep for a minute," I said, taking her hand and leading her along the hedged path.

We sat side by side on the stoop for a moment before I could think of anything to say.

"You don't know me, but I'm an old friend of your mom," I began.

"What's your name?" the girl said.

"Mary," I said. "If you'd like, you can call me Aunt Mary."

"Are you related to me?" she said.

"Yeah. In a way, I am," I said. "Your mommy's not feeling so well. We have to get her some fresh air."

"What's wrong with her?" the girl said. Her lip quivered the way Max's does when he's hurt.

"Nothing bad. I think she just ate something that made her a little sick," I said.

"Where is she? I want to see her," the girl said.

"She's sleeping in the car. My friend over there is taking care of her," I said, nodding to where Gina was standing. Gina waved at the girl, and the girl lifted her hand in a halfhearted wave.

"Is she related to me, too?" she said.

"No, she's not. She's my friend from Miami."

"Where are you taking Mommy?" she said. She seemed to be on the verge of tears.

"I don't know yet—what about the beach? Would you like to

go to the beach?" I said, blurting out the first thing that popped into my head. I suppose I thought of it because it was Max's favorite excursion. But this was not Max—this was a child who had no reason to trust me.

"If my mommy goes, I'll go," she said. She got up from the stoop. "I want to go see her now."

As we walked to my car, I worried that the throw had slipped, exposing the handcuffs. I didn't want the girl to see her mother in handcuffs.

"Is she cold?" I hollered to Gina with a nod that meant she should check the throw.

Gina glanced into the car and nodded.

"Mommy!" the girl squealed. "Wake up! I made you a present at camp."

But, thankfully, Bad Mary kept sleeping.

"Wake her up. I want you to wake her up," cried the girl, knocking on the car window. She was beginning to work herself toward a tantrum, something I wanted to avoid at all cost.

"Come on, let's go inside a minute. Your mom told me to give you something to eat when you got home," I said, reaching for the girl's hand. From my pocket I fished out the house key I had grabbed on the way out. I opened the door and let the girl in. "Why don't you go change into comfy clothes and I'll make some breakfast."

The girl ran off, seeming to have brightened a bit.

I rushed in to tidy up the kitchen. By the time she appeared, dressed in peach cotton shorts and a yellow tank top, she found a bowl of Froot Loops and a glass of milk. I sat with her at the country-style table and watched her take sips from her glass. Her eyes were red from crying.

"How was camp?" I said, trying to break the ice.

"Super fun," she said. "We had a race."

"What kind of race?"

"A race around the lake. It's a big lake in the woods. I loved it. I love to be outside," she said.

"Being outside is healthy for you," I said.

"Is that why you took Mommy outside?" she said.

"Yes, it is," I said, and I wasn't lying.

"The beach will be good for her," she said.

I left the girl to finish her cereal and I went to her room to pack a bag of clothes for her. When she asked why I brought it along, I said her mother had asked me to do so.

Twenty minutes later, I was driving across the deserted sand on a patch of Melbourne Beach as Natalie peered out the front window from the passenger's seat. Her mother continued to sleep soundly in the back.

"She must be really tired," said the girl.

"She is," I said, "but she's going to be okay."

The girl and I climbed out of the car and walked along the shoreline while Gina, who had followed us in her car, stood guard by the woman. I let Natalie tell me about summer camp, about the nature walks, talent shows, and popcorn movie nights. She told me about her best friend, Lauren, the one who wants to be a ballerina when she grows up.

"Does Lauren ever stay over at your house for a slumber party?" I asked her.

"No. Mommy doesn't let anyone stay over," said the girl in a level tone of acceptance.

"I have a little boy your age," I said.

"What's his name?" the girl said.

"Max."

"Where is he?" she said.

"He's at his dad's house," I said.

"Is he with his dad all the time?" she said.

"No, he's with me," I said, "and sometimes he's with his grandparents."

"Wow. He's so lucky. He can see his dad, his grandparents, and his mom. His whole family," said the girl, stooping to pick up a starfish. It glistened as if it had been dusted with white glitter.

We stayed on the beach for a little while longer, collecting odd-shaped seashells. The morning was particularly sunny, not burning hot like it might have been at another time of the day. No, the sun felt wonderfully and perfectly warm. I sat on the sand to watch the girl play in the surf. A dove swooped across the waves and it seemed to hover above her, a phenomenon that delighted both her and me. As I watched her, this beautiful child on the beach, I could not reconcile her vibrant and trusting spirit with the train wreck that was her mother. As carefully as I observed the girl, I could not find one thing that connected her with the Maria Portilla who caused such upheaval in my life. All the tension I had built up in the dark hours with her mother melted in the company of this child. I should have been in frantic mode or paralyzed with anxiety. But instead I felt calm and in the moment.

The girl ran back across the sand to show me her finds, a glimmering assortment of coquinas and cowries and cockles and zigzag scallops that put her mother's plastic bead collection to shame.

"They're beautiful," I said. I helped her scoop the shells into an empty cup I found on the sand.

"Does Max like seashells?" she said.

"Loves them," I said.

"Maybe you can take some home for him," she said, squinting in the sun.

We washed the sand off our feet and went back to the car, where Natalie gazed at her sleeping mother. The girl buckled her seat belt, ready to go. She seemed so calm and so assured of her safety that I prayed she wouldn't notice that I had no clue where

I was going next. I gripped the steering wheel firmly as if to give it all my decision-making powers, relinquish my navigational responsibilities, allow it to set our route along the most wisely chosen path. For all my rugged-individualist traits, I didn't want to map this journey. Not this journey. I didn't want to be responsible for separating a mother from her child, especially when I knew the depths of that pain firsthand. I had come here to get my life back. That's what I had told myself. Yet I knew that was no longer possible, for too much had happened. Too much had changed inside me. So why not simply return mother and child to their home, safe and whole, and cut my losses? I'd go home and try to work out my custody issues with Tony, find some kind of work, and be the best mother I could be. But then what would happen to Natalie? What if her father showed up? What if her mother was murdered? What if she was taken by force to Colombia?

As I buckled my seat belt and checked the back seat one last time, I noticed my handbag had fallen to the floor and some of its contents had scattered on the back rug. I unbuckled myself and gathered them up. But before I put them back in my purse, I stopped to examine one of the items that had spilled. It was a scrap of paper attached to one of the bank statement envelopes from the bead box. I unfolded the paper and saw it was a note, written by Maria Portilla/Sofia Villanueva to parties unknown. As I read the letter, I knew exactly where I had to go. I folded it up and returned it to my handbag. I turned on the ignition and gave Gina a sign through the window: *Follow me.*

Sixteen

FLORIDA ROAD—DAY 31

Mary's car travels on an open highway in the haze of another
sweltering day.

We rode in silence across a drab landscape of parched grass,
stretches of land not yet gobbled up by developers, not yet deemed
worthy of stamped concrete, waves of gabled roofs, or miles of
granite countertops. No, this was not yet a place where anyone
might hide.

Natalie gazed out the front-seat window, noting the types of
trees and birds along our route. We were going to visit Max, I had
told her, and she perked up at the thought.

"I think I saw a turtle," she said. She pressed a finger on the
window and traced the crooked path of a canal we were passing.

"Was it big?" I said.

"Not as big as a sea turtle. And not as old. Sea turtles can live
like eighty years," she said with some authority.

"That long?"

"Really amazing, I know," she said. "You know the mothers are the only ones who can swim to the shore? Fathers don't do that, just the mothers."

"I didn't know that."

"And they're also really smart. The mothers go back to lay their eggs in the same exact beach where they were born," said the girl, her eyes dimmed slightly now. "I wonder how they can even find it."

The girl's observation hung in the air as her gypsy mother continued to sleep.

Two hours later, I pulled off the road into a rest stop and signaled to Gina to do the same.

"Go on to the bathroom with Gina," I said. "I'll wait for you here."

When she was gone, I opened the back door and tried to nudge Bad Mary awake. She half opened her eyes and yawned.

"Maria, I have to talk to you. Wake up," I said.

She blinked and looked around, disoriented.

"Why are you taking me like this?" she said, rolling over on her side, still groggy.

"I didn't know you had a little girl," I said.

"Natalie. Where is she?" she said as if she had just remembered the girl's name.

"She's in the bathroom," I said. "She'll be right back."

"I have to see her," she said. She scrambled to the edge of the seat.

"You will in a second. But you and I have to have a conversation now," I said.

"What about?"

"I read your letter, the one you wrote about Natalie, the one you kept with your bank statements."

"What about it?" she said.

"I need to know if you really mean it," I said.

"Why would I write it if I didn't mean it?" she said.

"Then I want you to tell her," I said.

"No."

"You have to tell her."

"She's too young to know any of that," she said. She brought her cuffed hands to her face to wipe away tears.

"Then I'll tell her," I said.

"Don't you dare," she said. She stared at me for a long, angry pause, as if that one look would break me.

"You tell her, or I will. Your choice," I said.

Bad Mary thought about it for a moment. She looked off toward the restroom area. In the distance, she could see Gina and Natalie had started walking back to the car.

"Take these off," she said, holding up her handcuffs.

I reached into my handbag and pulled out the small key that unlocked the handcuffs. I leaned over to grab Bad Mary's wrists.

"I'm going to say this once: I have a gun. If you even attempt to run, or do anything stupid, I'll use it," I said. I gave her a glimpse of the Glock in my purse. I tried to keep my threat vague yet credible. "I will not think twice about it."

I unlocked the cuffs and tossed them into my purse just as Natalie bounced back to the car.

"Mommy!" she said, running into Bad Mary's arms. "Are you feeling better?"

My stomach turned with a nagging thought that Bad Mary had duped me—after all, a woman of her background might not blink before using her own daughter as a shield. But if that was the case, I was determined to shoot her in the leg, at the very least.

"Your mom has something she'd like to tell you," I said to the girl as I handed the letter to her mother.

Bad Mary took the letter and closed her eyes as if in prayer.

"Mommy, what's wrong?" said Natalie.

"I want you to listen to something I wrote. It's important," she said. She blinked back a tear as she prepared to read from the well-creased sheet.

" 'I write this letter as a mother who has had to make a most painful choice. I had to take my child away from her father, from her friends and her country of birth. I did it for her good. I had no choice. My husband is an abusive man who has threatened to kill me.

" 'If anything should happen to me, I want my daughter, Natalie, to know the truth about her father, so that she may seek safety. And I want her to know that, like every human being, I made my mistakes . . . but that I loved her more than anything in the world. I want her and everyone else to understand why I have been living a secret for most of her life. When you have something so precious, so completely yours, you do what you have to do to make sure nobody takes it away from you.

" 'You do what you have to do. And that's what I did.

" 'Sincerely, Maria Portilla.' "

Natalie choked up and buried her head into her mother's shoulder.

"Why did you write that, Mommy?" she said.

"Because it's true. Because I love you."

"But why do you have to tell me like that?" the girl said.

"Because we have to go live someplace else for a while," the mother said.

"Again?"

"I promise you that we are going to be okay. Please believe me," said the mother.

"I don't know," said Natalie. The girl then looked up at me with lost, reddened eyes. "I can't leave my friends."

She seemed to direct her words at me.

"You'll always have friends. And you'll always have new friends," I said to her.

"You mean like Max?" she said.

I glanced at her mother—she sat stone-faced in the back seat.

"Yeah, like Max," I said.

"Am I going to meet him?" said the girl.

Her words gave me the entry point I thought I'd never find.

"Of course you are, if your mom says it's okay," I said.

The mother gave me a hard look, one that told me she was as protective of her girl as I was of my boy. She looked at me as she directed her words at her daughter: "Yes, it's okay," she said. "I asked Mary if she would take care of you while I go to a meeting."

I let her words hang in the air between mother and daughter as I tried to grasp the enormity of what she had just said. I started up the car and signaled to Gina. Moments later, we were back on the road.

We traveled for about a half hour, saying nothing to one another. Natalie turned on the radio and clicked between the stations. She stopped at one song, a cover of an old Mexican bolero, one of those fatalistic standards. It was sung by a clear-voiced young woman who bent the ends of each line in a way that suggested her first language was Spanish. Natalie seemed to recognize the song.

> Yesterday I heard the rain whispering your name, asking
>   where you'd gone . . .

I knew the melody well. It was my mother's favorite Manzanero song, "Esta Tarde Ví Llover," one I hadn't heard in ages.

I let my mind wander with each verse as I tried to remember the words in Spanish. But just as the song was ending, a jarring noise brought me back to the moment. A siren. I looked in the rearview mirror to find the flashing light of a Florida state trooper. My hands turned clammy as I clutched the steering wheel. I didn't know what to do next, but the amplified voice coming from the trooper's car gave me a good hint.

"Pull your vehicle to the right side of the road," it said.

I slowed down and pulled over as Gina, whose car was behind the trooper's car, continued ahead at a moderate pace.

"Are we in trouble?" said Natalie. She grabbed the strap of her seat belt and slid down a few inches.

"No. We're okay. There won't be any trouble," I said. I pitched my voice to the back seat, where I hoped her mother took my words as a warning. Maria Portilla met my glance in the rearview mirror and looked away.

Seconds later, Florida Trooper Wes Baggett, a man in his late fifties, was leaning down to peer in my window.

"License and registration, please," he said.

"License is in my wallet," I said.

"Will you get it, please?" he said.

I reached into my purse and felt around for my wallet. I could feel the cold metal of the gun on the back of my pinkie, but I tried to remain as composed as possible. I managed to extract the wallet without fishing out any of the other contents, and I handed the trooper my license.

"The registration and insurance papers are in the glove compartment," I said.

"Get them, please," he said.

I leaned over Natalie as I clicked open the glove compartment. I had the urge to look back and see what Maria Portilla was doing, but instead I straightened up and gave the trooper the papers.

"Here you go," I said.

"You were going pretty fast there, Maria," he said.

"I didn't realize it," I said.

"I clocked you at seventy-six in a sixty-five-mile zone," he said.

"I'm sorry," I said.

The trooper was about to say something else, but he stopped when he saw Natalie leaning toward the window to get a closer look at him.

"Are you in trouble, Aunt Mary?" she said.

The girl's tiny voice spilled out the window and, it seemed, hit the trooper somewhere near his badge. He dropped his shoulders a bit.

"You must be about eight years old," he told the girl.

"Seven and a half," she said.

"How'd I know you were about that age?" he said.

"I don't know," said Natalie.

"That's my granddaughter's age," he said. "That's how I know."

Natalie let out a chuckle and I glanced back for a look at her mother. She sat upright, a polite smile pasted on her face.

The trooper handed the papers back to me.

"Just giving you a verbal warning this time," he said. "Mind the speed limit. You've got precious cargo over there."

"I do," I said. "Thanks."

I watched the trooper pull back onto the road, then make a U-turn into the northbound lanes. I continued my drive south, calling Gina on the cell to check her whereabouts. She had stopped up the road a bit. I passed her and she joined in behind me, and we rode all the way to Miami at the speed limit.

＊　＊　＊

I knew things would happen quickly upon our arrival in Miami, although I never could have predicted the succession of developments that occurred. Still today, I wonder how it is that a handcuffed fugitive wound up drugged in the back seat of my car while her young, innocent daughter chattered about turtles. Four hours after having left Melbourne Beach, I pulled into the driveway of my house. I let Natalie play in Max's room, in the care of Gina, while her mother and I huddled in the den. Bad Mary napped on the sofa while I pieced together a report of everything I had learned. Just before we headed to our destination, leaving the girl with Gina, the mother gave the girl a long, tearful hug. Then she straightened herself and sent Natalie back upstairs to watch TV.

"I'm ready. Let's go," she told me once she saw the girl disappear into Max's room.

I drove through the neglected backstreets leading to the center of Miami as she stared out the window at nothing in particular. We didn't speak because there was nothing left to say. What remained to be done was the painful but necessary act we both dreaded. When we arrived, I reached into my purse and pulled out the handcuffs. Maria Portilla lifted a wrist in surrender.

DEA FIELD OFFICE—DAY 31
Agent Green pours a mug of coffee. A bustle of activity surrounds him. A secretary approaches. Beneath the office din, she tells him something nobody else hears—something major. Agent Green puts down his mug and races out.

I reached the reception area just as Agent Green came running out from his office. He must have been astonished to watch those elevator doors open and find me standing there, handcuffed to a fugitive drug trafficker. Maria Portilla wept and slumped against the elevator wall in exhaustion and defeat. She had arrived at DEA headquarters without a single scratch, something I was happy to take credit for—and something I personally believed she should be thankful for.

I stepped out of the elevator, tethered to my nemesis, and I met Agent Green's disbelieving stare.

"Brought you a present, Agent Green," I said, lifting my hand to display my captive and, thanks to the handcuffs, also lifting hers. "Don't worry, Dan. Neither one of us is armed."

I went to unlock the handcuffs with my key, but Agent Green stopped me.

"Let me do this," he said, taking the key and unlocking our handcuffs. He directed us to a small waiting room tucked next to the elevator. "We'll have to interrogate you both, you know."

"I'm fine with that," I said, glancing at Bad Mary. She said nothing, only stared ahead.

Moments later, a second agent appeared.

"Which one of you is Maria Portilla?" said the agent, a salt-and-pepper-haired, business-like guy in nice gray slacks and a well-pressed white shirt.

Agent Green went to speak up, but he was cut off.

"I am, sir. My name is Maria Portilla," said the woman I call Bad Mary. "This woman here, she has nothing to do with what-ever criminal charges you have against me. She is a good, decent person. She is innocent."

Agent Green glanced over at his colleague.

"Go ahead and take her over to room C," he told the second agent, instructing him to escort Maria Portilla to an interrogation room. "I'll take this one."

As the salt-and-pepper agent directed Bad Mary toward the corridor, I felt a need to call out to him.

"Be nice to her," I said, "she has a child."

Bad Mary glanced back, and for the first time she smiled at me. It wasn't the kind of smile that could be perfected by cosmetic injectables, a surgeon's touch, or the right shade of red lipstick. It was a smile that relaxed her entire body. It was real.

For the next three hours or so, I sat in a quiet conference room and told Agent Green everything I had learned about the Cardenal cartel, while the second agent questioned Maria Portilla in a room very similar to the one where they had interrogated me on the day of the raid. I gave Dan Green the bank documents and the note I had found attached to them. I gave him the passports I had found in the black cat pillow and Natalie's unsent letters to her father. Out of concern that they might cast an unnecessary light on the child, I had debated over whether to turn them over. But in the end, I figured they would serve as proof that she was the daughter of a wanted, dangerous man and that she was worthy of the utmost care and protection by U.S. authorities.

I gave Agent Green the report I had put together, detailing the whereabouts of all the principals of the Cardenal drug cartel. And I gave him a written affidavit signed by Natalie's mother requesting that the child be placed with me until she was released from jail. I had no idea if such an affidavit would be considered a viable document or whether it would stand up under scrutiny in court. But the facts it listed were true, and they were easy enough to verify, so I drew it up as an additional layer of protection for the child with whom I had bonded in such a short period of time.

Despite all the above, I fully expected to get arrested that day. As someone who prided herself on living so cleanly within the boundaries of the law, I knew the things I had done in the previous week were anything but legal. It was more than simple subterfuge. Weapons were involved, as was coercion. I knew this.

But Agent Green didn't know it. He only knew that I had found and turned over Maria Portilla. And, to be perfectly honest, I don't think he wanted to know much more than that. And after gathering his own facts from the fugitive later, he concluded that she had come of her own accord.

At the end of a very long day, Agent Green emerged from his internal huddles and found me in the waiting room. Without too many words, he extended a handshake. This time I was happy to accept it.

Although I had delivered a fugitive, my mission was far from complete. When I left the field office that day, I wasted no time in finishing the task.

I drove to Tony's house.

Tony came to the door with his usual air of self-importance.

"It's past eleven o'clock. Would you like me to call the police?" he said.

"Go ahead. There's no restraining order against me," I said. "I'll tell them Victoria invited me. And then I'll tell them the candidate's crony, the shrink, has been allowed to drug my son—with the consent of his father. I'll leak it to the *Daily Press*. I hear they just love Victoria."

Tony glanced off, angry.

"We can do this the right way or we can do this the really embarrassing way," I said. "I say you invite me in and we work this thing out, you and me. No judge. No guardian. No shrink. No wife. Just you and me."

Tony stepped out of the way and let me come inside. He was alone in the house. Victoria was out at a late campaign meeting and Max was at a summer camp sleepover.

In the leaden quiet of his penthouse, Tony and I talked for a good while. I told him everything I knew about him, the financial records, the letter from Wharton, all the evidence that was yet to be presented to Judge Costello. He seemed distressed as he heard the litany of points I threatened to make against him, but more than this he seemed tired, particularly each time I mentioned Victoria's name. I sensed something was going wrong between them, although I couldn't pinpoint what it was, nor did I ask him. I wanted to keep the focus on our son. I had the feeling, however, that whatever was troubling Tony, it would work to my advantage. He didn't seem as fixated on Max as he had been days earlier, when he had seemed to be obsessed with forming the picture-perfect, campaign-worthy family.

Because I noticed an uncharacteristic slump in his shoulders, I didn't argue when he said he needed a while to collect his thoughts. I didn't push him. I left him in that lifeless penthouse to contemplate his options.

When I left Tony's house, I called Gina to check on Natalie. She was asleep, Gina said.

"We made some popcorn and watched a little TV. She hit the sack early," said Gina. "You coming home?"

"Later," I said. "Don't wait up."

I hadn't slept in three days and I smelled like a locker room after a football game. I could still feel the funk and dust of the road clinging to my clothes, the same pair of light summer pants and pale tank I had worn to Bad Mary's house. The top looked a few shades darker than its original ivory tone. But despite my condition, I couldn't go home without making one more stop. I took a drive to see Joe.

I found him at the Rapture Lounge, working in his office, alone. I watched him for a long while before he glanced up to find me in the doorway. Without a word, he rose from his desk and swept me into his arms. In his powerful embrace, I felt as if my heart was swelling like a great balloon that could lift me off the ground. I pressed my chest into his, my forehead into his, then my lips into his lips. With soft, deep kisses, and without uttering a word, I told him everything that had happened since the night we parted in Key West. I kissed the corners of his eyes the way I used to years earlier. He brushed his lips along my neck in a way that always made my eyes mist.

Taking my face in his hands, he gave me a look that told me he had something important to say. But I spoke instead.

"I know. I need a bath," I said.

He laughed and took my hand.

"Come on," he said. "I want to show you something."

He led me around his desk and unfurled a blueprint for some kind of house or business.

"What is it?" I said.

"It's a big surprise," is all he would say.

TV SCREEN—DAY 32
A series of news bulletins flash on TV across the city.

NEWS BULLETIN—CHANNEL 7
A redheaded local TV anchorwoman narrates a breaking news story over silent images of Mary speaking at a press conference.

ANCHORWOMAN: Drama in the suburbs! An international
    drug ring has been busted—by a Miami soccer mom,
    no less. Just weeks after being the victim of a wrong-
    house raid by the feds, Coconut Grove Realtor Mary
    Guevara hunted down the cocaine trafficker she had been
    mistaken for . . .

NEWS BULLETIN—CHANNEL 4

A dapper local anchorman broadcasts Mary's story over several scenes of federal agents leading away handcuffed suspects.

> ANCHORMAN: . . . a domino effect of drug busts ensued! Arrested in the statewide operation were longtime fugitive drug kingpin Juan Cardenal, his son Francisco, and their partner Jaime Paz . . .

NEWS BULLETIN—TELEMUNDO

An aging national Spanish-language news anchorman offers his take on the story of the day over a Mary montage.

> ANCHORMAN: . . . y señores, aquí la tienen, la extraordinaria María Guevara, la humilde ciudadana norteamericana que derrumbó el imperio narcotrafficante de Juan Cardenal. ¿Como la ven?

NEWS BULLETIN—CHANNEL 6

A stylish local newswoman delivers the breaking news glowingly as images of a smiling Mary flash on-screen.

> ANCHORWOMAN: And here's the remarkable kicker . . . On Thursday afternoon, Mary Guevara will be presented with a civilian medal of distinction by the very DEA agents who raided her home. And later that night, she will be honored by the PTA of her son's school. Pretty incredible story all around.

Seventeen

MARY'S HOUSE—DAY 38

Mary, in sweatpants and a tank top, tidies up in the living room,
fluffing pillows, straightening books, and plucking dead leaves
off the potted plants. She moves quickly and energetically.

I could hear my mother singing in the kitchen as I buzzed around
the living room, getting ready for the big, special occasion later
that afternoon. I had not heard her sing in so many years that
when I caught the first strain of her liltingly melodic voice, a
voice like a bell, I felt an old, sweet feeling wash over me. She
was belting out a song I hadn't heard in a very long time, one
of the favorites at our noisy family gatherings and Sunday sing-
alongs.

> *Those were the days, my friend*
> *We'd thought they'd never end . . .*

Wafts of roasting delicacies drifted out of the kitchen and filled the house with familiar, comforting aromas. Through the window, I could see Daddy outside doing his best to trim the hedges as neatly as he could get them. Random branches and twigs jutted out as he passed them by without notice. He was doing a nice job, I thought. And even Fatty was there, making himself useful in the den. He was at my laptop—his ankle finally free of the tracking device, thanks to good behavior—loading new music into my iPod.

"Gotta hear this joint, yo," he said, bopping in a pair of headphones. "It's gangster. Like you, my sis."

Gangster. That's what he started calling me the moment he saw my picture in the *Daily Press* next to the story of my "heroic one-woman operation." From then on, I became his idol, taking the place of that beret-clad simpleton in the pantheon of Fatty's demigods.

As I slipped on the headphones, a raw Cuban-style conga assaulted my senses. I hardly recognized Fatty's voice on the track. He wasn't just spitting out rhymes, as he usually did. His voice carried a depth I had never heard in him, the melodious tenor of an artist coming into his own.

Sweet, sweet Mary, so misunderstood.
Can't find justice.
Can't find right.
Got no choice. Gotta fight.
Te busca la policia, Maria, te busca.
Te busca la policia, Maria, te busca.
Quien tu eres, Maria? Dimelo.
Quien tu eres, Maria? Suenalo.
Quien tu eres, Maria?
Te andan buscando en las calles de Hialeah.

I handed the headphones back to him.

"Nice. Download some Toots and the Maytals while you're at it," I told him. "I'm gonna take my gangster behind upstairs to get ready."

I changed into a nice pair of no-name jeans and a simple V-neck T-shirt, slipped on some flats, smoothed a little clear gloss on my lips, a little lotion on my elbows, and brushed out the layers of my hair. I had cut my hair in bouncy new angles, and at times I didn't recognize my own silhouette in the mirror. Some days, I'd pass by and think, Who's that smokin' woman? But not that day. That day I was in a bit of a hurry.

I dashed into Max's bedroom and gave it a good inspection. Everything was in its place, toys stashed into their respective bins, Spidey sheets tucked perfectly into the edges of the bed, a dream team of basketball jerseys hanging neatly in the closet, the LeBrons next to the D. Wades.

I was wiping a little smudge off the dresser when I heard the doorbell ring. I dropped what I was doing and bolted downstairs, the same stairs I had raced down that day the feds came.

"I'll get it!" I said.

I rushed to open the front door, and when I threw it open and saw who was standing there, I nearly lost my breath. He seemed a little more formal than I had remembered him, his hair somewhat shorter, his clothes brand-new and different. But in his smile I recognized everything I so desperately missed. I flung open my arms and Max raced into them, gripping me as tightly as he knew how. Max, my beautiful boy, was finally home. More than five weeks after the federal raid, I swept him up and into the living room, where my parents and my brother waited with more hugs and kisses.

After a little while, I took Max up to his bedroom so he could change into his favorite jersey. After he had dressed, he took my hand and we plopped down on the floor together.

"Mommy," he said, "why did it take so long for you to bring me home?"

I didn't know how to answer his question, but I gave it a try.

"I tried very hard to bring you home, but the judge said I couldn't," I told him.

"So why didn't you just go get me anyway? Like, with a light-saber?" he said. He whipped the air with a make-believe sword. "I could have helped you beat up the bad guys."

"You are the silliest boy in the world, you know that?" I said, wrapping him in a giant hug. I laughed to myself at Max's super-hero ideas, and I realized how hard I tried each day to live up to his grandiose image of me. Perhaps that's why I went after Maria Portilla in the first place. Perhaps, on some level, I saw myself not as Mary Guevara, Realtor, but Max's Mom, Superhero.

We went back downstairs and joined the party. I was so stirred up with emotion that I had not even glanced at the guy who brought Max home that day.

"Hello, *chérie*," said Tony with an air kiss. "So nice to see you."

He seemed notably different than days earlier, when I had given him that ultimatum. He seemed meeker, remarkably grounded, albeit more pale than what is normal for him. It had taken every ounce of courage he had to go to family court and announce that he was no longer fighting me for custody, that he would observe our original custody agreement, that he would no longer take his son to therapy. The judge could have played hardball and tossed a few more obstacles into the process. But she didn't. Judge Jane Anne Costello was more angry at her favorite child psychiatrist for hiding his conflict of interest from the court. She closed the case before any of the shrink's political ties hit the press. I'm sure it helped that I also had some key factors weighing in my favor:

A) The truth

B) A resounding recommendation from Agent Green

C) An equally glowing one from the countywide PTA

D) The expertise and old-fashioned legal persistence of Elliot Casey

E) The crumbling election campaign of Victoria Ramonet

This last one was a doozy. In my brief absence from Miami, it came to light that Victoria had accepted generous campaign contributions from not one but three convicted felons, a trio of developers who had served time for embezzling public funds. Apparently, they were hoping for some plum construction projects to fall their way, thanks to a nudge from would-be commissioner Ramonet. And the scandal only got worse for her when the *Daily Press* published photographs of Victoria and one of the developers in the throes of a passionate kiss aboard the man's yacht.

I shouldn't have to explain how the revelation sucker-punched a proud chap like Tony. He was devastated. The worst part of the story was that he was aboard that yacht, sailing the Greek Isles, the day the photo was snapped. He was on the other side of the deck, sipping a Kir Royal, contemplating the jagged limestone cliffs of Corfu. Shortly after the paper published those photos, Victoria plummeted in the polls. She was forced to drop out of the race. In fact, she was doing just that on the day I went to deliver my ultimatum to Tony. What I had sensed that day was the anguish of a man on the verge of getting dumped. You see, as Victoria's political aspirations went out the window, so did her need for a ready-made family. She came home that night and packed up her jewels and her pantsuits and left Tony.

I had spent the next few days with Natalie at home, oblivious to all the drama. She'd slept in Max's bed and played with his toys, and at night she'd curled up on the sofa and watched movies with me. Her mother, I had told her, was arranging a trip for them into a great new neighborhood. The truth was that Agent Green had managed to arrange Maria and Natalie's "disappearance." As a valuable informant and witness to the crimes of the Cardenal family, Maria Portilla found an ally in the very federal agents who had sought her arrest.

Natalie stayed for five days, until the day Agent Green showed up at my door with word that arrangements had been made for the mother and child's passage into a "safe new place." As persuasive as I tried to be, he wouldn't let me escort the girl to where her mother was.

Natalie and I said our good-byes in the backyard, beneath a canopy of hot pink bougainvillea that spilled from a cedar trellis. She lay her head on my shoulder and cried for a long while.

"Why do I have to move again?" said the girl.

"After this time, you won't have to move anymore," I said, trying to comfort her.

"But it won't be home," she said.

There was such a depth of sadness in her eyes that I had a hard time coming up with the right things to say. She was too smart a child to be soothed by pat responses. Grasping for a language she might understand, I remembered something she told me the first day we met.

"Remember the sea turtles?" I said. "Remember how you told me the mothers are the only ones who go to the shore?"

"They are," she said.

"The mothers always go back to lay their eggs in the same beach where they were born," I said.

"I know. I told you that."

"How do you think they find it?" I said.

"I don't know," she said between sniffles.

"They find it because it's home," I said.

"I don't have a home," the girl said.

"You do. You know why that beach is home to the sea turtles?" I said. "Because that's where their mothers went. They were probably looking for their mothers. Natalie, the beach isn't the home. The mother is the home."

The girl embraced me one more time and then Agent Green took her away to the place where she would live with her mother.

The girl drifted out of my life as a strange new phenomenon was drifting in. When I ventured from home after those days I spent holed up with Natalie, I came to realize something curious: I had become a local celebrity. All of a sudden, random strangers recognized me. They stopped me at the supermarket, waved to me in rush-hour traffic, congratulated me on my daring mission. Letters, phone calls, and invites streamed in from out of nowhere, some from people I hadn't heard from in years.

Some days after Max's homecoming party, I received invitations to appear on *Good Morning America, Larry King Live,* and *Oprah.*

I also received an interesting letter from Ida Miller, gorgeously handwritten on Tiffany blue stationery. My former boss heaped praise on me, her protégé. This is what she wrote:

My Dearest Mary,

Not a day goes by that I don't remember you more fondly than the day before it. When I read about your act of bravery, I whispered a prayer of gratitude for you. "Thank you, Lord," I prayed. "Thank you for keeping my Mary safe. Thank you for having brought her into all of our lives."

Mary, how proud you have made your old friend! I always knew there was something extraordinary about you, from the first day you walked into my office and

asked if I needed a receptionist. A receptionist, you said,
not yet grasping the full scope of your talents. Do you
remember that? You took a look at my bookshelf and
asked if you could borrow my "Sales Techniques for
Winners" tapes. I never told you this, but it was that very
day that I placed the call to enroll you in the real estate
course.

I wanted to polish you the way one polishes a precious
gem. But now I know I didn't have to—you were always a
sparkling diamond.

I know we've been distant for a while, but please allow
me to be the first to break the silence and ask: When are you
coming back to work? Everybody misses you here. I miss
you most.

Please say you'll come back soon.

Warm regards,

Ida Miller
President
Grand Realty

I replied to her letter with a short, sweet handwritten note.
Here's what I said:

Dear Ida,

Thank you for your kind words. I miss you, too. Please
give my regards to all my friends at Grand Realty. As for
my work-related plans, I have decided to pursue other
opportunities.

All my best to you,

In eternal gratitude,
Mary Guevara

Those other opportunities I mentioned in the note involved starting my own real estate–plus business. I found a decent-sized, Old Florida–style bungalow in Coconut Grove and set up shop there with Gina, whom I didn't have to coax too hard. She quit her job at Grand as soon as I explained the concept behind the Take Me Home agency.

I called it "real estate–plus" because that was the best term I could think of to describe its mission, which extended well beyond the sale of real estate. The truth is, I couldn't open a normal real estate office because I was no longer the same kind of saleswoman I used to be. In the weeks that followed my return from Malabar, my life seemed to flow on a different kind of momentum. I no longer cared about outselling my real estate colleagues, or breaking commission records, or pitching the heck out of listings I knew were all wrong for the buyer. I no longer felt a need to work the pole. Instead, I made it my mission to help my customers find their special nook in the world, a place to truly feel safe. Perhaps this is because I had begun to attract a different kind of clientele, one less interested in property speculation and more concerned about longtime security.

The headlines generated by my hunt for Maria Portilla also brought a curious flow of new visitors to my office door: desperate people, lost souls, wronged lovers, abuse victims, regular folk who wanted their lives back, victims of injustice all. They brought me stories few people had wanted to hear, cases few law enforcement officers would or could take, long-forgotten dreams and dying wishes.

Can you help me find who's stalking me?

Can you help me hunt down the man who tortured my father in prison?

Can you help me find my teenage daughter?

Although at times I've failed, Gina and I have tried to help every one of them. In turn, these anonymous souls helped me find new meaning in life. In them, I saw pieces of myself and of my family. I saw the kind heart of my father, the determination of my mother, the dreams of my brother. I saw fragments of places I had been and emotions I had felt—desperation, anger, conviction. I saw my own flaws. And like these "clients," I had come to redefine the meanings of "normal" and "dysfunctional."

DULCE MARIA CIGARS—DAY 70

An intimate cigar shop of distressed terra-cotta walls and dark wood details. Tony Bennett tunes and chocolate leather chairs in the smoke lounge. Paperback Western hours in the cigar-rolling room. And Joe Pratts. He's arranging boxes of Arturo Fuente Gran Reserva cigars in a display case.

Of all the times I've seen Joe at work, I don't remember ever seeing him looking as handsome as he did on the night he opened his shop. He wore a crisp linen, long-sleeved guayabera, sugar white, and loose-fitting, tan linen slacks. There was a glow on his cheeks and a fine sense of self-confidence in his stride. His longish hair had that clean, casual, finger-stroked quality, and whenever he laughed—which was often that night—it would brush lightly against his temples.

And now, as I dropped by the shop, I noted that the glow still lingered. Of course, he had every reason to be in high spirits. He had brought to life his all-time dream, to open the cigar shop of his grandfather's inspiration. It was the place he had envisioned on those dim nights at the Rapture while cloistered in that lifeless back office of his, running numbers and knocking back shots of Chivas. What had stopped him from chasing his dream was never a lack of money—he had managed to scrape together quite a bundle with high-volume liquor sales and low overhead expenses. What had stopped him was basic inertia and a fear of the unknown.

But something had shifted in him during our time in Key West. I'd like to think it was the fact that we fell in love again, but I think it was something more complicated than that, a new awareness triggered by that incident in the alley. It was that night, as he stood over the crumpled figure of that derelict, that Joe realized who he was not. While his pistol-whipping actions may have suggested something else, he realized he was no thug, no killer, no deadbeat. So why was he there, in that alley, when he simply could have ditched the bum after a couple of scrapes and moved on? A few days after the incident, the answer to that question hit him hard. He wasn't there because it was the valiant thing to do—he was there because it was the easy thing to do, the thing he could do with his eyes closed. He wasn't a bona fide delinquent, but he did nothing to separate himself from the derelicts and thugs. It was easier not to. The more difficult thing to do would be to plant himself in a different environment, even if that environment better reflected his true identity.

But once he returned from Key West, he felt like an alien in his own bar. He walked out one night, leaving it in the hands of Eddie, the bartender, and he called me. He asked if I could show him some available storefronts. He had an idea for a new business.

Two months later, he opened the shop of his dreams, a reality created from those blueprints he had shown me at his office. Cozy, warm, eclectic, casual, and extraordinarily Cuban, the place was an extension of Joe's most distinctive qualities. Of course, my favorite part of the shop was its name, which he did not unveil until opening night. When he climbed atop a ladder and yanked the tarp off the sign, I couldn't believe the letters spelled DULCE MARIA CIGARS.

As a double-whammy honor, he whipped up mango sours for his guests and customers, printing up a large copy of my favorite drink recipe and hanging it up in a nice black frame. It read:

The Dulce Maria Special

Mango juice
Vodka
Fresh key limes
Superfine granulated sugar

Squeeze three key limes into a cocktail shaker half-filled with ice. Add four tablespoons of sugar, two shots of vodka, and a half cup of mango juice. Shake well. Serve in sugar-rimmed glasses. Salud!

Now, as Joe entered his second month at the shop, I had gotten quite used to stopping by on my way home from the office to catch a glimpse of him at work.

On a recent night, I watched him stack cigar boxes on a tall mahogany bookcase.

"Sell any Dulce Maria robustos today?" I asked him.

"Sold out," he said. He came over and gave me a kiss on the lips.

"Kidding, right?"

He was not kidding. Apparently the luster of my celebrity had spilled over to the cigar business. At least that's what I decided to believe, and Joe didn't rebut it. He just enjoyed watching me count the rapidly disappearing inventory and tally up the Dulce Maria profits in my head. I did it for a hobby, mind you, not out of any desire to outsell my beau. I wasn't that kind of saleswoman, not anymore.

I leaned across the counter and gave him another kiss, this time lingering a little longer.

"I'll be over in a couple of hours," he said, and by that he meant he was allotting time to go home, see his father, and wait for the night nurse to arrive.

"Give Papo a kiss for me," I said. "See you later."

And with that, I was off to pick up Max at my parents' house. I stepped into the Miami night, a mild and balmy night, and turned to contemplate the sign above the cigar shop as it glowed bright against a clear tropical sky.

Minutes later, with Max in the car, I headed home to 416 Hibiscus Lane. As we pulled into the driveway, the headlights of my car illuminated a path of newly planted gardenias and the fresh, ocean-blue paint on the door frame. What had begun as a series of home improvement projects to boost the house's curb appeal had segued into something more fulfilling as I discovered my house all over again. It was filled with lovely, subtle details, hidden gems to be polished and enjoyed for years to come. I was so busy dreaming of my next house—in essence, someone else's house—that I had never stopped to notice them. And now, as I stood at my front door, admiring the ocean-blue color on the frame, I wasn't sorry at all that I had passed on the "dream house," the one with the enormous yard and pool and gourmet kitchen. It was beautiful, yes, but it was too damn big. Besides, it looked just like every other house on the block.

ACKNOWLEDGMENTS

Sweet Mary came to life one Fourth of July to the sounds of firecrackers bursting outside my window. The novel was born, thanks to the contributions and support of many to whom I owe a debt of gratitude.

I thank Johanna Castillo, my editor at Atria, for her inspiration, for believing that this newspaper columnist had a novel in her. Many thanks to Judith Curr for creating a literary space where inspiration is possible, and, also at Atria, to Amy Tannenbaum for her steadfast diligence.

I thank Raul Mateu of the William Morris Agency for his guidance and unwavering support in my creative endeavors. Thanks to Eric Rovner, also at WMA, for the spirited flow of ideas and possibilities.

I am forever grateful to Andy Garcia, *Sweet Mary*'s poetic godfather, who fostered this story in its first incarnation, as a screenplay.

Special thanks to Bill Greer for his thorough editing and generosity of spirit throughout the years. I thank him for nurturing my love of writing and for reminding me, daily, why journalism continues to matter. I am also grateful to my editors at *The Palm Beach Post* for their courage and commitment in times of uncertainty.

Thanks to Claudia Forestieri for her valuable feedback, to Dario Acosta for his beautiful portrait photography, to Lilly Blanco for her inspired technological assistance, to Joe Cardona of KIE Films for his creative support, and to my niece, Lauren Alatriste, for putting her boundless imagination to work for *Sweet Mary*.

I also wish to thank Richard Sharpstein and Elizabeth Schwartz for their expertise and friendly ears.

I extend particular thanks to Virginia Garcia-Perez for sharing with me the true story that inspired this novel. I also thank my friend, Joan Fleischman, for reporting the news item in her "Talk of Our Town" column in *The Miami Herald*.

I am grateful to Dr. Pedro Jose Greer and his family for their kind hospitality in Islamorada.

Never least, thanks to my loving family. And to my boisterous choir of angels above—Mami, Abuela, Abuelo, Mara, Tere, Elly, and Nenita—my deepest gratitude for lighting my path with all those splendid butterflies.

SWEET MARY

LIZ BALMASEDA

A Readers Club Guide

Introduction

Mary Guevara is a successful real estate agent on her way to buying her dream house. She works hard to afford a decent lifestyle for her and her beloved son Max. Then, disaster strikes: after being mistaken for the drug queen Maria Guevara Portilla, she is taken away in handcuffs while her son and neighbors look on. Despite being cleared of the charges, all those around her remain suspicious as tabloids scream that the evidence in her favor was "murky."

Mary decides that she only has one way to reclaim her life: she must find Maria Guevara and bring her in. Her quest will force her to revisit her past, confront an old flame, and lock horns with the scourge of the Florida underworld. With the help of old friends and new allies she meets along the way, Sweet Mary will take Maria Guevara down. In the process, Mary will create an entirely new life for herself and her son.

Sweet Mary is an epic tale of a woman's struggle to get her identity and her family back. In the end, however, it is Mary herself who will be the most affected and come out a completely different person than she was before.

Questions and Topics for Discussion

1. Mary claims her life is pockmarked by times when she gets thrown back into the "emotional pit of my childhood in Hialeah" (p.28). Why does she choose to try and forget her past? Does she ever really obtain the healthy level of detachment she claims to need to survive?

2. The opening page of *Sweet Mary* is a quote from one of the characters in the book: "People run away from who they

really are—they do it all the time" (p. 68). Discuss this quote and its relationship to the following characters: Mary Guevara, Maria Guevara Portilla, Tony, and Joe Pratts.

3. When does Mary begin her "quest for justice" (p. 91)? How does her quest change over the course of the book?

4. When we first met her mother, how was she toward Mary? Why? What course of events cause Mary's mother to be sympathetic toward her? What does Mary say is the reason for this?

5. The author chose to start many of the scenes in the book by "setting the stage," much like in a movie script. Why do you think she opted to do this? What, if anything, does this contribute to the overall flow of the book?

6. Mary seeks the assistance of her old flame Joe Pratts in getting her connected with the Cardenal drug ring. She claims Joe "had no right to draw conclusions about my life, no right to assume he knew the independent person I had become . . ." (p.121). Does Mary ever let Joe see the woman she has become? Or does she transform into an entirely different person while she is with him?

7. Mary professes that no one else "could affect me the way Joe Pratts could affect me. That is why I had left him years ago" (p. 133). What does Mary mean by this? Does Joe still have an effect on her? Why did she marry Tony and not him?

8. Discuss Mary and Maria's confrontation. Do you agree that Mary knew "who I used to be before you [Maria] ruined my life" (p. 187)? When does Mary finally discover who she really is?

9. Mary experiences a number of changes in the book. We learn about the person she was and the person she is; then we get to see the person she starts to become. Which one did you like the most? Why? Do you think the Mary at the end of the book is the person she is meant to be?

10. Why do you think the book is entitled *Sweet Mary*? Would you define Mary Guevara as "sweet"? Were you surprised to learn that "Bad Mary" was not as bad as she was made out to be?

Tips to Enhance Your Book Club

1. Food plays a tremendous role in Mary's cultural background and upbringing. Experiment one night with some of the tasty foods from the book and bring some to share with your book club!

2. Make your own Dulce Maria special for book club night! You'll need:
   ½ cup mango juice
   2 shots rum
   3 fresh key limes
   4 tablespoons superfine granulated sugar

   Squeeze key limes into a cocktail shaker half-filled with ice. Add sugar, rum, and mango juice. Shake well. Serve in sugar-rimmed glasses.

3. Bad Mary has a craft hobby. Have some of your members who are into crafts come and share their works with the book club.

Printed in the United States
By Bookmasters